CAST THE FIRST STONE

CAST THE FIRST STONE

Ray Woodward

The Book Guild Ltd
Sussex, England

This book is a work of fiction. The characters and situations in this story are imaginary. No resemblance is intended between these characters and any real persons, either living or dead.

This book is sold subject to the condition that it shall not, by way of trade or otherwise, be lent, re-sold, hired out, photocopied or held in any retrieval system or otherwise circulated without the publisher's prior consent in any form of binding or cover other than that in which this is published and without a similar condition including this condition being imposed on the subsequent purchaser.

The Book Guild Ltd
25 High Street,
Lewes, Sussex

First Published 1996
© Ray Woodward, 1996
Set in Meridien
Typesetting by Poole Typesetting Ltd, Bournemouth

Printed in Great Britain by
Antony Rowe Ltd.
Chippenham, Wiltshire

A catalogue record for this book is available from the
British Library

ISBN 1 85776 052 5

... whichever of you who has committed no sin may cast the first stone ...

(John. 8:7).

ACKNOWLEDGEMENTS

Thanks are due to a number of people for their considerable help in the production of this manuscript. During my research, Vanessa's information on the Spanish section was priceless, and my lawyer, Neil, provided invaluable help with the legal passages. I must also express my great appreciation to my secretary, Joan, for her unrivalled word-processing skills and the many corrections and suggestions she made.

Many friends and relations have read the manuscript and I thank all of them for their comments, but it was mainly due to the encouragement, proof reading and criticism provided by my wife Marion and our dear friends Richard and Valerie that I decided to continue. I dedicate this book to them.

For Marion, Richard and Valerie

CAST THE FIRST STONE

PROLOGUE

He sat quite still on the bottom bunk of the narrow cot, with his head in his hands and his shoulders slumped. He was the picture of dejection and his upper torso expanded with each intake of breath that preceded the sobs that racked his body. After a while, he raised his head slowly and for the thousandth time he ran his eyes over the four green and white glossy painted walls. The cot opposite which unusually was unoccupied, now seemed to reflect his mood of deep depression as his eyes ran over its stained mattress. He fell back onto his cot and his forearm dropped across his eyes, partly shutting out the glare of the fly-blown light attached to the ceiling above his bed.

He knew that he should make another effort to climb out of this abyss of self-pity but each time he tried, his thoughts turned back to the events of the last year. How many times had he said 'if only', knowing that this useless negative brooding only drove him deeper into the pit of despair. He hated prison, the woman who had caused his arrest, and most of all he hated himself.

Somehow, those few short years ago when he had divorced his first wife, he was sure that he would at some time in the future end up with Marie. She was still happily married at the time, but he felt he could be patient. He was sure her love for him would override her feelings of loyalty for her husband.

His thoughts were interrupted by the sound of a large key being inserted into the lock. The heavy steel-lined door swung outwards, and an overweight moustachioed warder almost filled the opening with his immense frame.

'You'll be eating in your cell for the next few days until things quieten down a bit.' He placed the tray of food on the small bedside cabinet and left the room, re-locking the door after him.

The prisoner raised himself slowly, still conscious of the pain around his ribs and back. His anus was still very tender where the three long-term prisoners had recently beaten him and attempted male rape on only his second day in the prison. His present depression was as much a result of his revulsion as to the events of the last few months.

He toyed with the food. The thick gravy was already congealing and forming a dark brown ring around the edge of the plate. His thoughts returned once more to the woman. The pain of knowing that he would almost certainly never see her again added further fuel to the burning fire of his despair. He knew that he could never survive his 25-year term and his thoughts turned again to ways of ending his life. He returned to his food that had become cold and encrusted. The cutlery was plastic and he realized that it was too fragile to inflict real damage. His eyes cast languidly around the room again and came to rest on the cot opposite. He reached across the small gap and lifted the dirty mattress. The frame below was made up of smooth metal angle-legs with a wooden board platform. He had hoped to find metal springs that he could force open to make a sharp point.

He let the mattress drop back into place and returned to his tray of food. He picked up the plastic spoon and his eyes searched in vain for a rough surface to grind the edge into a sharp cutting blade. He sighed and went to the toilet in the corner which was partly concealed behind a small wooden modesty screen projecting from the wall. There was no seat or cover but he lifted the plastic cistern lid, thereby exposing the works below.

At last! He knew he could fashion an implement out of the thin arm which held the ball valve. He went back to his small bedside table and pulled a pad of lined paper towards him. He wrote slowly and carefully.

'I cannot take the pain and fear of loneliness and solitude of this place. The mere thought of spending the next several years locked away for a crime that I did not commit is unimaginable. I am quite innocent, and so to a lesser extent is Marie. I still love her deeply and it is partly for this reason that I cannot go on. I'm very very sorry.'

He signed it without emotion and left the pad on the table. As he had now made up his mind he felt strangely calm.

He went back to the toilet and removed the cistern lid once more, placing it carefully in the corner. He reached into the cold water, and grasping the plastic ball valve he levered the arm upwards against the split pin connecting it to the valve. When he had forced it up and down a few more times, it came away in his hand. Without the restraint of the float, the valve was fully open so water gushed into the already filled tank until it reached the level of the overflow outlet. He placed the partly flattened and roughly burred end of the arm on the floor and put the full weight of his heel on it. It made very little difference, but by now he thought that he had enough. He wanted to end it all now. It would hurt but only for a short time.

He took a deep breath and placed the ragged edge to his wrist. Turning his eyes away he tried to drag the rough metal across his skin. The water was still running. The improvised blade stung and he flinched, automatically drawing his arm back. Tears stung his eyes as he staggered back to the toilet and plunged his left hand into the water. After a short while it felt quite numb and he tried again. This time he opened a sizeable gash in his wrist, but he knew he must find the artery below. He dug away but he was unable to slash at the skin sufficiently to open the blood vessel. With a huge sob, his frustration, fear and deep depression burst forth. He raised the crude dagger far above his head and stabbed down with all his might onto his wrist.

He was surprised at the apparent lack of pain and also the fountain of blood which spurted over the wall and into his face. He had done it. He raised his dagger again but felt his head swimming and collapsed back onto the spare cot. His injured arm hung over the edge touching the floor. His life blood spread quickly into a pool on the floor tiles. His last conscious impression was of the gushing sound, but he didn't know whether it was the running away of his blood or the water.

1

His eyes flickered once and opened wide. Like a cat, he was instantly fully awake and totally aware of his surroundings. He lay quietly for a few seconds while trying to establish the source of the disturbance to his sleep. It was only the sparrow nestlings in the honeysuckle below the bedroom window that had begun to quarrel again over the breakfast supplied by their busy mother, so he relaxed, problem solved.

Sensing his master's wakeful state, the white toy poodle, strangely named Rambo, stepped delicately from his basket and stretched luxuriously. With a wag of his small stumpy tail, he jumped nimbly on to the bed and carefully avoiding the entangled limbs below the covers, he gently approached his master's face. He gave one quick good morning lick to the cheek, and then sat down to scratch vigorously.

Matthew Du Bois carefully raised his head, and leaning on his elbow he studied the face of his wife still lost in sleep alongside him. She would later argue vigorously that she was not snoring as 'ladies don't do such things', but he could hear a gentle whistling sound through her partly opened mouth. He could just see her small perfect white teeth that contrasted sharply with the slightly twisted upper right molar, the result of a rotten wisdom tooth left too long before extraction. This did however lend character to her near faultless features, by giving a slight lopsidedness to her ready and attractive smile.

At 27, she was eight years his junior and they had just celebrated their sixth wedding anniversary. To the obvious joy of their parents, she had announced four months ago that she was pregnant for the first time. They said it was about time too! Among their many friends, Matt and Marie were thought to be the most stable of couples and they were both very happy. Therefore it was odd that he sometimes felt twinges of jealousy caused by involuntary and unwelcome thoughts that occasionally crossed his mind. Although it had been some time since he last had serious doubts about her relationship with one of her work colleagues, his mind still occasionally returned to that theme.

*

Marie had always been good at work. This derived not only from a natural ability to grasp quickly and understand problems, but also from apparently boundless energy. Even mundane tasks were tackled with enthusiasm and zeal.

Her early years had been very tough but in spite of everything, they had been fairly happy. Her father had been killed in an industrial accident when she was very young, and her mother, at the tender age of 27, had been left to raise her and her two older brothers. 'God,' Matt thought, 'she was the same age as Marie is now!' Throughout her schooldays, she never had much as there was not much to be had, but she was always clean and well clothed and she had sufficient to eat.

As a result of her mother's training she had developed a very sensible approach to the material things in life, and hating waste, she would even now still squeeze the very last drop from the toothpaste tube or the shampoo bottle. This was one of the many sources of private jokes between Matt and Marie.

Like most young girls, Marie had always wanted to be something glamorous like a ballet dancer or a hairdresser, or to work in films perhaps as a make-up artist, but her mother's practical insistence upon her taking a shorthand typing course had led to her first job in an insurance office.

Although she was very shy, she was attractive to males of all ages, so she soon settled in and discovered that her prettiness and ready smile could often make up for the occasional spelling mistakes or grammatical errors.

Marie progressed well and enjoyed working in London. It was only after marrying Matt on her 21st birthday that she decided to work part-time. Their plans were to enjoy each other for five years or so before sharing themselves with children. Matt's business as an architect was now beginning to pay off and although her extra income was useful, Marie could afford to look for work that gave her pleasure and self-satisfaction.

It later seemed that fate had influenced her decision to work as a temp with Baldwin Norris & Co., a firm of publishers in central London. She had taken the job on a three-days-a-week basis with limited hours from 9.30 a.m. to 3 p.m. over six years ago but she had left just one week ago due to her pregnancy.

Her original boss had been a tall, thin, ageing woman called Miss Downs, who took on the role of personal assistant to the chairman, Mr Norris. Marie acted as her secretary, and she shared an office with her. On very rare occasions she also took dictation from Mr Norris himself. Miss Downs insulated all of the staff from Mr Norris, allowing only the rarest of visitors to pass her desk into his office. Marie had worked there for over a year and had been allowed into the inner sanctum only twice.

He was a rheumy old man, long past retirement age, with a chronic prostate problem, and he appeared never to notice Marie. He was kept at the firm in a non-executive role out of sentiment and respect for his long-lost dynamic leadership back in the very early days. Marie was always aware of an unpleasant pungent smell which emanated from his office. Once, when he and Miss Downs were both out one day, she ventured into his office to leave some letters for signature. The awful smell was stronger than ever, and she tracked it down to a large Victorian twin handled mug below the desk. It had obviously been used for a number of years as a urine receptacle, and it looked and smelt as though it had not been washed for all that time.

Letting out an involuntary screech, Marie picked up the mug with a piece of blotting paper. Then, holding it at arm's length, she scuttled down the corridor to the kitchen and dropped it, paper and all, straight down the refuse chute. She then went to the ladies' toilet and scrubbed her hands for a full five minutes while her nose was wrinkled with the effect of the unpleasant odour. She then returned to Mr Norris's office to set a fresh blotter on to his pad.

The following morning at about 10 o'clock just after Mr Norris arrived, Miss Downs took him his first coffee of the day, and just as they had for the past eighteen years, they went through the day's post together. Miss Downs returned 15 minutes later to dictate a short memo to Marie, when suddenly an animal-like bellow ensued from the chairman's office. They both looked up in alarm. Fearing a heart attack or something similar, they leapt towards the door to the chairman's office. Mr Norris was slumped back in his chair, his face purple with anger and a large wet stain spreading around the centre of his trousers.

'Which stupid bastard's taken my bowl?'

Miss Downs was distraught, and with great presence of mind she snatched the pristine blotter from the pad and spread it on Mr Norris's lap. She then stood in front of him, spreading her voluminous skirt, as if to hide his embarrassment from the world.

'It's that stupid little cow! isn't it?' He leaned over to glare round Miss Downs's meagre buttocks. 'Get rid of her! Tell her to mind her own bloody business! Get out, you! Get out!'

Miss Downs glowered hatefully at Marie and looked as though she wanted to strike her. However, as her hands were full of skirt, she gathered her mouth and spat a globule of spittle at Marie.

After the initial shock, Marie strove to maintain her self-control, but failed. The sight of this pathetic old man having pissed himself, being protected by his spinster assistant, was so bizarre as to cause her natural sense of humour to bubble over. However, his aggression together with Miss Downs's venomous attack replaced Marie's desire to laugh with a sense of self-protection and indignation.

'How dare you, you filthy old man! You should get a proper receptacle, or at least keep it clean! You're a walking health hazard! You are as bad, you old cow for letting it get like that! Don't worry. I'm leaving, and I bet that's the first time you've ever had your skirt up for any man!'

Close to tears, Marie spun round to stride out of the office when she collided with Stephen Murray, one of the senior line managers. He had heard the commotion and dashed in to see what the problem was. He took in the scene immediately and turned calmly to Marie.

'I suggest you go down to my office and wait there. My secretary will look after you,' he said, gently pushing her out into the corridor.

She had never noticed him before. He was just one of the many men who said 'Good morning' or 'Goodnight', and whose eyes she felt following her whenever she passed. About three weeks later, they met again.

Mr Norris had left the office on that unfortunate day and he had not been seen since by any of the staff. Miss Downs would find it difficult to attend to anyone else after all those years with one man. The new chairman, who had been working for many years towards this appointment from the board, decided to rearrange the office at senior level, so she left. He appointed Stephen Murray as his personal assistant, and at Stephen's request, Marie was asked to stay on a full-time basis. She would act as joint secretary and personal assistant to Stephen and the new chairman, Martin Bowers. Mr Bowers was, relatively speaking, a young man in his early forties full of energy and ideas. He felt that the firm had stagnated over the years.

'Just like my predecessor's pisspot,' he said to Stephen and Marie, 'and your dealing with it and him in the way you did is just what was needed to precipitate the situation. I have every intention of restoring this firm to its previous high standards and I hope to be able to rely on your help.' Although she thought it a somewhat corny speech, Marie was happy to run with the proposal.

Stephen had begun to work long hours, and his marriage of four years was proving to be a tragic mistake. Initially, Marie was concerned that she should spend more time at home setting up their new home, but discussions with Matt dispelled any doubts that she had. He was very busy with his practice and often worked a twenty-hour day. The house looked after itself and they both agreed that if she was going to work at all, it should be at a worthwhile and interesting job. Marie therefore threw herself into the task wholeheartedly, and in retrospect she thought that they had been the most fulfilling years of her short life.

*

Matt slipped carefully from beneath the duvet, and his place was immediately filled by Rambo who settled into the small of Marie's back. The dog knew he had about twenty-five minutes before Matt reappeared from the bathroom to let him out into the garden, after which he would have half a cup of milky coffee and some of his master's toast and marmalade for breakfast.

Feeling guilty about his doubts over Marie, Matt stepped into the shower and turned the valve on full without waiting for the 'dead-leg' of cold water to run off. The jet of water that felt like liquid ice hit him full on the back of the neck, but he forced himself to take this self-inflicted punishment. Slowly the temperature increased, and after about 30 seconds he was luxuriating in the steam-filled cubicle. Ten minutes later, he was towelling himself down vigorously. He caught sight of himself in the full length bronze tinted mirror at the foot of the bath and once again praised himself for the choice of shading. It certainly gave him a healthy looking tan! He consciously straightened, holding in with ease the slight bulge appearing at his stomach. 'Not bad,' he thought.

He was still very fit due to three strenuous games of squash each week and regular Saturday morning rounds of golf. Last year he had been forced to retire from his first love, football, after a fairly serious back injury that he was told could cause permanent damage if aggravated. At 5 foot 10 inches, he was of average height but his considerable width of shoulder and overall powerful frame gave him an appearance of stockiness. He had always been naturally fit and although his suppleness was somewhat reduced by his build, he was agile, well-balanced and well-co-ordinated. He was aware that he would probably need extra dietary care when he was older, and that the inability to pursue explosive sports would slow down his metabolism.

In his very early years, he had taken life just as it came. He was easy going, having inherited the trait from his parents. His brother, James, was two years older and of a very gentle nature which predictably resulted in Matt taking on the lead. In circumstances where they were in a one-to-one situation, Matt, being the extrovert, would invariably take over, and to a certain extent he would bully James. However, if any of their friends –

they were the 'Woolwich Road Gang' headed by the Larkin twins – either took James for granted or teased or threatened him, Matt would wade in, regardless of the size or rank of his adversary. At the age of seven he broke a 14-year-old's nose, and the secret pride that he sensed from his father while being scolded by him, set the pattern for the next few formative years.

He spent a lot of time with his Dad in horseplay and wrestling for fun, which developed his muscles and an in-depth knowledge of close combat. He was a fighter from an early age, and through his late teens and early twenties he took on a sometimes overly aggressive attitude born from the 'angry young man' image that had been popular in the mid-seventies.

He had developed a deep sense of fair play which often led to an impulsive over-reaction on many occasions, resulting in physical violence. By the time he was twenty, he had scars on his knuckles which bore testimony to this; but strangely enough his face was quite unmarked, apart from a small scar on the bridge of his nose.

It was curious that his only real pasting had come from James. Matt had been taken quite by surprise one cold winter afternoon when he was sixteen and James was eighteen. They had been talking about girls in general when in order to impress his older brother, Matt made a typical dirty-minded sixteen-year-old's disparaging comment about one of the girls at the Youth Club that they both attended. He did not know that James was secretly very sweet on her and had written anonymous poems to her. James set his jaw and walking purposefully over to face Matt, he said nothing but punched as hard as he could into Matt's midriff. Taken completely by surprise, Matt doubled over gasping for air, as James continued his attack with both fists about Matt's head, ears and neck. It was only when Matt was curled in a pathetic ball on the floor, arms around his head and knees drawn up to his stomach, that James stopped, and taking several deep breaths he walked from the room and gently closed the door.

No words passed between them for a week until Matt could take the tension no longer. He knocked on James's bedroom door and entered without invitation. He simply said 'Sorry'. Then he turned on his heel and walked out. The incident had never been mentioned since and the bond between them was as firmly cemented as ever, and they had had no serious conflict since then. Matt's respect for James's quiet strength had been reciprocated by his brother's admiration for his ability to take his punishment.

*

Matt stood in front of the handbasin, carefully brushing his teeth, 24 of which were his own and 6 of which had been gifted by a talented South African dentist. He reflected on the small length of loose tiling grout above the mirror. He was more cross over this than he should have been, mainly because he had laid every single tile himself. In fact, the whole of the bathroom had been designed and built by him during his spare time, over a period of twelve weeks.

As a competent, practical and experienced architect, the design had been quite a simple exercise, apart from a need to explain and sketch each detail to Marie. He had always said that she was his most demanding client. However, fulfilling some of her demands was one of his greatest pleasures!

After completing the designs and plans for the DIY work, the enthusiasm and skill that he had demonstrated in carrying them out – the plumbing, carpentry, electrical work, glazing and tiling surprised them both. Marie took on the role of his able and willing 'gofer' and she also proved to be a very capable and careful decorator. He found this physical work therapeutic, and he had observed that his manual dexterity was of great benefit when criticising unacceptable work by so-called tradesmen on some of his building sites. It also gave him a greater appreciation of those tradesmen who did first class work that was up to his very high expectations.

After having carefully selected his clothes for the day in the adjacent dressing room, and then giving his jacket a final brush, Matt stepped back into the bedroom just as Marie sleepily opened one eye. This was Rambo's cue to leap off the bed and stand expectantly by the door, his tail wagging furiously.

It was only half past five, but Matt was ready for a full day's work and he hoped to be back in the house by half past six that evening. His gentle peck on Marie's cheek led to a full, lingering kiss on her mouth. 'Don't go,' she mumbled. Although this had been a standing joke for many years, he would indeed willingly have stayed if she had pressed the matter any further.

'Have a nice lie-in and I'll see you this evening,' he said, quietly closing the door.

Rambo was waiting in the dining room by the patio doors and danced out into the garden when Matt slid it back to its full extent. The morning was glorious; the birds were singing and a multitude of insects were already busy at work, buzzing about and pollinating the flowers. The sun shone into the east-facing room, casting a dappled effect on the paintwork as it filtered through the gently swaying tops of the Norwegian Maples on the boundary. Early July was his second favourite time of the year, the first being the Spring when everything was coming to life and Mother Nature was prodding her progeny to rouse themselves after a winter's sleep below ground.

By the time Rambo returned, the coffee had been made and the toast had popped out of the toaster. He prepared one round each with a layer of butter and a coating of marmalade. Rambo was pleased with the extra treat of thick chunks of butter, as Marie had left the dish in the cold part of the fridge again, making it impossible to spread. Not many years ago, he would have been severely irritated by such a small thing but he had mellowed with age. He wondered when the change had happened. It certainly had not started with the beating he had received from his brother, which only made him aware that sometimes you have to get hurt in order to win, and that you just have to make the other man hurt more. It was more likely that he had changed as a consequence of the only time that he had really lost his temper in the last ten years.

Since that one incident, he seemed to have calmed down considerably, and had also lost a great deal of his aggressive nature when he qualified as an architect. This was after ten years of hard study at evening classes while working in various architects' offices. Perhaps he had subconsciously felt that he was now one of the 'elite', a 'professional man', or it may have been that he then believed or hoped that he would have more time to enjoy himself. It was possibly a mixture of both, as well as the fact that he could afford the luxury of more than four hours sleep each night.

He had started studying on a part-time basis immediately after leaving school, having taken his GCE examinations a year early. He had had a single-minded desire since the age of 11 to be an architect, and he left school as soon as possible to start work in a large architects' office in London. He was very green, and wet behind the ears, so he was often taken advantage of in those early weeks, but he was quick to learn and very willing. Consequently, he was soon receiving help and guidance from his immediate bosses. On his first day at work he was wearing his father's only blazer and a pair of old but freshly pressed trousers. He arrived at work with ten pounds in his pocket. After buying the week's lunch tickets from the canteen, paying his joining fee for the Union, contributing to the office biscuit box club and several other things which he was too embarrassed to refuse, he had only 12 pence left at the end of the day.

He had not yet established the best form of travel from his parents' home at Greenwich in South East London to Aldgate, where the office was located, so that morning he had caught the bus to Tower Bridge and walked from there. Then, after work he was left stranded in London, and being too nervous and proud to ask one of his new colleagues for help, he started to walk home. It was only about 14 miles and he calculated that if he stepped it out, he could get to the Greenwich Naval College in four hours, and his 12 pence would go on the bus ride for the last three miles.

He arrived home that night feeling hungry, foot-sore and weary and with a resolve never again to be without money in his pocket.

*

Matt's last job as an employee was in local authority, with the architects' department of a London borough. There, the times of his normal working day were strictly set to accrue the exact weekly number set down by the Union. The office hours were incongruously accurate from 9.00 a.m. to 5.07 p.m., and most of the 120 members of his department used to stand by the door to the lobby waiting for the minute hand to click over onto the seven when there would be a dash for the lifts. Those were good, if very busy years. He had made many friends at Croydon (and a few enemies too), and in his role as Social and Sports Secretary he got to know by name most of the 1,800 employees in the twenty-storey municipal offices. He revelled in his considerable popularity and reacted to this by gaining the reputation for being friendly, cheerful, helpful and full of confidence in dealing with all people, regardless of age, colour, creed and sex.

Matt's warmth and friendliness during his six years at the Council led to four fairly serious involvements with members of the opposite sex, two of them embarrassingly took place at the same time, and one of the women was married. At that time, he had also met Marie for the first time, at a cousin's wedding, and although she was very aware of him, he took little notice of this very pretty and fairly adult sixteen-year-old.

He received notification of his success in the final part of his examination in June 1984, and he immediately handed in his notice to the Borough Architect at the Council. For the past seven years while being employed, he had executed a number of private architectural projects for various clients, often working deep into the night to meet deadlines. His need to study and keep a full-time job as well as do private work left very little time for play, but he often forsook the luxury of regular sleep to achieve both. His reward was not only the extra money he was earning from private commissions, but also the considerable satisfaction in producing a good job under extreme pressure. He was also building up a client base for the day when he knew he would be working for himself.

On the first of August 1984, his practice of 'Matthew Du Bois, Chartered Architect', was founded and he took a compact one-room office with a flat overhead in the centre of a small market town in Kent. His first year was very busy as his old clients were even more willing to place commissions with him now that he was able to give full-time attention to their various projects. The reputation that he had for sensitive work to Listed Buildings ensured a good workload from the many owners of historical buildings in the area. One of his 'private job' clients from the Council days, Brian Sailon, had been instrumental in his move into private practice. Matt had first worked for him on office unit conversions in London in 1982. Over the next three years, Sailon Ltd had built up a large portfolio of property and Matt's workload had grown with it. Slowly, as greed took over, Sailon's attitude changed to all of his professional advisors including Matt.

Having made his first million by honest hard work, Sailon decided, probably sub-consciously, that he was paying too much for the services of the likes of Matt, so he endeavoured to get his next million partly at their expense. Gradually, the regularity with which Matt's fees were paid diminished, despite his increasingly applied pressure. This eventually led to confrontation on one of Sailon's building sites late one February afternoon. Although Sailon was a very tough businessman, he was a coward at heart, and as he was anticipating trouble, he had engaged two villainous-looking minders who hung around when the two men met. The structural conversion of the office suite on the second floor was almost complete but the building was very cold. The plastering had only just been finished and second-fix electrics and plumbing was underway.

Matt had called the meeting on site to coincide with his preparation of a valuation of the work done for Sailon's bankers. He was hoping he could persuade Sailon to pay his outstanding fees of £14,000 accumulated over the last year by threatening to withhold the issue of the certificate. After about ten minutes of heated discussion, it was obvious that things were going to turn nasty. Sailon called in his heavies, ordering them to 'teach this prat a lesson!'

Matt's sense of fairness was severely affronted, and he could later recall what had happened only through a red mist. The first punch to the side of his head was only a glancing blow, but it was strong enough to stimulate a considerable violent aggression which had lain dormant for a few years. As he was grabbed from behind by one and pummelled by the other, Matt knew he had to break free or else be badly hurt. By now, Sailon had joined in, kicking at Matt's legs but ensuring that he didn't get too close.

Matt lunged out with both feet, catching the first villain

squarely in the midriff, causing him to collapse gasping. The momentum of the kick propelled the yob behind him backwards into the partly open door. The force ripped it from its hinges and the leading edge of the door split the back of the yob's head; blood spurted over the freshly floated plaster. Matt was immediately on his feet and he caught the first of the villains while he was trying to get up. He helped him up, with a well-placed kick to the head and punched him three more times before he hit the floor again. He then wheeled around towards Sailon with the single intention of hurting him as much as possible. Seeing one minder prostrate and quite unconscious, and the other sitting on the floor, moaning in a pool of blood, a very pale Sailon was shaking and whimpering at the sight of Matt's still unvented fury.

'Remember me, Sailon! I'm the little prat that you were going to teach a lesson!'

Without waiting for his turn, Sailon leapt through the broken doorway, but as he looked over his shoulder, fearful of Matt following, he slipped on the sticky pool oozing from his man's head injury. He was propelled in panic to the open and unprotected stairwell. He fell screaming through three floors and landed in a grotesquely twisted heap in the ground floor lobby.

At this sight, Matt's fury evaporated and he rushed down the stairs, three at a time towards the crumpled shape below. Sailon was still breathing, although erratically. Matt did not want to move him so he covered him with his overcoat. His first thought was to call for medical help when a shout came from above.

'It's okay mate. I've phoned for an ambulance and the police!' Matt looked sharply up to see two electricians leaning over the stairwell at second floor level. 'Don't worry, we saw it all! We'll give a statement confirming it was self-defence, and by the way, if you don't like any of our work, we'll do it again – no argument!'

Matt smiled weakly at their attempt to lighten the situation with humour, but for the next five minutes he was shaking uncontrollably. He knew his shivering was not only due to the coldness of the building and the fact that he was lightly dressed.

The ensuing investigation took a full six months to complete.

It was based mainly on the testimony of the two electricians, and Matt was completely exonerated. The two villains were jailed for common assault, and Sailon, having broken his back, was to spend the rest of his life paralysed from the waist down. The judge ruled that this was sufficient punishment for his crime.

2

By the time Matt was ready to leave for work, there wasn't a cloud in the sky and the sun was casting long shadows over the front lawn. The promise of another fine summer's day was in the air. He did like these early summer mornings and found it no hardship to leave his bed on such days. Even in the dark winter mornings, it was not too difficult, despite the lure of Marie's warm back which was the greatest obstacle to overcome.

He opened the garage door electronically from the switch inside the house, and once again he admired the sleek lines of the white Jaguar XJS V12 glistening alongside Marie's Mercedes 380E Drophead. Although she professed to not have any firm views on cars, he still remembered her obvious delight when he gave her the keys last Christmas.

He had always had cars of some character since his early days of driving, and somehow he had managed to afford to change as and when he wanted. He was the first person in the whole of his family to own a car, although one of his uncles once had a motor cycle combination, and he had derived great pleasure from ferrying his mother and father around in the car. This pleasure was reflected in their obvious pride in their little boy who looked as though he had made good.

The throaty chuckle of the twin $2^1/_2$ inch exhausts echoed off the rear wall as he eased out of the garage onto the gravel drive. Taking care not to spray the surface all over the lawn, he enjoyed the quiet crunch of the tyres as he drove slowly down the driveway to the front gate. When he was fifty yards away, a press of a button that he had installed on the dashboard signalled to the receiver on the gate and it swung gently away from him. Judging his approach to perfection, he smiled to himself as he had just enough room to pass through without adjusting his speed while the gate continued to open fully. Although he knew it would shut automatically after 30 seconds, Matt gave a further press of the control button and he saw the gate start to close in his rear view mirror.

By the time he reached the A21 Sevenoaks By-Pass, the temperature gauge was reading normal and he enjoyed the rush of air through the open sunroof as he pushed it through the gears, using the J-gate as a clutchless manual, to a comfortable speed of 110 mph. Closing the electric sun roof which was now buffeting, he switched to a local radio station, and with some difficulty he sang along with Whitney Houston, *I Will Always Love You*.

Ten minutes later, he swung off the main road and in through the entrance to the office car park. The barrier was already half-raised and Matt was sure that George Adams, their chief security man, had spies at the end of the road to forewarn of his arrival.

'Morning, Mr Matt. Another nice one.'

George called everyone by their Christian names, except Matt and his partner Chris, both of whom were prefixed with 'Mr'. George was particularly fond of Matt who was always friendly and polite, and never omitted to say 'Good morning', 'goodnight' and 'thank you'. Chris, however, was sometimes a bit gruff and surly, particularly late at night and rarely made time for small talk. George's Christmas gift from Matt of a case of Famous Grouse Whisky was his most welcome, and with care he could eke it out for the whole year, limiting himself to a bottle a month.

At 62 years old, George was a retired Metropolitan Police sergeant who found controlling the security of this Architectural and Project Management Practice something of a restcure after 40 years of druggies, villains, drunks and yobs. It was okay in the early days of his career when a clip around the ear or a kick in the pants would do the trick, but he had lately seen too many of his colleagues knifed and shot. The shift work for the Marten–Du Bois partnership supplemented his pension nicely and the three alternating weekly shifts of 5.00 a.m. to noon, 11.00 a.m. to 6.00

p.m. and 5.00 p.m. to 11.00 p.m. suited his interests of snooker, golf and bridge.

He had been devastated last year when his wife died suddenly and mercifully quite quickly, within five weeks of being diagnosed with stomach cancer. She had suffered in silence for three months before pain overcame her fear of the truth, forcing a visit to the doctor. After the funeral, George had been drunk for a full month. During that period he drank the equivalent of almost two complete Christmas gifts. It was only after Matt had shared the last month's supply with him one evening and deep into the night that he returned to work for the middle shift the next day looking spick and span. He was clean shaven and he had a fresh haircut. His eyes showed no sign of the past 28-day-binge and only an occasional frown gave any indication of the lasting pain. Neither he nor Matt had found it necessary to mention that night, but both were aware that a bond had been forged between them. George's gratitude and friendship would endure for the rest of his lifetime.

Matt parked in his reserved space under the cover of the cantilevered first floor and smiled at the slate plaque by the entrance doors: 'Architect – Matthew Du Bois, 1990'. Although not terribly proud of some of the members of his profession, he was extremely proud of himself and his own achievements. He often thought back to the comments of his tutors at College and knew that they had been correct. Architecture was not just wearing orange rimmed spectacles and pink corduroy jackets and 'building pretty', but rather it was achieving the difficult balance between aesthetics, materials, construction, function and economics. Too many architects leaned towards the first with little consideration for the others, and builders and clients often ignored the components other than those that they considered important.

The design of MDB House did, in his view, maintain the architectural equilibrium, and as he had been at once architect, builder and client, he was sure of the sincerity of his view. He was very pleased with having won the battle with the planners which allowed him to build the office on this sylvan site, replacing an existing derelict warehouse four years ago. Ever self-critical, he could find little to fault in the scheme apart from his own and Christopher's need to pander to their egos, and this was reflected in the sizes and finishes of their personal office suites.

However, it was their money and they had worked hard to achieve it, so why not have a little self-indulgence? They had taken the same view when buying the company's house in Florida. 'So what if we only use it once a year – we can afford it' had been Chris's opinion, endorsed wholeheartedly by Matt.

Matt let himself through the smoked glass entrance, cancelling the burglar alarm by feeding in the code on the panel beneath the beech and spun aluminium reception desk. He took the lift to the top, the seventh floor, and dropped a dictation tape onto his secretary's desk as he passed through the lobby. The beech panelling and hessian covered walls gave an air of pristine luxury and the light from the atrium overhead was soft and dappled by the barely visible plants on the roof garden.

Entering his office, he immediately felt comfortable as the sunlight enlivened the autumnal colours of the decor, firing the oranges and browns of the seating area into contrast with the functional drawing area which always, he admitted, looked slightly scruffy. The T-shaped arrangement of his black ash desk and table provided a good conference facility for eight people and with his matching drawing board and plan chest, it all occupied almost half of the large 750 square foot room. The remainder was taken up with a corner seating unit for six people with low, comfortable upholstered easy-chairs and two coffee tables.

The filing cabinets, bar and coat hanging space were cleverly concealed in built-in units behind hessian-faced 'jib' doors that opened to a touch on concealed pressure pads. A private shower room led off one corner, and Matt had a small wardrobe with two suits, one light and one dark, a couple of white ready-ironed shirts and two ties, all for emergency use.

The rather angular form of the furniture was softened by a number of modern floor-mounted self-watering plant troughs and bowls. The walls were carefully hung with artists' impressions and photographs of some of his larger and more impressive completed jobs.

Matt's certificates which displayed membership to the Royal Institute of British Architects, The Chartered Institute of Arbitrators, The South Eastern Society of Architects, The British Academy of Experts and the Association of Project Managers, were hung with some pride on the wall at the back of his desk in matching black frames. Marie's photograph smiled at him from a beach in Turkey on the corner of his desk.

As he was always in the office early, he occupied the southeast corner of the top floor, while Christopher took the southwest corner to enjoy the evening sun. Although he was never at his desk before 10 o'clock in the morning, Chris would often still be there at 10 o'clock at night, so the spread of senior partners' cover was about 16 hours per day. This not only kept demanding clients happy but also impressed the staff and their competitors. They operated a no-smoking policy throughout the office and provided a room on the ground floor for those unable to go completely without nicotine.

The remainder of the top floor was taken up by an imposing board-meeting room which also doubled as an executive dining room for entertaining up to 18 visitors. The offices of the four salaried partners and their respective secretaries took up the rest of the floor space. The reception area, interview and staff, rest and smoking rooms, together with a janitor's closet occupied most of the ground floor and gave access to the dead filing store in the basement. The boiler and plant rooms were also at the lower level with a loading door providing access to the outside at the rear for future boiler or plant replacement.

The rest of the building was taken up by personnel, administration and accounts on floors one and two under the control of the partnership secretary, Adrian Bullock. Floors three to six inclusive were occupied by two floors of quantity surveyors' and project managers' teams and two floors of architects' groups alternating floor by floor. Each floor had three associates to control the teams who were directly answerable to the salaried partners.

The total staff complement was now over 200 and this was something of a meteoric achievement for Matt in ten years. He remembered chatting to his accountant when he first started in practice, saying 'Quite frankly, if in ten years' time I am still working in one room as a one-man band with a part-time secretary, I'll be quite happy.' His accountant advised him that if he tried to steer a level course he would certainly go downhill. The aim must be for gentle growth at least, with the view that staying level would be the very worst that could be achieved.

3

Christopher Marten had always worked in big organizations. When he qualified as a Chartered Architect in 1979, he had been working in the same large London practice for the eight years since leaving school in 1971. His loyalty and his exam success had been rewarded by his mean bosses with a meagre salary increase and a promise of a company car in a year's time. Much to his wife's concern, he immediately handed in his notice and told the senior partner to 'stick the job up your ass – I'll remember this when one day you come to me looking for employment!'

He had always been a very hard worker. When he moved to London from a small village near Plymouth, in Devon with his parents as an only child at the age of nine, he spoke very little and even then with a broad accent and he could barely write. As a result of a considerable amount of effort and time spent by his mother and the local parish priest in South London, he gained a scholarship two years later to a Roman Catholic academy, and then went on to a secondary school in Southwark where he finally gained eight GCE O levels.

Having taken one thing at a time, he was then at a loss as to what to do. A friend of his father had a small jobbing building company and suggested that 'with all his exams, Chris might consider the professional side of building'. After a trip to the Youth Employment Office in Blackfriars, Chris secured an interview with Matthews, Colley, Jones & Partners in Bruton Street where he started as a trainee architect the following week.

On the advice of his group leader, he started a correspondence course with the Kingston College of Art, but lacking the self-discipline to study alone, he joined a Day Release Class at Brixton School of Building the following year. He eventually passed his Part I and II Final Examinations and qualified as a Chartered Architect in 1979. His achievements in 15 years were remarkable and the pride generated in his family was justly deserved. From that day forward, he affected the pose of what he thought an architect should look like and always wore a bow tie.

He had prepared drawings for small house extensions on a moonlighting basis through those years but although he liked the extra cash, he was not very enthusiastic about doing the extra work. In 1978 he married Jennifer, a pretty nurse born and living in Stepney, East London. They were both 23 and shortly after, Jennifer fell for their first child, Ben. When Chris left Matthews, Colley, Jones & Partners, Ben was two and with his baby brother Thomas, who was three months, not only was Jennifer kept fully occupied at home but their limited resources were strained to the limit. Jennifer was a very homely girl and did not find the lack of material things a problem. Her fairly frugal upbringing demanded only good health and happiness and she found that the former flowed naturally from the latter, which ensured having a happy and healthy family.

When Chris stormed out of the firm of architects, he knew that he would fairly easily find work but he decided that life owed him more than just a job. He had made enormous strides since his late development and unlike his wife, his desire for the good things in life spurred him into planning for the future.

On a few occasions he had carried out private jobs for William Belton of Belton & Co., a small firm of architects and surveyors in Woolwich. Chris sensed that the old man had a liking for him. Mr Belton had only one son who had failed his law exams at the third attempt and who was now travelling the world as a Hippy in a Cult Group. He knew that Mr Belton had taken over the firm several years ago and as the sole proprietor, he would see it all fall apart following his impending retirement in a few years' time, unless he took on a partner. Chris asked for a meeting and put his cards on the table. He said that he had no money to buy in, only a great deal of energy for hard work and several contacts from his years at MCJ & Partners. He also pointed out that although Mr Belton was a first class General Practice Architect and Surveyor, as a result of clients becoming more and more cost conscious, it was in project managing that the future lay. Through aggressive marketing, quantity surveyors were being appointed as project managers, dictating the role and functions performed by architects, structural engineers and building surveyors. He felt that his organisational abilities could redress the balance to secure such commissions for the practice.

After a fairly short period of deliberation, Chris was appointed as an associate partner in the re-named W Belton & Associates. He threw himself wholeheartedly into the practice and built up his section of the firm. He took only a liveable salary and his small share of the profits were left in the practice in his capital account for future use. He employed a very good practical building surveyor and concentrated hard on building up the project management side of the firm, as well as forming a quantity surveying section.

After five years of association, William Belton knew that he could now comfortably retire and offered Chris the opportunity to buy him out for an agreed figure. The deposit would be found from the capital sum in Chris's account. The total price could be paid over the next five years, after which time Mr Belton's private pension plan would have matured. Chris agreed without hesitation. The desire to own his own business had grown since he joined the practice. The agreement was finalized, signed and sealed within six weeks. Mr Belton would continue from then on a consultancy basis until Chris could afford to complete the buy-out.

With some trepidation, due to his fear that clients would fail to recognize the well-established old name, Chris changed the name of the practice to The Marten–Belton Partnership. However, his ego won through and all his concerns proved unfounded, as in that first year the practice grew from strength to strength. Jennifer often recalled how they had been poor, then quite rich, suddenly poor again and now well off enough to be comfortable if not yet entirely rich again. Chris was certainly well off enough to re-indulge himself in one of his early loves, that of motor cycling.

When he was 17 years old, he could only afford a BSA Bantam 125 which barely reached 50 miles an hour downhill. The development of motor cycle engineering due to Japanese influence had resulted in an enormous increase in power output from the same size engine. One day, after having visited a site in Deptford Broadway, on impulse, Chris called into the Suzuki dealers in Trafalgar Road, Greenwich. The salesman was very good at his job and convinced him that the modern machines were so much more easy to handle than the oldies, even though Chris had not ridden for ten years now. Chris still had his full driving licence covering bikes so he borrowed a full-face crash helmet and set off for a trial spin on a Suzuki 500, having left his car keys with the salesman as security against his return.

He took it carefully and somewhat hesitantly through the traffic, negotiating the one-way system by the Naval College with some trepidation. He was pleased to gain the relative quiet and safety of Greenwich Park, and he climbed the hill past the observatory and through the gates at the top onto Blackheath. Gaining in confidence all the while, he accelerated smoothly through the gears and was astounded when he glanced down at the speedo as he dropped into fifth gear to see he was doing 95 mph.

He immediately slowed down and revelled in the thrill of a superlatively engineered piece of machinery pulsing between his legs. He smiled at the unintentional pun in his thoughts, although secretly he was equally proud of his sexual equipment. Swinging left at the one-way system at the Royal Standard, Chris accelerated past the rows of shops and parked cars at the top of Westcombe Hill. As he glanced behind at the traffic merging from the right, he did not see the door of the parked car that had begun to open to allow an elderly lady driver to get out. He turned round just as his front wheel collided squarely with the leading edge of the door, catapulting him through the air, his left arm tearing badly on the top sharp corner of the door. He landed squarely on his back, having turned one and a half somersaults, and was at once in agonizing pain from his damaged arm but quite numb in his left leg which was twisted at an ugly angle beneath his body.

His recovery was slow, and several operations later he was

finally allowed home from hospital after four months. He had a small scar on his lip, a badly scarred but nearly fully functioning left leg and only a very slight limp. However, his left hand would always be useless as the nerves in his forearm had been severed by the impact of the door. Although the skill of the surgeons had saved the limb, no feeling could be generated in the hand. Since then, he wore a black leather glove and carried the hand across his chest most of the time.

*

The insurance payout was considerable and Chris's lawyer made the most of the fact that Chris could not now fully pursue his chosen profession. In fact, having a staff of 16 by that time, Chris spent very little time in architecture pure and simple. His role was at once accountant, marketeer, salesman, procurer and office manager.

The settlement had been sufficient to allow Chris to finally clear his debt to Mr Belton, buy the automatic Jaguar car that he had always wanted and move to the house in Beckenham for which Jennifer had yearned for many years. His ability to drive an automatic car had been unimpaired. The only conversion needed was a knob on the top of the steering wheel allowing a one-handed operation.

Secretly, Chris rather liked the sinister air that his black leather gloved hand created. He even found that some women were fascinated by it and in some perverse way would get great pleasure from using it in sex play. He sometimes suspected they were trying to put some life back into it! Together with his slight limp, his hand was the subject of many conversations. One thing he did extremely well was to talk about himself, and over the years the story of the accident was embroidered almost beyond belief. He grew a droopy moustache to hide the small scar that caused a slight misshaping of the right corner of his mouth. This was the one blemish on his dark Roman good looks, and he always kept the moustache neatly trimmed and brushed.

Christopher's reputation both in the building industry and in the professional world was growing rapidly, and by 1986 he had a thriving and very successful practice. His one disappointment had been his inability to break into the field of Conservation and work on Historic Buildings. This had always been reserved for architects experienced and skilled in that discipline and he had, of course, no track record. The rewards in the form of high fees were considerable due to the excessive cost of top quality building work.

His attempt to employ on his payroll such specialist architects had met with no success – they were at a premium and would only come in on an Equity Partnership basis. Chris was jealous of and would not give away any of his hard earned shares in the practice. The next alternative he tried was to sub-contract the first Heritage contract for which he was at last invited to tender, to a specialist firm of architects as a sub-consultant. This was doomed to failure when the firm he used claimed the need for direct dialogue with the building owner and then poached his client. The only other alternative appeared to be to find a practice successful in its own right and with conservation experience, but ripe for expansion, and either to purchase it outright or amalgamate the two. It was as a result of keeping his eyes and ears open for such an opportunity that Chris latched onto Matthew Du Bois, when they first met at a corporate golf day in 1987.

After a period of co-operation working on a few jobs together, where they got on really well, they amalgamated their practices in January 1988, trading under the name of Marten Du Bois & Partners on a straight 50/50 basis. Although they both agreed that a 51/49% split would be better so that one person had the ultimate say in any dispute, neither was willing to relinquish total control. They therefore agreed that it would work as they would be performing differing functions in the practice.

Not only did their personalities dovetail, but being very similar in looks, colouring and stature, they were often taken for brothers. Although they each ran their own sides of the business, they promoted existing associates to salaried partners and Chris and Matt took on an even greater management role. It suited Chris to pass over the 'hands-on' function to his partners, but Matt found he increasingly missed the design and management of building projects. As a result, it was agreed that Chris and his admin team would take on the overall management function and financial control of the practice, releasing Matt for those duties for which he was best qualified, and indeed more suited.

Matt was not only a very talented and quick designer, but his presentation to clients and personal friendly approach invariably resulted in forming relationships of confidence. On occasion, he needed to take great care to not get too involved with clients' wives as many were physically attracted to this personable, good-looking and enthusiastic young man. He had a healthy appetite for female company and he often reciprocated their attraction, but he had never been caught in bed with a client's wife – only a daughter on one occasion!

Matt was delighted to unload the responsibility for accounts, bills, PAYE, salaries and financial matters and happily entrusted this to Chris. He would only be called upon from time to time, to sign the odd document that required both their signatures. He trusted Chris completely and his copies of the annual accounts showed a healthy balance for them both in their respective capital accounts. They had each built up over the past six years a reserve approaching one million pounds, as well as having taken out sufficient cash in the form of partners' drawings to give them a very comfortable lifestyle. They had achieved this despite the current three-year recession that had been the worst in the history of the building industry. They had also managed to buy the site and build their own offices, financed through a mortgage they had taken out four years before.

*

Matt was therefore quite unconcerned but a little curious that morning to find an unopened letter on his desk. It was stamped 'strictly private and confidential. To be opened by addressee only'. The back of the envelope bore their banker's logo and it was addressed to Chris and Matt personally.

Slitting the top of the envelope, Matt frowned as he read. Thinking then that there must be some mistake, he read again more slowly. The letter was from the manager of their branch of the bank at Fenchurch Street. It pointed out that as they had again exceeded their overdraft limit of £500,000, all further cheques would be stopped. It went on to ask what were they going to do to rectify the situation. Apparently their last draft accounts received by the bank only a few days previously had painted a sorry picture, and although they appeared to be very busy, cash-flow was a considerable problem. The bank was willing and able to support them while they were in a healthy position but their balance sheet showed their personal capital accounts now depleted to only a few thousand pounds each and the bank's exposure had reached unacceptable levels.

By now, Matt was sure of a mistake. He opened one of the wall panels at the rear of his desk revealing his filing cabinets and a safe built into the wall. When he fed in the digital combination to his safe, the door swung open and revealed five shelves packed with private and confidential papers, insurance policies and ten thousand pounds in cash, which he kept for serious emergencies. It also had a typewritten sheet giving the location of various private and confidential files in his cabinets.

He located the file holding his copies of accounts over the past six years and he flicked through it. They all bore his signature and he recalled from time to time signing at least half a dozen copies at Chris's request for sending on to their accountants or bankers. He took out the last set of accounts and his eye went to the bottom line on page four, which showed a gross profit which had increased steadily each year to over £600,000 at the end of last year. The capital accounts on page five showed Matt's balance of £987,000 and Chris's of £1,000,200. He recalled having taken out a little more than Chris in drawings last year. Relieved, he knew then that the bank had definitely made a mistake, and he replaced the file. He was confident that he and Chris had a good financial buffer for any future business disasters that may occur and knew that their taxes had been paid by the partnership from cash-flow as and when needed. On this year's projected profits, they would both have a tax bill of about £150,000, but their reserves more than covered this.

They had been lucky over the past three years. However, this luck had been made up of good fortune, good management, foresight and a great deal of hard work and talent. They had weathered the recession well, mainly through their spread of work both in the UK and abroad. This allowed a diversification of human resources, keeping their staff fully employed and on a multitude of varied projects. They had extended their fields of expertise and had gained a particularly good reputation for being experts in sports stadia design. They had successfully designed schemes for 37 of the 92 English Football League clubs, leading to improved safety of the grounds after the Taylor Report that followed the Bradford and Hillsborough disasters. As the funding for these projects was through the government financed Football Trust, their fees were secure and always paid on time and in full.

Matt was now so busy on architecture that he was grateful that Chris had taken on the office management role, but regular interruptions for Matt to sign papers was almost a pain. He was sure that it was unintentional, but documents requiring his urgent signature were always thrust under his nose by Chris at times when he was right in the middle of an important task or nearing the resolution of a difficult design problem. Chris was always apologetic – 'Sorry about this, if you could just cast your eyes over this and sign all six copies whilst I wait,' he would say, before hurrying off to the bank, lawyer or accountant. Matt would quickly read the document and sign.

Matt then remembered the previous year's accounts and balance sheet being brought in by Chris during an important team meeting to resolve a design problem at one of the London Football clubs' grounds for a new Stand. He had read the proffered copy which seemed in order. His capital account showed the appropriate increase and profit was over £600,000 so he signed all six copies on the last sheet. Chris countersigned one copy for Matt and took the others off to his meeting, as usual with sincere apologies for the interruption.

4

Matt decided to ask Chris to deal with the bank when he came into the office later that morning to sort out this obvious mistake. By now, it was half past seven in the morning and his coffee had brewed in his small private kitchen that doubled up as a bar. He took his first coffee of the day at his desk while he reviewed the decisions taken at the previous day's meeting and checked his diary for the new day's appointments. A team meeting scheduled for 9 o'clock would need to be condensed into two hours. He had a meeting with a client at 12 o'clock noon in Maidstone and it would take three quarters of an hour to drive there. Anticipating lunch afterwards, he had kept the afternoon free of meetings. Although he had already dictated two full sides of a tape for his secretary, he knew that she would be free of urgent work by mid-morning, and he settled down to dictate notes of yesterday's meetings and several letters dealing with day-to-day matters on those contracts that he was still handling personally.

He found it increasingly difficult to find the time to take any one project from its inception to completion entirely on his own, and he glanced across the room to his drawing-board. He knew he had nearly resolved the planning and design problems for a major marina and villa complex on the island of Menorca in the Balearic Islands.

Although he was an early-to-bed, early-to-rise individual, inspiration would often come to him in the middle of the night and he would need to slip out of bed, go to his study and quickly sketch the idea before it had been lost in the depths of his subconscious. It was for this reason that he dispensed with any drawing tools at home apart from a sketch pad. He knew that he would be awake and working all night if facilities were there. This would be to the detriment of his plans for the following day, and probably his marriage as well. He had worked those silly hours for 20 years, and he now accepted that he didn't have the energy nor indeed the desire to carry on at that pace.

By the time Cathy poked her head around his door after a discreet knock, it was a quarter to nine and he had a further two full tapes for her.

At 23, Cathy Steiner was a remarkably mature young woman, extremely efficient and willing to work hard. She took pride in her appearance and presentation which was reflected in her approach to her job. She hated criticism and had learned that the only way to avoid it was to be above it. Swedish by birth and still having a recognizable accent, the attractiveness of her voice and first-class telephone manner provided just the front that Matt needed.

Strangely, although there was an obvious mutual attraction, neither of them had made any romantic moves towards the other in the three years that she had worked for him. Possibly they both realized the importance of their business relationship, and neither wished to put this at risk. After three years, they had formed a solid team and Matt relied on her to take some of the administrative load from his shoulders and to insulate him from persistent nuisances on the telephone or from the office. She would often resolve staff problems without his even having heard about them.

'Cathy, please can you ask Group Four to come up to the meeting room in five minutes, and bring the sketches I left on Tim's board yesterday morning.'

Matt picked up his papers and left for the meeting room across the lobby. He dropped a scribbled note on Chris's secretary's desk. 'Chris, can we have a chat about banks!' as he passed. Wendy's pale smile told him she was having personal problems again.

Wendy had been with Chris as his secretary for over two years. She had replaced his previous secretary of eight years standing. It was a difficult act to follow and he worked her very hard which she didn't mind, but she found it almost impossible to cope with their on-off love affair. Chris was very demanding when things were not going well with his wife at home, but being completely insensitive to Wendy's feelings, he felt no need to let her down gently when he had occasional periods of tiredness with her. She was a divorcee, and although her ex-husband had been forced to leave the matrimonial home to her, she found the mortgage an increasing drain on her resources. When she had cried on Chris's shoulder after their first bout of love-making, he had quite wrongly thought that this was through a sense of remorse.

Wendy told him of her problems, and in a fit of unusual generosity and possibly as a result of his freshly sated body, he promised to speak to Matt about a £10,000 interest free loan from the practice to be repaid over a period of years. He assured her that he would not mention their involvement, and would say it was just because she was his secretary that he wanted to help her out.

However, when he spoke to Matt about the loan, he boasted of his conquest thereby demonstrating a considerable lack of maturity and sensitivity. He was surprised at Matt's suggestion that he should show a little more compassion. Someone had once expressed their opinion of Chris's degree of sensititivity, saying to him in Matt's company, 'You have as much compassion as a mule!'.

When they were discussing Wendy, Matt reminded him of that later, adding 'He maligned the mule – I think he meant that you are as considerate as a dead donkey's bollocks! Yes, of course we can lend her the money but for God's sake, don't tell her I know about your affair. At least leave her with some dignity.'

Matt thought that secretly, Wendy knew that he knew and she always thought of him as the 'human' side of the partnership. Her feeling of being emotionally trapped for the second time in her life seemed to grow with each day.

The team meeting was unusually lively. A heated discussion about the balance between the time taken to achieve the refinement of the design and the money and man hours available resulted in Matt reminding the team that they seemed to need three times as long to do a job as he would. He underlined again that targets of fee accounting must be met if they were to stay profitable, and that of all the professional building consultancy firms that he knew, MDB was the only one that had expanded over the past two years. Many of their competitors had failed due to the recession, and in his mail each day he said he had at least four applicants for jobs.

When he left the meeting with a suitably phrased pep talk he went directly to Chris's office. Chris was not in yet and Wendy was not expecting him for another half an hour or so. Chris was very casual these days about his office hours and it was a source of a slight irritation to Matt that he neither accounted for his time nor informed Wendy of his movements which would pose a problem if he was needed in an emergency. On impulse, Matt decided to pre-empt the problem with the bank.

'Wendy, I need to look at the certified accounts for the past three years. Have you got the keys to Chris's confidential files cupboard?'

'I am sorry, Matt. Chris is particular that I don't let anyone into that cupboard. Even you!'

Matt's eyes took on a cold staring look that he held for a full five seconds. Cathy was not at her desk, so what he had to say would be private between them.

'Wendy, I'm not getting at you. You have a job to do, and as Chris's personal assistant and secretary you must of course protect him and act on his instructions to the full, but I'm not just anybody. I am 50 per cent owner in this business and Chris's equal partner. So if I ask you, or anybody else for that matter, to do anything within reason for me, I expect immediate and unquestioning response. Your loyalty to Chris is laudable but it doesn't stop there. I also expect and even demand loyalty from all of the staff, and even more so from the likes of Cathy and you. So as long as I am not asking you to do anything that would harm Chris, please please, accede to my wishes and do as you are told. Please give me the keys.'

He had judged his tirade to perfection and stopped his attack just before she burst into tears.

'Yes Matt. Of course,' she said, and reaching into her desk she drew out her handbag and handed him a bunch of six small keys.

Matt went directly to Chris's office and opened the rosewood panelled concealed door at the rear of Chris's desk. This exposed a wall safe similar to his and a bank of filing cabinets marked STRICTLY PRIVATE, and Matt wondered why. Each cabinet was marked with a small coloured tag stuck to the lock plate. Matt scanned down the labels: Staff Files, Banking, Property, Florida, Clients' Personal Details, and so on. Then he found 'Accounts and Balance Sheets' in the third cabinet. Matching the blue colour of the tag on the key to that of the lock, he slid open the drawer and removed the file. Chris was meticulously tidy in the management of his office and Matt knew that the file would hold in chronological order the accounts and balance sheets for the past six years.

The last year had been filed on the top of the stack and they had all been neatly wire-bound by the accountants. Looking at the year ended 1994 which was the previous year, Matt at once saw his signature with Chris's below it. He then went to the bottom line on page five. He frowned when he saw his capital account at £1,080 and Chris's at £7,200. This was crazy! The previous year showed similarly low amounts and he again checked his signature. He moved to the small A4 copier in the corner of the room, and took a copy of the last three pages of each of the last six years, each bearing both partners' signatures and the accountants' certification. He then carefully replaced the sets of accounts in the files and closed the drawer.

As he was just about to lock the cabinet, his eye caught the label on the drawer below. It was marked 'Pink copies of Accounts'. They had a system within the practice of producing an extra copy of every letter written in the office on pink paper and put on a Day File. These were circulated on a weekly basis to the partners to give them an overview of what was happening within the various groups. 'Pink copies of Accounts' however was most strange.

Matt turned back to the cabinet and opened the drawer, removing the file. There were two pages from each set of Accounts, and although they were on white paper they had been marked with a pink high-lighter pen in the top right-hand corner. On page five, the figures on their capital accounts were shown as the healthy total that he knew it should be. None of the pages had been signed.

Matt replaced the file and locked up. As he was walking back to the lobby he picked up his hand-written note to Chris that was on his desk. This was on the top of the pile of the day's mail for Chris's attention which had already been opened and date stamped, and which was ready for distribution to the other partners and associates. There was also a pile of private and confidential and personal letters that remained unopened. Matt leafed through these until he found one from the bank, knowing from the format that it would hold their weekly statement. He would check their current situation for himself. He made a note of the numbers stamped on the back of the six keys and slipped the letter into his pocket and returned the keys to Wendy.

'I'm very sorry that I lost my rag. You are probably correct and should keep those keys safe from everyone, including me. I certainly won't embarrass you by asking for them again and I won't mention to Chris that you were bullied by me into passing them over. In fact, if I am asked, I'll say that you refused point blank to give them to me on his instructions.' He squeezed her hand gently and knew that the matter would never be mentioned to Chris.

Matt went back to his own office and asked Cathy to ask Tim to take on his lunch appointment if possible, and to hold all calls and make sure there were strictly no interruptions for the next few hours.

He went into his office, locked the door and took the phone off the hook. This was a fairly regular procedure when he was in the middle of a particularly complicated design problem requiring his total concentration. It was the only way that Matt could keep 200 staff and several demanding clients at bay for a few hours.

He firstly went to his own private and confidential files and compared his copy of the accounts over the past six years with those taken from Chris's office. They were identical apart from pages four and five which dealt with the capital accounts. A note had been appended to Chris's certified copies. This indicated that a transfer from Matt to Chris of the bulk of his share of profit had been agreed and that the adjusted balance in the first year showed Matt with £828 and Chris with £137,338. A further entry showed that payment had been made to Chris of £136,000. Matt's signature confirmed agreement to these money movements. Matt felt quite cold. Each subsequent year showed a similar transaction, and his mental arithmetic calculated that a total of about £900,000 had been transferred from him to Chris, and that payments of about £1,750,000 in all had been made to Chris from the practice accounts.

Without doubt, the signature was his with the distinctive capital D in the middle obscuring half of the names on either side, but how had it been done? His mind again went back to the times when he had signed documents at Chris's request and once more recalled that they were always wanted urgently. However, he had always read, even if somewhat quickly, the document before signing. He then realized what had happened. He had read the top copies, signed them, and then signed the remaining copies without reading them fully. The accounts generally ran to seven pages and as only two were different, he had not picked up the con trick that had obviously been played on him.

His emotions ran at once to anger, deep disappointment and an unidentifiable feeling in the pit of his stomach. The feeling was so strong that he felt the need to rush to his private shower room and splash cold water on his face before he threw up. How could Chris do this? They had not only been partners but Matt thought they had been friends as well. Their families met every few months at dinner parties, and Matt and Chris played golf together on a regular basis. They were even booked to go to Florida in a few weeks' time for their annual golfing holiday with two of their friends.

With some difficulty Matt managed to control his anger and thought back to the Sailon experience. He still had some regrets over the injuries suffered by Sailon, and that experience would stay with him until the day he died. However, it had served to help him control his emotions. Consequently, the only other time in his career that he had been purposely tricked by a client, he had taken an entirely different approach to effect retribution.

*

He had worked for a developer, Charles Randall in his very early days while he was still with the Council, and had built up a good relationship with him over a period of several years. However, when Randall took on an accountant partner who later proved to be dishonest, things slowly changed and he lost almost everything on a phoney deal setting up a ski resort in France.

At the same time, Randall's business had moved into a catering and leisure activity, opening several free house pubs and clubs throughout the south of England. Matt did a great deal of work on these projects but his fees were never paid in full. Randall was robbing Peter to pay Paul in order to balance his books. Matt would never understand Randall's stupidity, especially when he personally knew so much of Randall's business. After all, they had virtually lived in each other's pockets for eight years and Randall had boastfully confided to Matt about some of his shady business deals. Over the last year or so of their relationship, Matt had kept careful notes of all of their meetings. He had no desire to be connected with anything even slightly illegal and felt that he might, at some time in the future, need tangible evidence of his innocence. He always ensured in his dealings with Randall that his activities were confined to the architectural side of the projects. On two occasions, he even secretly took tape recordings of the meetings that he had anticipated could be difficult.

Randall had increasingly ignored Matt's fee accounts and was obviously finding him a continuing irritation. Having seen Randall's methods of dealing with sub-contractors and contractors in the past, Matt took out the insurance of recording the conversations, knowing that Randall would almost certainly make some comment about his irregular activities. Eventually, Matt stopped work for Randall until his outstanding fees were paid. Finally, he resorted to seeking legal advice.

Randall laughed when he heard of this, which strengthened Matt's resolve to get even. He would not choose physical violence as before; instead he would use the courts to fight his case.

It was with a great deal of pleasure when he later heard that the Fraud Squad were investigating Randall's operations anyway, so he contacted the officer in charge and made his considerable knowledge available to him. Although Randall tried to hide behind bankruptcy, eventually he was arrested and charged. Matt's evidence, which ran to 47 pages in the form of his statement, had proved crucial in Randall's conviction. His fraudulent activities led to his imprisonment for four years.

*

Matt sat at his desk thinking back over the two times that he had been conned. The first crook was now in a wheelchair and the second in prison. Although he felt some satisfaction that justice had been done, in neither case had he recovered the money out of which he had been swindled. Would he get his money back this time? It had obviously been salted away somewhere safe and Matt grew determined that he would not get turned over for a third time; he would recover what was rightfully his and exact retribution in his own way. The damage that the publicity would do to the practice would be intolerable if he pursued Chris through the courts.

Matt went to his bar and took from the top shelf an unusually shaped bottle of amber liquid. He had bought himself the bottle of Hennessey XO brandy two years ago for 130 pounds. It was a very expensive indulgence and he kept it only for very special occasions or dispensed it to privileged guests. He poured a sizeable measure into a large balloon glass and with his freshly made jug of coffee at his elbow he sat and started to plan.

Two hours later he slowly sat forward and eased the muscles around his neck. A smile touched the corners of his mouth and he knew that the scheme he had in mind could work. He carefully poured the untouched brandy back into the bottle and returned it to its place on the top shelf. The coffee was cold. He tipped it away in the sink and set up a new jug on the machine to brew.

Matt telephoned the bank in Fenchurch Street and asked to speak to the records clerk. As one of their larger customers, MDB were well known to most of the staff of the bank and when Matt explained that one of his girls had unintentionally dropped their bank statement into the shredder, the clerk immediately agreed to send another copy to them.

Matt took the envelope that he had picked up from Chris's desk and examined the seal. Unlike most modern envelopes, this was stuck down with gum making it almost impossible to open without tearing. He plugged in the kettle at his kitchen bar, and when the steam was sufficiently fierce he ran the flap over it until the glue was softened enough to allow him to carefully slide a pencil in the corner and turn it as it ran under the flap, so he was able to open it without tearing the paper. He removed the statement which showed £528,487.48 overdrawn, after payment of the monthly standing orders and direct debits.

Ignoring his rising anger once more, Matt put the statement into his pocket and carefully smoothed down the envelope on his blotter. When it was quite dry, Matt placed the original letter from the bank manager into the envelope, refolding it so that the address showed at the window with the private and confidential stamp fully on view. He then carefully resealed the flap with paper gum and dropped the enveloped into his jacket pocket.

Matt replaced his phone on the handset and unlocked the door. He told Cathy that he was now back in action and asked her to bring in his list of calls. There was nothing urgent apart from a call from Marie and he phoned her back immediately. There was no reply; she had obviously gone out.

Crossing the lobby, Matt signalled to Wendy that he was going into Chris's office. She was speaking on the telephone to what appeared to be a difficult client so she just waved to him as he passed. He pretended not to understand her signs that Chris was not in his office and entered, closing the door quietly behind him. Chris had been in for a short while but he had gone out again. Matt glanced at his diary and saw that Chris had an appointment in London at 12.30 p.m. and would not return until later in the day.

The second delivery of post was on Chris's desk and alongside the opened and date-stamped mail, a further small pile of private and confidential envelopes were there intact just as before. Matt slipped the bank letter in the middle and quietly left the office.

Wendy was still on the phone and pulled a face as Matt smiled at her. The first part of his plan had been executed and he felt strangely quiet, but he knew that if he was to take this through to its conclusion, he would need a strong nerve and considerable resolve as well as help and support from Marie.

5

Marie stretched languidly and enjoyed the luxury of lying in bed with the warmth of the sun streaming through the window directly onto her face. Rambo would be happy to lie there all day. She gave him a gentle shove to allow her to lift the covers. She carefully swung her legs over the side of the bed and sat up slowly. It was pure luxury not to feel sick in the morning. She marvelled at the miracle growing slowly inside her. She was very conscious of the slight bump appearing and was not looking forward to those last few months, hating the thought of developing a waddle like some of the girls at the ante-natal clinic who were more advanced in their pregnancy.

She really did look quite radiant and was one of those lucky women who blossomed with pregnancy. She had never smoked nor had she drunk very much alcohol, and she had always kept extremely fit. Even now she played netball competitively and had at last agreed, after some cajoling by Matt, to make the game she had arranged this coming weekend the last until after the baby was born. She couldn't imagine herself as a 'mum', and although she was looking forward to the event, she was determined that she would not sit at home all day and that she would engage in some satisfying pastime as soon as she was able. This was not to say that she would shirk her motherly duties, but she expected, having been promised help from Matt, that she would not be tied to the house 24 hours a day.

At the moment she was enjoying a life of near luxury being able to relax at home. So far, the summer had been glorious, and as she was a sun-worshipper, she had already turned a beautiful golden tan all over, which enhanced her near blonde hair and startling grey eyes. It was still almost like being on holiday. She had left work three weeks ago and felt a small pain as she remembered that that facet of her life was over. She had cried all the way home on the train and for the rest of the evening after her last day. Although Matt had been sympathetic and comforting, she knew he couldn't fully understand, for it was not only her job she was leaving but it also meant that she would no longer see Stephen Murray every day.

Their relationship had taken some time to foster. He had not been the easiest man in the world to work with and having personal problems at home, he had often been moody and morose, particularly on a Friday afternoon when he knew he would be unable to lose himself in his work for the next two days.

It was only after they had shared an office for six months that they talked about anything other than work. Marie's natural friendliness and compassion had led her to offer her company for lunch whenever he wanted a good listener. Thereafter, they lunched about once a week, then twice and after a further six months or so, they ate together all the time. She was astounded that someone for whom she had had so little time initially she now thought of as very attractive, and at the same time dangerously available.

During those months of discovering each other, Stephen introduced Marie to poetry, classical music and other 'high brow' entertainment that had hitherto been slightly beyond her understanding. For his sake, she tried hard to appreciate the virtues of the likes of Wagner, Bach, Verdi and Shakespeare, and they often went to lunch-time concerts at The Temple Gardens off the Embankment.

For some reason she had never mentioned Stephen Murray to Matt in the early days, probably because he was just not important. She kept him secret later on for more obvious and understandable reasons.

As time went on, it was obvious to everyone in the office that they were having a love affair, but no one knew if it was active or passive. Stephen was being patient, understanding the turmoil he had created in Marie's life. Marie had confessed her feelings to him but had claimed that any love she felt for him in no way diminished her love for Matt. He could not believe that this was possible but he didn't argue.

When she looked back, Marie could not believe their mutual self-control while they had hourly contact. It could have been the denial of the ultimate act had enhanced the electricity there was between them when their fingers touched while passing a file or a piece of paper.

Their boss was obviously aware of the predicament but having more important things on his mind, he decided to ignore the situation. Also, it was having no apparent effect on their work. However, when it became necessary for Stephen to go to Glasgow to attend a seminar over a long weekend, he allowed Stephen to take Marie with him.

When she mentioned this trip to Matt, he found it difficult to hide his fears. She was so attractive; they had been married only three years and she was obviously desirable to any man, let alone a fairly young recent divorcee. However, he had been no angel in the past and felt he could not refuse. To have done so would have been a statement of mistrust. He therefore thought long and hard and agreed that she should go. He said he trusted her completely and saw no reason why she could not have a perfectly normal platonic friendship with another man. He hoped that this little speech would serve to prick her conscience if temptation came her way.

*

Marie and Stephen travelled to Glasgow on a day train and held hands all the way. They had left Euston Station at 7.05 a.m. and they were both bubbly and excited about the weekend ahead. She was sure that they would sleep together that night and felt her neck go red just at the thought. However, the further they got from London and the closer to Scotland, the more quiet and pensive she grew. By the time they had arrived at Glasgow Central, Marie's mood had slipped into one of being completely still and Stephen's attempts at jocularity did not even bring a smile to her face. When they left the train, Marie asked Stephen if they could sit and have a cup of coffee in the buffet, and they found a quiet table in the corner. The room was shared only by a large black woman sitting by the door.

'Stephen, I'm so sorry, but this won't work.' Her face was pale and she looked quite ill. Her hands were clenched tightly on her lap to stop them trembling although the waver in her voice exposed the strain which she was feeling. He began to protest but she touched his mouth with her hand, and continued:

'I love you, you know that, but I still love Matt and I also owe a duty to him. He has trusted me to come away with you – maybe he thinks something will or will not happen – I don't know – but he has trusted me. If I betray that trust now, just once, that will be the end of our marriage. I still hold the state of marriage dear and if I end with Matt, it will never have the same meaning ever again. The same would apply if we were together. What would I do then if someone attractive in the future came along – would I have no respect at all for the vows that I would have made? I'm sorry. If it was just a physical thing we could jump into bed together now, but it is far, far more dangerous than that.

'It also means that without sex, our affair would never be complete, so we must finish it now. I'm going to go home on the next train. I'm sure you can make excuses at the seminar for me. I can bear the pain of being loved by two lovely and loving men, but I just could not cope with being hated by one of them and that is what it would lead to. Matt would never, ever forgive me.'

By now her cheeks were wet with tears and he was looking down at the small mound of spilled sugar on the table that he was pushing into different shapes with his fingernail. His face was drawn and his voice strained as he looked up at her.

'Okay Marie, I won't say anything now except that I won't give up. I will always be there if you need me. I won't even express my love for you – you know that already. I had hoped that this weekend would be the start of our life together, not the end. I will only say one more thing – if your marriage relies on a feeling of duty rather than love, it could be fragile – I know, I've been there. I'll go now and I'll see you on Tuesday at the office.'

He rose and walked slowly away. Marie had needed all her self-control to stay seated and not to run after him.

She caught the next train back and arrived home at about 10.30 p.m. She didn't know if Matt believed her story that she had felt unwell on the train but he was delighted to see her and pampered her for the rest of the weekend. He was even more delighted than she knew. He had received a telephone call earlier that day from one of the women who worked in her office informing him that something was going on between Marie and Stephen. He had told her quietly and simply to 'fuck off' and put down the phone.

*

Marie slowly showered and dressed and was about to sit down with her morning toast and coffee to read the newspaper when the telephone rang. Her heart jumped slightly as she recognized Stephen Murray's voice. He had just phoned to see how she was coping with her life of leisure and to tell her he missed her. Although they were still very close, the past eighteen months had been something of a turmoil but nevertheless they had coped well. It had only been on her last day that she realized how her life would change completely now with her leaving work and not being able to see him on a regular daily basis.

Stephen had divorced 18 months ago and was living in a small flat in Croydon. She had resisted the offers to visit fearing that her strength of character and resolve might crumble if tested for a second time. They had chatted for about ten minutes, and afterwards she felt strangely guilty so she phoned Matt at the office. Cathy told her that he was locked away and wondered if he could call her back when he was free.

Marie finished her light breakfast and took the six vitamin and iron pills that she had been told were good for her. She was going to take Rambo for a long walk, and then she had the month's household shopping planned for the afternoon. By the time she returned home at half past four, she was surprised to find Matt's car in the driveway.

6

Having called the bank, Matt looked up the phone number of the local Margolis filing cabinet supplier. When he got through, he explained that his house, car and office keys had been stolen over the weekend and if he gave them the key numbers to his filing cabinets could they provide spares. The supplier said that of course they could and after checking he found that in fact they had them in stock. Matt suggested that he could pick them up in half an hour or so on his way home. He also wondered about the wall safe in Chris's office, and although he would soon have access to the papers in the filing cabinets, he was sure that the safe would hold further secrets.

Chris was a creature of habit who had always been rather transparent to Matt, particularly when he was doing something slightly devious. He recalled that the code on their burglar alarm was 16 03 59, which had been chosen because it was Matt's birthdate. On impulse, he went back into Chris's office, telling Wendy he was leaving a note as he passed, and went directly to Chris's computer set adjacent to his desk. The IBM held all manner of financial and management information, and because of this it was locked behind a personal code to access the information. Matt switched on and waited for it to invite commands. He glanced out of the window just at that moment while waiting for the machine to warm up and saw Chris's Aston Martin pulling into the car park. Matt followed the commands given by the computer until the machine requested the entry code. He keyed in Chris's birthdate of 07-11-55. Bingo! The screen came alive: 'Good morning Christopher, we are ready for work'.

Matt speedily went through the exit procedure, and had just parked the heads when Chris walked through the door. Matt was standing over his desk scribbling a note.

'Oh hi, Chris! You saved me the trouble – I was just leaving one of my little notes to say I'd see you tomorrow morning – I'm off to see a client at Sevenoaks.' He screwed up the piece of paper that only had the words 'Dear Chris' on it and lobbed it accurately into the bin.

'I'll be here until 10 o'clock tonight,' said Chris, 'so I won't see you very early in the morning.'

Surprised at the ease with which he had concealed his growing hatred and how simple it had been to lie, Matt left the office. He would check the safe combination tomorrow hoping that Chris had used the same easily remembered code as for his computer.

Matt diverted to Tonbridge on his way home and picked up the six spare filing cabinet keys. He sat in the car and stuck the coloured tags that he had previously noted to the appropriate numbers. When he arrived home it was still warm and sunny, and he was slightly surprised that Marie's car was not in the garage. He parked in front of the house and was greeted by Rambo who leapt into his arms as he opened the front door. Going straight through to the rear terrace he opened the patio doors wide and stepped out. The pool looked inviting.

He hung his jacket on the back of a chair and went into the small changing room next to the kitchen and removed all of his clothes. After taking a quick shower, he stepped quite naked straight out on to the paving and dived into the pool. He swam two full lengths under water and then he surfaced and swam a further four with a powerful crawl. He had always been at home in the water and was a fully certified scuba diver. He was still trying to persuade Marie to join him in this interest but they would have to wait now until after the baby was born.

He climbed out and taking a fresh towel from the pile in the changing room, he towelled his hair dry and gave his firm body a good rub down. He had just put on his bathrobe to return to the terrace when Rambo announced Marie's arrival home. He went out to the car and hopping on the sharp stones of the driveway, he carried 15 bags of food and groceries from the boot back into the house.

'You're home early,' she smiled and gave him a warm kiss full on the mouth. He wrapped his arms around her.

'I couldn't stay away – and I've nothing on under this robe!'

'Well, I've very little under this dress,' she said with an impish grin, and they walked hand in hand back through to the poolside.

They had been most careful in setting out the garden so that the pool and terrace were fully screened while being completely in the sun all day to allow sun bathing and swimming *au naturel*. The added benefit of making love in the open air on a sunny summer's day had not been fully appreciated until the last few months. The spontaneity of it heightened their considerable pleasure. Matt thoughtfully spread the mattress from the swinging couch on the paving to save Marie's back but these days she wanted to be on top. He was again surprised at her energy in lovemaking and she laughed at his concern for her safety and that of the baby.

They both had a gentle swim afterwards and it was while they were relaxing on the loungers sipping an early evening glass of Chablis that he told of Chris's deceit. Her reaction when he explained that they had been fleeced of about a million pounds in transfers to Chris's account, and that Chris had stripped the practice of that reserve, was one of utter and downright fury.

'I knew you should never have been mixed up with that little fart! He's useless and he has just preyed on your abilities! What shall we do? Tell the police?'

Matt had anticipated her anger and allowed her to continue without interruption until it was fully spent. He then told her of his plan.

'Let's look at the facts. Firstly, he isn't stupid, or if he is what does that make me? He is very clever, and indeed very talented. Since our amalgamation we have both done extremely well. Last year alone, we took about 100,000 pounds each in drawings, our taxes have all been paid and we should have a reserve of about two million between us. That's not all down to me. Chris's side has contributed as much.

'His trouble is his greed and I find that inexplicable. He must have known that he would be found out eventually. My signature might well have provided a defence for him in law but it is all a bit fragile. Perhaps he feels that he can now afford the best legal minds to extricate him and that I, having nothing, can't. I can't explain what has gone on in his tiny mind, but he is positively and definitely not going to get away with it.

'As far as that goes, forget about the police. I've been turned over twice in my life by two villains – the first is in a wheelchair and the second is in jail. I got nothing from either and when the second one gets out in a year or so he will live the life of luxury on the proceeds. No, we can't rely on the law and it seems that the legal system of this country is there to protect the guilty. We will have to do it ourselves.

'I do have a plan. I think it is a good one but it will need nerve and resolve on our part and complete trust and secrecy. Eventually, it might well lead to some considerable sacrifice as well. Initially I will do all the work, and in your condition I hope that you can take the strain. I'll tell you my scheme and see what you think. Basically Marie, Christopher Marten is going to murder me.'

By the time he had finished, the sun was sinking low in the sky, and both Matt and Marie were feeling slightly chilly beneath their bathrobes. As they got up to go indoors Marie gave a slight shudder and she knew that it was not entirely due to the drop in temperature.

*

Matt set his alarm for even earlier the next day and it was still dark when he tiptoed downstairs already fully dressed. He smiled to himself when he opened the dining room patio doors, disturbing the birds in the honeysuckle. It was his turn to wake them early today!

He eased the car out of the driveway, and when after a short time he pulled into the car park at the office it was still only four o'clock. He used his key card to open the barrier, the first security shift not being expected for another hour. He then let himself into the building, and after cancelling the burglar alarm, he relocked the front doors, leaving his key in the lock so that it could not be opened from the outside. He took the lift to the seventh floor and going straight to his office he opened the vertical blinds wide and turned all the lights on. He then pulled a pair of tightly fitting white cotton gloves from his pocket and put them on.

Next, he went across the lobby to Chris's room. He wedged the door open and closed the blinds in their fully shut position. He did not want anyone outside to know that he was in Chris's office. Using a small but powerful pen-light, he went immediately to the cupboard, and switched on the photocopier and the IBM as he passed. The slight glow from the screen and the digital displays would not penetrate the sun blinds. Opening at a touch, the doors to the filing cabinets compartment swung back silently on their hinges. Matt did not need his light for the combination on the safe which was glowing green. It was the same model as his, needing a six digit code. Taking a deep breath, he punched in Chris's birth date 07 11 55. The top panel lit up with its distorted computer script: 'wrong code – try again'.

This model of the safe allowed only three attempts before lighting up 'tamper', and he could not afford for there to be any enquiries as to who had tried to open Chris's safe. Matt was sure that Chris would use these figures and tried to get inside his mind for a possible variation. He tried again, pressing 'reset', and then reversed the figures to 55 11 07. The same 'wrong code try again' lit up.

Matt had only one more chance. Could it be a complete number reversal of 70 11 55? It then came to Matt in a flash of inspiration. Just at the time that they had moved in, Chris had remarked on the American system of dating things by preceding the day on the date with the month. This would give a code of 11 07 55. But what if he was wrong? He had the answer – he would go to his safe, punch in the wrong code three times and when 'tamper' lit up he would leave the office with both his and Chris's doors wide open. At least then the finger would be pointed away from him with an attempted petty theft having been thwarted by the technology of the safe maker. He punched in

11 07 55. The digital display panel changed to 'safe open', and the door swung gently towards him. He breathed out slowly, realizing that he had been unconsciously holding his breath.

The safe was the same size as Matt's and it held a number of documents, mainly brown A4 envelopes with white labels on the front printed in Chris's immaculate writing. Taking careful note of their position in the safe, Matt removed them one by one and lined them up on Chris's desk in that same order. He glanced at his watch which showed 4.15 a.m. He would have liked to switch on the desk lamp but could not take the chance. Holding his pen-light in his teeth he proceeded.

The first three envelopes were of no interest to him, holding details of pensions and life assurances. The fourth, labelled 'Fun' surprised him. It contained polaroid photographs of Wendy, quite naked, in crude and compromising positions and then prints of Chris in 'Mr Muscle' poses. Further copies that had been taken on a time delay switch showed them both together. The photographs were hard porn, and Matt was surprised at the stupidity of Chris keeping or even taking such photographs.

He returned them to their envelope in the same order and turned to the fifth envelope. This looked more interesting. It was entitled 'Dollar Account – First Alliance'. He carefully removed the contents and spread them on the desk. There were a number of bank balance sheets showing deposits and withdrawals in a numbered account at the First Alliance National Bank, Fort Street, George Town, Grand Cayman BWI. It bore the name of Christopher David Marten, followed by a 12 digit account number. The address in Petts Wood, Kent, was unknown to Matt. The account had been opened in May 1989 with a deposit of £136,000 sterling converted to $US231,200. There were mainly deposits, but a few withdrawals had been made over the next five years. The last deposit had been in June 1994, about six weeks ago. It was of $US850,000. The total credit balance was shown in both figures and script, and Matt slumped back in the chair when he read $3,867,502. A note advised that this was inclusive of interest.

Matt carefully took a photocopy of each page. There were only fifteen in all. He had returned the statements to their envelope and was about to look at number six when he jumped as he heard the shrill call of his telephone in his office. He left the papers where they were and strode quickly across the hall. 'Hello,' he said, slightly breathlessly.

'Oh hello, Mr Matt. George here – saw your light on and was just checking that all is okay. I couldn't get in the front door, did you know that you had left your keys there?'

'Fine. Thank you, George. I am just getting a few things sorted out before the rush starts. I couldn't sleep last night so I came in extra early. Thanks for your help. Yes, I did leave my keys in the front door – I thought it was safer until security arrived. I'll collect them in a few minutes.'

George made a note in his security log of the time and the conversation. Matt went back to Chris's office and as it was now 4.55 a.m. he decided that he could take only a further 15 minutes.

As he entered Chris's office, he realised that it was now light enough outside, so he angled the blinds to let in some daylight. Putting his pen-light in his pocket, he picked up envelope number six. This was the only one of them all that had been sealed, and although it was of the modern type which could be easily opened, it bore Chris's signature across the flap. The front bore no label but the words 'Access' in capitals in Chris's script. Matt was sure therefore that the contents were of some importance. It also indicated that they were examined fairly frequently as Chris had not bothered with a label. He would simply replace the envelope each time after opening it and damaging the signature.

Matt needed to look inside this but he would have to wait for a safer time. He replaced the envelopes carefully in the safe and after closing the door he waited for the signal 'closed' followed by 'key in code' to light up. He then closed the cupboard and went to Chris's IBM.

Chris had the only Pinwriter printer in the firm due to his need to produce documents such as cashflow, targets and workloads on A3 format, which the NEC laser printers couldn't manage. His machine was therefore unique in the typeface produced and easily recognizable. Matt could use this to his advantage. He keyed in the code to get him in to the computer and called up the menu and directories to ensure that he would erase nothing, nor give any clue of this visit to the machine. He then started to type, using the internal memorandum template and dating it three weeks earlier.

> From: Chris Marten
> To: Matt Du Bois
> Subject: Insurances
> Date: 14th June 1994
> I have been looking at our partnership agreement and particularly the insurances clause. As you know, if either of us died, the practice would be in severe financial trouble in continuing, due to the loss not only to the practice but also in needing to find enough cash to pay off the estate of the deceased. Can I suggest, therefore, that we each increase our life cover from the existing £500,000 to £3m. each. This would mean that if I die, the practice will get £3m, part of which, say half, would go to Jennifer. The same applies to Marie in the event of your untimely death. Perhaps we can discuss this further.

He typed the reference at the bottom as CDM.

When he had finished and gone through the spell-check function on the computer, he printed the memo on a standard form that he had collected from Wendy's desk, taking the usual copy for Chris's file.

After six years of reading Chris's signature, Matt was fairly sure that he could forge it quite accurately, helped by the fact that Chris always used the unusual purple coloured ink to be found in Pentel ball pens. He knew there was a supply of these in Chris's desk. Taking one, he signed the letter to him 'Chris', and the file copy 'CDM'. He then went back to Chris's filing system and using the green tabbed key he opened the 'Partnership and partnership agreement' filing cabinet. There were several notes and memos between them, and Matt filed the copy of the memo in the correct order. He closed up and locked everything away carefully. He knew that his plan could work only if he was meticulous in his preparation. He then switched off the photocopier and went through the procedure for shutting down the computer and printer, erasing the date, time and content of the memo from the memory. With a final look round he returned to his office, went to his private cupboard and filed the memo from Chris into his partnership agreement file. The first stage was now complete.

It was now a quarter past five, and as George was in position he felt safe in returning to the ground floor to unlock the front door and retrieve his keys.

*

By 9.30 the office was buzzing and Matt was surprised to note that Chris was already at his desk. Chris liked to work with his office door open, except when he had meetings or very personal telephone conversations. Matt was fairly sure that Chris would be on the phone to the bank manager, as his door was closed.

Chris had opened the second post letter from the bank the previous evening on his return from his London meeting. God! he was lucky that Matt hadn't seen the letter first – it was addressed to them both. He spoke to Alan Cardew, the manager at Fenchurch Street.

'Look Alan, sorry about the hiccup, you know we have had a few problems with cashflow. However, I am expecting a big cheque from one of our American clients today. It will be paid into our dollar account in Sevenoaks and I'll arrange for transfer to your branch as soon as possible. It's in the region of 250,000 dollars so it will drop us well below our overdraft limit.'

Having exchanged pleasantries, Chris said goodbye after promising to arrange a lunch together some time next week. Then he went to his safe and dialled in his American birthdate and the door swung open. Leafing through the A4 envelopes, he selected the one marked 'Access' and slit the top open. Inside were four sheets of paper. There followed, in Chris's immaculate handwriting, the complicated security pattern required for Chris to gain access to the numbered bank account in the Cayman Islands and to execute transactions by telephone.

He had a specially dedicated telephone number to dial and when the phone was answered he had to ask for a Mr English. He then had to give his account number followed by the letters CDM, his date of birth in the American version and then

BRITISH, all in that very strict order. Then after the response 'Go ahead, Mr Devon,' he would give his access code. This random eight digit number changed with each transaction. It was printed on his statements sent through to confirm the latest transaction. He had set up this complex procedure with the help of an Irish lawyer when he opened his account five years before, and his statements were sent to his mother's house in Petts Wood. Chris noted all of the information needed on his scratch pad ready for use later.

He would phone the bank at three o'clock that afternoon, knowing that First National opened at ten, and as they were five hours behind GMT, he hoped to be first in the queue. With luck, a telegraphic transfer would get to Sevenoaks before close of business and then an immediate transfer to Fenchurch Street would keep Cardew quiet.

He knew that he had been lucky this time but would need to keep a closer eye on cashflow so that the bank wouldn't rock the boat. Cynically, he thought the 250,000 dollars would merely be a loan to the practice, and he knew that he would get it back at the end of the year.

*

Chris had not started out to rook his partners. He had always been basically honest, which was a trait that had been instilled in him in his early days in Devon and throughout his teens and early twenties. He had always been straight, honest and truthful in all of his dealings. He had never really been a gambler either. The only money that he possessed had always been earned by honest hard work; that is until he went into the London Casino in Duke Street as a guest of a builder one evening six years ago and won £400 at roulette. It had all seemed so easy and during three further visits as a guest he had won twice. He had obviously enjoyed himself immensely, and after asking his builder friend, he was proposed, seconded and accepted as a member of the club.

He soon found he had started to arrange his meetings in London so that he could go into the club for lunch or for an early evening session and each time would visit the tables. He started by taking only £50 in cash but then found that he was changing cheques to buy more chips which inevitably, as he was chasing a win, he lost. As his references were exemplary, being a senior partner in a very successful professional practice with a healthy bank balance, he was allowed to gamble at the club on credit. In six months he lost £18,000 but as he was able to pay this from savings and income, his credit account was left intact. He knew that he was eventually going to win and continued to gamble with fanatical enthusiasm. When his account reached his limit of £50,000 in only one month, he knew that he was in serious trouble. He wondered how he had let this happen and what he could do.

The practice accounts had just been published in draft. The profits for that first year after amalgamation were tremendous. They were approaching £260,000. Both he and Matt had taken £40,000 in withdrawals throughout the year which left about £90,000 in each of their capital accounts. They had agreed that this money would be left in to fund the practice, but Chris needed to settle his gambling debt within three weeks. Otherwise he would be in very serious trouble. He though of talking to Matt and asking for a loan from the practice or even taking his capital out at that stage. However, he had his pride and a very real fear of ridicule. He also knew that Matt would frown on this suggestion and his stupidity. Besides, they needed at least £65,000 tax reserve and some working capital for the practice.

An idea came to him when four sets of building contract documents were signed on one of their Housing Association projects. He noticed that even though each party had read the top copy carefully, they only glanced peremptorily at the remaining copies before signing.

The accounts for the year had been duly prepared by the accountants and six copies were sent through to Chris for signature by the senior partners. Chris extracted the fourth and fifth pages from five sets, and having taken photocopies he added the type-written note to them:

'As agreed between the partners, Christopher David Marten and Matthew Ronald Du Bois, regardless of their shareholding in the

Partnership, the totals of their capital accounts shall be redistributed as 95 per cent to Christopher David Marten and 5 per cent to Matthew Ronald Du Bois. This Agreement has been made to reflect the purchase price paid to Mr William Belton by Christopher David Marten when he purchased the practice.'

The capital account figures were then adjusted accordingly, giving Chris a balance of £197,338 and Matt just £828. A further statement noted that £196,000 should be paid to Chris at once from practice funds. He rebound these two pages into the five copies of the documents, leaving the first unadulterated set on top. He chose his moment carefully. Waiting until Matt was in the middle of what he knew was a boisterous team meeting, Chris entered his room.

'Sorry to interrupt this design work Matt. Can I ask you to join me in my office for half an hour or so – I need some signatures urgently?'

Matt replied as expected. 'Chris, can it wait? We must get this problem solved today to meet deadlines. The last thing we want is a claim by the contractor due to late information.'

'I'm very sorry Matt. I'm just on my way to the bank with the accounts – can you read these now while I wait – then sign them and I'll get out of your hair?'

Matt saw the pile of papers which were wire-bound, and with a grunt he picked up the top copy and read.

'There seems very little difference from the draft we had last week,' he said.

Taking five minutes to read fairly speedily, thinking he already knew the drift, he signed the top copy. He quickly turned to the last page of the remaining sets and he signed them too.

'Thanks, Matt – sorry for the interruption – see you later.'

Chris took a deep breath as he closed the door to Matt's office. Now he was not only able to pay off his gambling debts, but he also had a good buffer against future extravagances. He resolved never to gamble again, but he felt pleased with only a slight prick to his conscience by the ease with which he had fooled Matt. He also realized that he would be unable to rectify his fraud and knew that he would continue to rob Matt of his share. It only remained for him now to ensure that he was not found out and to build up a big enough well-protected reserve to be able to fight any claim that might be brought against him.

He spoke to his Irish lawyer, and with the help of an international accountant he resolved to set up a numbered bank account somewhere. He first thought of Switzerland as being the obvious place, but as he and Matt had talked of buying property in Florida, he finally decided on a bank in Grand Cayman in the West Indies.

*

The next morning, Matt was again in Chris's office at four o'clock and having taken the same precautions as before, he opened the safe and extracted the 'Access' envelope. He noticed that the lettering on the front was in a slightly different position and knew that Chris had used it the previous day, probably as a result of the letter from the bank. Matt had practised Chris's distinctive signature over several hours using the unique purple ink, and he was confident that it would pass scrutiny when he came to sign across the flap of the envelope. Matt slit open the envelope and read with great interest the complicated formula required for Chris to gain access to his money. He took a photocopy of the procedure and made a note that he would need knowledge of the revised code from the confirmation of transaction statement.

He then returned the papers to a new A4 envelope taken from Wendy's desk and carefully wrote 'Access' on the front with Chris's purple Pentel. The result was identical to Chris's. Finally, he sealed the envelope and signed with a flourish Chris's signature. He was very satisfied with the result and returned the envelope to its place in the safe. Matt again scanned through the envelopes in the safe and noticed that one of them at the back was entirely blank and unlabelled. He took it out and emptied the contents onto the desk. Again, there were pornographic polaroid photographs. He was astounded to see that this time there were photographs not of Chris and Wendy, but of the partnership secretary, Adrian Bullock, in equally revealing and compromising poses with a girl who was unknown to Matt. At the back of his mind, Matt had had a niggling doubt as to why Bullock had not picked up Chris's fraud but he now knew the reason.

Matt then scanned the rest of the filing cabinets and contents of the safe, but seeing nothing of further obvious interest he replaced everything carefully, shut down the computer, locked up and returned to his own office. He had retrieved his keys and was busy at his desk before the first security shift arrived. He knew that over the next few weeks, he would need to spend many early hours at the office completing his plans.

The foundations had been laid with the insurance memo, and he had since taken the opportunity to discuss with Chris the possibility of increasing their life cover to £3 million. Chris had agreed and they had already arranged for the necessary medical examinations. Subject to satisfactory results, their proposal forms had been accepted by their insurers. Matt knew that if anyone had cause to investigate the matter, they would discover that the plan to increase their life cover had been at Chris's instigation. Matt also felt a need to provide further evidence that Chris would like to see him 'out of the way' in order that he could benefit from insurance payouts.

*

Not wishing to draw too much attention to any change, Matt had not been at the office very early for a few days. However, after a while he again came to the office at four o'clock and sat down at Chris's computer. He set up the template for internal memos once again and typed a memo from Chris to himself, the heading being 'Nigerian Projects':

> 'Matt, I have been looking at the possibility of obtaining work in the Third World and particularly in Nigeria. I understand that there is a distinct possibility that we can secure contracts for design work with hotels in the Calabar region which is about 400 kilometres from Lagos.
>
> I have spoken to the Nigerian High Commission in London who have agreed that a visit could be of great benefit.
>
> Could you as a matter of some urgency please arrange a flight to Lagos and a five-day stop-over. I understand that hotels are readily available in Lagos, and when you arrive just ask the taxi driver to take you to the nearest and the best. You can arrange

meetings and internal flights once you are there through my contact, who will send you a list of possible work sources. Perhaps we could discuss this in the next few days.'

Once again, Matt signed the memo 'Chris' and initialled the file copy CDM. He filed the copy in Chris's 'Potential Clients' file, and he would ask Cathy to open a Nigeria file for him later.

Matt had recently read articles describing the corruption and considerable personal dangers prevalent in visiting Nigeria, and he knew of the significant precautions that were needed. If he acceded to Chris's request, it would be tantamount to committing suicide which, on the face of it, was just what Chris wanted.

By now, Matt was confident that his plans to incriminate Chris were proceeding nicely, but his patience was being sorely stretched by the need to prepare so carefully, and at all times the need to act quite normally. The foundations had now been laid, and by chance he already had an escape route through his Menorcan project.

*

Some months ago, when he was approached by his client, a Spanish developer, to prepare sketches for a major scheme in Es Grau on the north side of the island of Menorca, Matt of course agreed. He had worked for Señor José Maria Maldoras on another project in Calpe on the mainland of Spain, when he was disappointed to discover that Spanish law insisted upon all schemes being submitted for approval by Spanish architects. Through Señor Maldoras, a Barcelona-based architect was employed to ghost the work, and as a result Matt felt that he had lost control of the detailed design.

In view of this, Matt asked José if he could pull any strings to enable him to carry out the total architectural service on this new scheme. He knew that this Spanish entrepreneur of Greek extraction sailed fairly close to the wind on some occasions, and Matt was sure that he was involved in a number of shady deals. José thought about Matt's request for a few minutes.

'First you must become a Spaniard. Please let me have six passport-size photographs and two million pesetas and I will see what I can do,' he said.

With Chris's knowledge, Matt arranged for the practice to deposit £12,000 in an account in a bank in Barcelona, which converted to 2.34 million pesetas. It was shown in the books as operational expenses for the project in Calpe. Matt made a special trip and withdrew 2 million pesetas in cash, and with only slight misgivings he passed this over to José. In order to slightly change his appearance, Matt had put on a pair of clear glass spectacles for his photographs.

Three weeks later, José asked Matt to join him in his London office and slid a large manilla envelope across the desk to him. Matt carefully opened the flap and removed a number of official looking documents. The first was entitled 'Libro De Familia'. It showed that his formal name was Alfredo Perez Gandia. His legal name was Alfredo Perez and Gandia was his mother's maiden name. The document showed that he was born on 4 March 1955, that he had been married to Neus Rosas Florit on 11 January 1977 and that he had one son, Jonathan, born 12 November 1980. It also showed that both Neus and Jonathan had been killed in a road accident on 11 November 1984. Alfredo Perez had been the sole survivor of the accident, having been badly injured and left completely deranged. However, the family history did not show that this Alfredo Perez had committed suicide in 1985. Matt's photograph was bonded below a laminated plastic film on the bottom right hand corner and had been overstamped by the Spanish Home Office. A number of official stamps and seals appeared alongside each entry.

Additionally, there were three identity cards. Firstly his fiscal ID card, then his national ID card and finally his health ID, together with a Spanish driving licence which was valid until 4 March 2015. Matt signed everything with his new name. These documents would allow Matt to work, live, eat, drink and pass back and forth in the EEC countries as a Spaniard, and being fully fluent in the language, he could carry it off well. They would also allow Matt to obtain a Spanish passport if he wanted to travel outside the EEC under the cover of Señor Perez.

Later, he was amazed at the simplicity with which the passport had been obtained from Madrid, by merely completing the form and sending this together with his ID and extra photos to the local office in Mahon for onward transmission. By 10 May 1994, he was quite literally, though totally illegally, a Spaniard. Señor Maldoras would never reveal the source of these documents, nor indeed did he inform Matt of the circumstances surrounding Señor Perez's death, except to confirm that he would never be confronted by the Perez family.

Matt had been investigating the possibility of entry into the Spanish Institute of Architecture as an associate member in order that he could submit planning applications under his pseudonym, when the matter of Chris's dishonesty took precedence.

7

Exactly two weeks after his discovery of Chris's fraud, Matt felt that his plans were now well laid. However, there was still a little preparation needed.

Leaving the office early one afternoon, Matt told Cathy that he was going to look at a development site in Croydon. Finding a parking meter in Catherine Street by the old town hall, Matt went immediately to a small shop on the upper level of the shopping precinct. Matt had often browsed there in his early days with the council and had once bought a replica of an original long-barrelled Colt 45 six-shooter for a fancy dress party when they were popular, back in 1979.

The shop displayed models of boats, planes, trains and every conceivable make of remote-control car, but Matt's interest lay in other directions. He knew that at the back of the shop there was a fine display of replica guns from the famed Winchester '73 Repeater rifle to very modern semi-automatic machine pistols and all types of hand-guns.

He told the salesman that he was starting a collection and asked to see what was available in automatic pistols. After inspecting many, among them a Beretta 38 and a German Luger, he finally settled on a silver coloured Colt automatic with black bone-handle inserts. Remarking on the realistic appearance of the replica, Matt was warned by the salesman that the model could only be used for display and that it was a criminal offence to use it as a make-believe piece of armoury.

Matt went straight back to the office with his purchase. He was sitting at his desk when Chris came in with a bundle of travel documents related to their forthcoming trip to Florida. He paled visibly when he caught sight of the gun on the corner of Matt's desk.

'What the hell's that for?'

Matt smiled. 'Don't worry, Chris, I'm not going to shoot you! It's only a replica – I'm starting a collection. Here, have a look.'

Chris picked up the Colt and balanced it in his hand. 'Heavy, isn't it? and so much like the real thing – it would have fooled me.'

'Oh yes, most of the mechanism works as well,' said Matt, taking the gun back and operating the loading slide – 'look though, the barrel is solid – if you look down it the front inch or so is hollow but after that it's plugged.'

Chris admired the workmanship and when he questioned the legality, Matt told him of the salesman's warning and said that it would only be displayed in a proper glass case in his study at home.

Later that night, when Matt took Rambo for his walk, he went deep in the woods and as it had served his purpose, he buried the gun where he was sure it would never be found.

*

Both Matt and Chris were very keen golfers. Even with his disability, Chris had developed a successful, if ungainly, effective one-arm swing. His current handicap of 14 was quite respectable, and not many could beat him at match play. Matt had not started playing golf until he was well into his twenties, but having a natural eye for the ball he was soon playing competitively. He was now very keen and played whenever possible. Unfortunately, this was generally only once a week on Saturday mornings. The week long trips to play in Florida, at which Matt and Chris entertained two of their friends, had been most successful over the past couple of years, and now that they had their own house it was even better.

Only six months ago Matt had replaced his clubs with Pings and had bought a new large black and white Ping bag. Later that evening, he took the bag into his workshop at the rear of his garage and carefully removed the stitching that held the bottom of the bag to the leather cylindrical body. He had called into the builders' merchants on the way home and purchased a 12 inch wide roll of the lightest gauge lead that they had.

Using the bottom of the bag as a template, Matt carefully fashioned a shallow dish from the lead with sides 2 inches high, and hammered it into shape while warming it gently over a blow lamp. Matt then fashioned a lid to sit inside the bowl, which when assembled formed a container of about eight inches diameter and two inches deep that fitted snugly into the bottom of the bag. He then drilled a hole through the top and bottom of the lead to correspond to the drainage hole in the plastic bottom of the bag. Next, Matt took a piece of soft foam rubber and placed this in the container. He replaced the bottom of the bag and with some difficulty, riveted the plastic and leather together in eight places and placed a 2" wide band of white tape over the seam. Although he was not too sure of the long term strength of the joint, he knew this would certainly survive the short period of time necessary for his purposes. The bag would always be on a caddie-cart in Florida and should therefore not be under any undue strain.

Matt slid his shallow lead cylinder down the shaft of the bag and pressed it in position with one of his clubs. When he had finished, the bag looked as good as ever, and viewed from above the drain-hole lining through belied any suggestion that the bag was anything other than it should be. He replaced the clubs and as they were now projecting a further two inches from the top of the bag, he adjusted its strap so that it was still balanced when he picked it up. A further piece of the jigsaw in Matt's preparations was now in place.

*

By now, both Matt and Chris had been thoroughly examined by the insurance company doctor and were accepted as good risks. The insurance documentation had been completed in a very short time and the first premium had now been paid.

According to the policy, in the event of the death of either one of the insured, the practice would receive £1 million and the estate of the deceased £2 million. This last sum would release the practice from the need to support the dependants, and their share of the value of the assets of the practice could then be negotiated. This arrangement would allow the firm to continue without the burden of needing to find liquidity immediately, and it would buy some time for the lawyers and accountants to resolve the best and fairest settlement for all concerned. A suitable clause was drafted by the lawyers and added to their partnership agreement.

At the same time that this was being put in place, Matt had a long meeting with his personal accountant who, at Matt's request, introduced him to an agent experienced in setting up off-shore numbered bank accounts. Matt had explained to his accountant that he might be in a position in the near future to have some money transferred from an off-shore company for whom he was working on a one-off basis without it appearing in anyone's books. He admitted to the accountant that he knew he would be breaking all sorts of tax laws, and for this reason he agreed that he would not involve him, nor tell him any of the details.

Acting through the agent, Matt set up a numbered account in the Commercial and Merchant Banking Company in St Helier, Jersey. He initially deposited £5,000 in cash that he had taken from his safe, and he set up a simplified procedure for gaining access to his funds by telephone.

When the administration had been completed, he informed the manager dealing with his account that he anticipated a deposit of a large sum of money within the next month or so. He also arranged for subsequent regular transfers of money to an account in a bank in Mahon registered in the name of Alfredo Perez Gandia.

*

It was now mid-September and over the past few days Matt had noticed a child-like excitement about Chris. This was due to their impending golf trip and Matt played along with it, knowing how much Chris enjoyed these golfing holidays.

On the Friday morning before their Saturday departure. Matt again went into the office very early. The security procedure that he had adopted was now quite familiar to him. He went straight to Chris's safe and removed the 'Access' envelope, and blessed the fact that he had bothered to check when he noted that there had been a further transaction. $250,000 had been withdrawn and a new access code had been printed on the bottom of the statement. Matt took a photocopy and returned the papers to a new envelope, signing and sealing it as before.

Earlier in the week, Marie had taken on a secretarial role. She had booked a return ticket with Cayman Airways from Orlando to Grand Cayman on the following Tuesday in the name of Chris Marten. The tickets would be collected and paid for at the airport. Once she had confirmed the times of the flights, she telephoned the First Alliance National Bank in Grand Cayman. Using the procedures detailed by Matt, Marie made an appointment for 'Mr Devon' with their 'Mr English' at 2.00 p.m. that Tuesday.

Even though there were many things that Matt could just as well have done himself, he thought it was important for Marie to be involved in the plot although for her own protection, he did not tell her the full detail. He therefore asked her to make a shopping trip to London and she travelled up by train from Sevenoaks to Charing Cross.

She first took a taxi to a theatrical costumiers and suppliers in Tottenham Court Road where she purchased a top quality drooping black moustache with the necessary gum fixative. Although it was very expensive, the salesman explained that it was the type used on TV for presentations that needed to be authentic enough to pass the exacting test of camera close-ups. He explained how it should be fitted and the use of the spirit gum.

Marie next took a taxi to Marble Arch and walked a few yards up Edgware Road to a shop providing medical and surgical equipment. With some embarrassment, she asked the assistant if she could purchase syringes and needles for taking blood samples. She was sure that the assistant thought that she wanted them for herself when she offered her a simpler alternative for home pregnancy testing, but Marie refused and bought a standard box of three sterile syringes and needles.

The assistant offered Marie a bottle of anti-coagulant solution, telling her that the blood would clot very quickly without its use. Not wishing to arouse her suspicions, Marie accepted it although she knew Matt would not use it. He had already told her that the blood samples would have to be pure and free from any additives. Marie returned home, pleased with herself and the purchases she had made.

The following Saturday morning, Matt was collected from his home at 9.30 by the courtesy limousine provided along with his 'Upper' Class flight ticket by Virgin Atlantic.

As it was their intention to play golf every day and to socialize during the evenings, Matt packed two suitcases, one for golf clothes and the other with smart casual gear. He also brought a dinner suit in case it was needed. In addition, he had packed a slim document case that held all the information relating to the numbered account in the Grand Cayman bank.

His bag of golf clubs and golf shoes were packed in a large leather flight bag, zipped from bottom to top and secured with a small padlock. He and Marie joked that it looked like a bag for transporting dead bodies.

Marie had always hated goodbyes, even for a very short week's separation, but she was putting on a brave face as Matt's driver swung down the driveway. Cuddling Rambo, she waved as he disappeared round the curve and two large tears rolled down her cheeks. Rambo immediately licked them away, either for the salty taste or from compassion, she did not know which.

*

She felt slightly sore between her thighs and she knew that she had caused Matt some concern that morning with the aggressive and forceful way that she had made love to him. She had woken up early, and starting with the top of his head, she slowly ran her tongue down his cheek, pausing momentarily at his mouth and then on down his chest. By the time she reached his navel he was fully awake and ready for her. She took him in her mouth and her hands worked gently around his buttocks and across his stomach, tickling and relieving the tingling at the same time. He groaned in ecstasy, and reaching down for her he pulled her body lovingly but forcefully up to him. He kissed her long and gently but her vigour overtook his relatively passive manner and she forced her tongue into his mouth. Then, climbing over his body, she forced his full length deep inside her. Matt was both totally excited by the violence of Marie's love-making, and at the same time he was concerned because of her condition.

She laughed out loud at the frown on his forehead and sitting astride him with her legs behind her, she continued to ride him even harder. At last his passion over-rode his concern and he exploded inside her as the waves of frenzy shuddered through his whole body. Marie collapsed on his chest and a wicked smile of satisfaction touched her mouth.

'There, that should last you for a week. Don't you dare to think about using it again until you get home!'

*

Matt's driver called into Sevenoaks to pick up Tony Grace on the way. They arrived at the airport at exactly the same time as Chris and his guest, Tony's brother Richard. They went immediately to the Upper Class check-in desk, and having completed the formalities they went through to the specially reserved lounge to await departure. Tony and Richard were partners in their own professional practice of structural engineers. They had been friends of both Chris and Matt for the past five years. They all played golf together on a regular basis, and Tony and Matt were part of the normal Saturday morning pairings. They all got on well, being of similar ages and in allied professions, and they were able to afford the luxury of this once a year extravagance without too many qualms.

The flight aboard VS047 was fairly uneventful, apart from Chris doing his usual chat-up job on the air hostess. Matt was always slightly embarrassed by this, not because of Chris's fairly juvenile approach but from the girl's obvious (to him but not to Chris) distaste, thinly veiled by her need to be pleasant to the customer. Although it was probably not his place to do so, Matt always found himself quietly apologizing later for Chris's behaviour in such situations.

When they landed at Orlando, they were whisked through immigration very quickly and taken by courtesy bus to pick up their Lindos hire cars. Due to the amount of baggage and golf clubs, they had decided that two reasonably sized cars would be better than one large one or a mini-bus, so they agreed on two Thunderbird convertibles. Chris was quite happy for the others to share the driving, as the cars obviously had no special steering adaptations to cater for his disability.

They drove straight to the house on the Buena Vista Lakes development, and established their priorities by calling into the liquor store on the Ventura Downs Shopping Mall to stock up. Both Chris and Richard were vodka drinkers. Tony drank only Scotch and Matt had always preferred gin. They collected a litre bottle of each spirit together with the mixers, a number of bottles of red and white Californian wine and two cases of Budweiser.

Although it was their intention to eat out most of the time they would eat breakfast at the house, so they stocked up at the supermarket with the necessary provisions. Also, one of their previous visitors had bought a gas barbecue as thanks for the use of the house, and they promised to use it on at least one of the nights. As the 'chef' of the party, Matt chose four 16 ounce rib-eye steaks together with a selection of fresh salad vegetables and four large baking potatoes.

The house had four double bedrooms, two on the ground floor with en-suite bathrooms, and two on the galleried landing at first floor level which shared one shower room. The rest of the ground floor was taken up with a large kitchen/breakfast room, a dining and living room, a family room, a utility and cloakroom and an enormous double garage. The main ground floor rooms opened out on to a sundeck and a heated swimming pool enclosed by a fine-mesh mosquito-proof screen. The view to the rear was in a south-easterly direction across a large man-made lake.

The house was maintained by a local agent who kept everything sparkling. He arranged for a contractor to cut the lawns on a regular basis, and Matt and Chris were delighted with the standard that had been maintained throughout. When they had bought the house, having selected the plot and then the style of house from a brochure, Jennifer and Marie had spent two weeks in Florida choosing furniture, furnishings, fabrics and curtains, and the whole effect was one of subtle good taste.

After a quick night-cap, everyone was tired and ready for bed as it was well into the morning British time. Chris immediately took one of the ground floor bedrooms that he always used. Matt's offer to Richard or Tony for the other was graciously refused and they all retired to their respective rooms.

When the house was being built Matt had arranged for a small wall safe to be installed in the walk-in wardrobe off one of the bedrooms. This was the bedroom in which he was going to sleep. Just before getting into bed he collected all the passports, return flight tickets, various wallets and money belts, and locked them away so they would have no worries about carrying them around and possibly losing them.

8

The next morning, Matt woke before his alarm at six o'clock. He had already swum, showered and dressed before any of the others stirred.

Knowing that Chris had pre-booked their tee-off time for nine o'clock at Lake Nona Golf Club which was 15 minutes away, Matt made two large mugs of coffee for the two brothers and a cup of strong sweet tea knowing this to be Chris's preference. Matt took the drinks to their respective rooms and took their breakfast orders. The result was a majority demand for thickly cut honey-roasted ham straight off the bone with fried eggs, and toast for everyone. By a quarter to nine they were all fed and dressed and ready for the day's golf.

The golf course was in magnificent condition and all four played their best golf for some time, with Chris and Richard just winning at the 18th hole. After a light lunch, they played a further nine holes at which Matt and Tony recovered their morning's losses and they arrived back at the house before seven. They had agreed that rather than play for silly stakes, the losers of each match would each put 100 dollars into the kitty, which would be used for such things as food, green fees and petrol. Chris was appointed kitty master.

After a quick swim to cool off, they showered, changed and were ready to go out to eat by the early evening. The others resisted Chris's suggestion that they go to the all-male club on Orange Blossom Trail, where the girls danced quite naked on your table, with the essential parts of their anatomy at just above head height! Instead, they went for a quiet meal in the Olive

Garden in Kissimmee. As it was their first full day, they were again in bed fairly early.

They had a full day's golf booked the next day at Grand Cypress, and in order to honour their obligations to their previous guest, they decided to have their barbecue that night. Matt had hung the steak in fly-proof mesh bags in the garage through the day to de-frost and ripen.

That evening, Matt donned an apron from the kitchen and served everyone with their pre-dinner drinks. They joked about Matt and Tony having a bottle of booze each whereas Chris and Richard were having to share their vodka. Matt lit the barbecue, and while it was warming he replenished the drinks. Then he went into the kitchen, and ensuring that the others could not see him he poured a tumbler almost full of gin and topped it up with a little tonic. He slipped through to his bedroom and left the drink in his en-suite bathroom. He then tipped the remainder of the bottle of gin down the sink and washed it away, leaving only a touch of alcohol in the bottom. He topped the bottle up to almost full level with cold water and then poured more drinks for everyone.

The barbecue was now ready for cooking and Tony opened two bottles of Napa Valley white wine, nicely chilled, and two bottles of Californian red. The food was a great success and Matt surprised them all by refusing wine with his meal, drinking only several 'gin' and tonics. By the end of the meal Chris, Tony and Richard were decidedly merry having had the best part of a bottle of wine each and two sizeable pre-dinner drinks. Matt seemed to be paralytic; he was slurring his speech, falling around and trying to persuade the others to go skinny-dipping in the lake.

Chris was amazed. He had never seen Matt like this before, and it was only when Matt staggered out from the kitchen with the gin bottle in his hand that they realised that he had drunk almost a litre

'Has anyone seen my glass?'

Matt slurred as he staggered over to his seat, but as he lowered his body on to it his feet continued to walk of their own accord, and before anyone could catch him Matt fell with a huge splash, fully clothed, into the pool. He broke the surface, coughing and spluttering, and surprisingly still clutching his bottle. He managed to grab the side rail, and the others pulled him out onto the deck where he sat, still coughing and staring vacantly at the pool, with his clothes hanging on him like rags.

Tony and Richard lifted him gently to his feet, and with Chris's help they half dragged and half carried him into the house. They took him straight to his bathroom, stripped his clothes off and wrapped him in two large bath towels.

Matt was a pathetic looking figure with his hair stuck to his forehead. He was obviously feeling decidedly sorry for himself, sitting on the closed toilet seat wrapped up like a papoose. He was repeating the same alternating refrain.

'Never again, no never again – can you pass my drink please, Chris?'

Chris caught sight of Matt's glass on the shelf by the hand basin. 'I don't think you really want this, mate,' he said with a smile. He smelt the mixture and quickly turned his nose away in disgust.

'Jesus, what have you been drinking? Taste this Richard, it's almost neat gin – no wonder you feel rough!'

They dried him off and put him to bed, and as Matt was in such a bad state Tony decided to sleep in the other bed in that room, in case he was seriously unwell in the night. Matt lay quietly, letting out the occasional moan or jumble of words to impress on Tony that he really was quite drunk. Only when he was sure that Tony was asleep did Matt allow himself to nod off. He was quite pleased with his acting display, and he hoped that he could carry it on further with equal success in the morning.

*

Although he woke as usual before six o'clock, Matt lay quietly waiting for Tony to stir. As he was still sleeping soundly half an hour later, Matt decided to give a little help so he let out a long, mournful moan. Tony opened one eye and saw Matt sitting on the side of his bed, his head held in both hands, rocking gently from side to side and moaning.

'How are you?' he asked quietly.

Matt looked up and immediately appeared to be sorry that

he had moved so quickly. 'Fucking awful mate. Fucking awful! What happened?'

'You drank a full litre of gin and went for a swim. Don't you remember?'

'I remember nothing, except putting that bloody apron on!'

'I'll get you some coffee – you'll be okay when you get some air in your lungs. We're playing Grand Cypress today.'

'I don't think I'll be playing anywhere. The thought of trying to hit a golf ball in 85° of heat is frightening, to say nothing of bending over a putt or stooping down to pick the ball out of the hole. No, I'm sorry, but I think you'll have to play a three-ball today. Sorry to let you down but I think I'll stay here by the pool with a large glass of Alka Seltzer.'

Tony roused his brother and Chris, and they decided that as Matt was feeling so fragile they would stop for breakfast at Day's just up the road on the way to the golf course. They left at eight o'clock.

As soon as he was alone, Matt quickly showered and dressed in a light tan pair of slacks, a white short-sleeved shirt and a navy blue blazer. He took 1,000 dollars of his own money out of the safe, as well as several travellers' cheques and Chris's passport. He then went to his toilet bag and removed the black false moustache from a silver talcum powder container.

He sat in front of the mirror and applied it carefully in the same way that he had practised several times at home. He combed the sides to curl down, which seemed to improve the realism. He looked in the mirror at his reflection and then at Chris's passport photograph. Yes, he was sure it would pass more than a casual glance; in any case he only wanted to give an impression, to create an image. He was not going to expose himself to close scrutiny, so he thought it would do.

Matt went to his chest of drawers and took out his document case from underneath the shirts. He checked that he had all the papers he needed and also the black left-handed glove. He went to the garage, operated the automatic door opener and drove out. It was just after nine o'clock. As he was very conscious that the local police enforced the speed limit rigidly, Matt drove slowly down Osceola Parkway and turned left onto Highway 441 towards Kissimmee. The booklet entitled 'Kissimmee and St

Cloud' at the house had told him that there was a sporting shop on Vine Street, which he found with no trouble.

Putting on the black glove and folding his left arm across his chest, Matt went in. The place was jam-packed with all manner of gear for coarse and sea fishing, rifles, shotguns, hunting knives, tents and camping equipment. The owner was at the back of the shop, counting small change into a till. He looked up as Matt came in, slowly rolling a damp cigar stub from side to side in his mouth.

'G'day sir. How can I help?'

Matt walked towards him and made a play of needing to put his document case down before proffering his right hand.

'Good morning, I want to buy a small hand gun. We have had a number of muggings and break-ins in the Buena Vista area lately and I want some protection. What do you have?'

'Well, sir, I think you're English. Are you a permanent resident?'

'No, but does that matter?'

'Well sir, I can't sell a firearm to anyone who either is or appears to be under the age of 21, or anyone who isn't a full US resident or anyone who lives out of the state.'

Matt smiled. 'I am over 21! Actually, I own a house here. I pay taxes on that house and I am quite willing for you to register the sale to me. The gun will stay in the house, locked away when I am not there and I can guarantee it will not be used by anyone else.'

'In that case sir, if you are willing to sign a standard registration certificate, I'll let you have one. Do you have ID?'

Matt produced Chris's passport, and with the salesman's assistance he completed a form. He gave Chris's name and the Buena Vista address. The shopkeeper spent the next ten minutes extolling the virtues of various handguns, and eventually Matt settled on a Smith & Wesson 38 Special, Model 63 – 'Accurate and a stopper, but light enough and easy for a woman to handle,' according to the shopkeeper.

The details of the gun, including the code number stamped on the barrel, along with information related to Chris were entered on the registration certificate. Matt signed it Christopher Marten with a flourish.

'That's a nice colour ink, Mr Marten. Most unusual. Now, you can pick up the gun in three days.'

Matt frowned. He hadn't expected this and might find it difficult to get away again in three days' time.

'I've got a little problem, there. I leave the USA tomorrow. Is there any way around this?'

'Well the County needs three days to check you out when I file the application, but quite frankly they rarely do anyway. There are over 15,000 dealers in the States and a further 270,000 licensed as dealers – but really amateurs. If each of them sells only ten guns a week, that's a total of nearly three million applications every seven days – the authorities can't cope. I guess if I date the sale today and collection in three days' time, no one will know if I don't file the application. The other way round it is to sell you the gun, not as a dealer, but as a collector. I'd be selling you part of my collection then, but that would be about 100 dollars more.'

'Can I go for the first option please? If you post-date the collection for, say Saturday, I'll pay the extra 100 dollars anyway for your trouble.' Matt didn't realize what a stroke of luck this would prove to be.

Matt paid cash and taking two boxes of ammunition, he left the shop. He locked the gun and the ammunition in the glove compartment and drove down the Beeline Expressway to Orlando International Airport. It was now ten o'clock.

Parking the car in the short term car park, Matt took his document case and went directly to the Cayman Airways desk on the upper concourse. The West Indian girl at the desk greeted him with a radiant smile, the colour of her skin emphasising the whiteness of her teeth.

'Good morning. My name is Christopher Marten. I believe that you have a ticket for my collection. It was pre-booked for me from England a few weeks ago. I'll pay you by cash.'

'Certainly, Mr Marten,' she said punching his name into her computer. 'Fine, you are booked on CA 006 to Grand Cayman, departing 11.00 arriving 13.15. They will be boarding from Gate B at 10.35. Do you want to confirm your return?'

'Yes please. I believe it's at 16.00.'

She punched a few more buttons. 'That's correct – CA 0011

leaving 16.00 arrives Orlando 18.20. The round trip cost is $275. Do you have any baggage?'

'No thank you, just my briefcase as hand luggage.'

Matt passed over the cash, and taking his tickets he left immediately. By the time he reached the departure gate, the passengers were boarding the 737.

Before he left England, Matt had discovered that although the Cayman Islands are in the British West Indies and a British protectorate, no passport or immigration control exists between the Cayman Islands and the United States once entry formalities on arrival at Orlando have been completed. Despite not needing a passport, he maintained the disguise.

The aircraft was only about one third full and Matt was able to choose a seat at the front by a window. The flight down the east coast of Florida, skirting Miami and out into the Caribbean over Cuba landed ten minutes ahead of schedule.

Having no baggage to collect, Matt was whisked through the entry formalities and emerged into the brilliant sunshine of Grand Cayman. His immediate impression was that the words 'mañana' and 'maybe' were common expressions there. As no one seemed very keen to do business, he strolled over to the taxi rank. The first in the line was an ancient, rusting transit mini-bus that had once been white. A huge black woman was sitting in the driver's seat and Matt was unsure whether she was in fact delivering goods, as surely passengers could not be expected to get in! However, she leaned across and almost sang the question.

'Where you want to go, mon?'

'First Alliance National Bank, Fort Street in George Town please.'

With some trepidation Matt slid open the side door and climbed into the back of the van. The seats were dusty and torn, and the floor was covered with old sandwich wrappers and empty coke tins.

The old woman started the ancient engine at the third attempt and immediately pulled away in third gear with considerable clutch shudder, without a thought of glancing behind. She drove the short distance to Fort Street in under ten minutes, not changing gear once and not even slowing down at 'stop' signs. Meanwhile she ignored all the angry honking from other drivers. Matt was quite literally on the edge of his seat and relieved when she shuddered to a halt outside the bank, stalling the engine as she did so.

'Four dollars US or five Cayman please,' she sang.

He passed over an American five dollar note. 'Keep the change.'

Matt then went into the bank to the sound of further angry hoots as the driver pulled back out into the traffic again.

Matt entered the cool interior of the bank, and introducing himself as 'Mr Devon' to a young white receptionist, he said he had a two o'clock appointment with 'Mr English'. She disappeared through a solid oak doorway and reappeared a few minutes later.

'Please follow me, sir. Mr English will see you right away.'

Matt followed her down a short corridor and into a large windowless office, which had been cleverly lit and decorated to convert a rather austere space into a comfortable and welcoming room.

Mr 'English' was a short, rotund white Jamaican who had been in banking all his life. The attraction of warm weather the whole year round and a more relaxed approach to life had tempted him back to the Caribbean, after a series of appointments in London, Zurich and Lichtenstein. At 55, he was very experienced and somewhat blasé about the huge amounts of money that passed through his hands every day.

'Good afternoon, sir. Please can we just go through a few procedures?'

'Yes of course,' said Matt as he reached into his document case and retrieved a single sheet of handwritten text.

'Account number 3870018472/07. CDM. 11.07.55. British.'

'Go ahead Mr Devon.'

'Access code 13722471.'

Mr English checked off this information on his computer console as Matt read it out. There was also a detailed description of Chris including the deformed left hand.

'That's fine, Mr Marten. Thank you very much. My name is Nigel Johns and I'll be happy to help in any way that I can. What can I do for you today?'

'Well Nigel. I need to move a substantial amount of cash in three weeks' time to my alternative numbered account in Jersey. I'll give you the details.'

Matt reached into his document case, and as he pulled out a notebook, Chris's passport fell out with it and dropped to the floor. Matt had placed his return flight ticket in the page that held the photograph, and as the passport fell to the floor it naturally opened at that page.

Nigel bent and picked it up and could not help but notice the picture and automatically glanced at Matt's face.

'Good likeness,' he said as he passed it back to Matt.

Matt handed over a typewritten sheet to Nigel on which he had set out details of the bank's name and address and the numbered account to which funds were to be transferred.

'I believe my account here stands at somewhere approaching $4,000,000. Can you give me the up-to-date figures?'

'As at opening of business this morning, Mr Marten, the account was $3,651,150. That takes into account the $250,000 drawn last month and overnight interest to date.'

'Right. In three weeks' time, the interest should have boosted that to about $3,670,000, so I would like a telegraphic transfer on 4 October of $3,660,000 to Jersey. The remaining $10,000 or so will keep the account open, and I hope to build on that once my deal is completed.'

'As it is such a large transaction, I will need to just get director level ratification. Can I leave you for a few minutes?'

Nigel left the room and while he was on his own, Matt gently massaged his left hand through the glove which was now getting slightly cramped and uncomfortable.

Nigel tapped on the door of the office next to the room where Matt was seated. The name 'J J Richards, Director', was inscribed on the panel.

'Hi J J. I have a client who wants to move $3.66 million in three weeks to another numbered account in Jersey. Can you ratify it? It all checks out on codes and description, and by chance I have also seen his passport. He is next door.'

J J pulled back the drapes over a dummy window, and switching out the lights in his office he had a full view of Matt through the one-way mirror.

'Give me the code please Nigel.'

Nigel read from his notepad and J J punched into his terminal. After a short search, a replica of the information on Nigel's VDU appeared, and J J read the physical description of Christopher David Marten, including his deformed hand while glancing occasionally at Matt next door.

'Okay, looks fine, but you know how I like to have a little fun Nigel. I'll come back with you. We'll give him one last little test.'

Nigel took J J into his office and introduced Matt.

'Well Mr Marten. This all looks fine. I'll just endorse the transaction.' He tapped his pockets.

'Damn! I left my pens in my office – may I borrow yours?'

Matt passed over his Pentel and J J initialled the transaction printout as 'approved'; then he dated it. Getting up, he shook hands with Matt.

'Nice to meet you – if we can be of any help at any time, speak to Nigel or me direct – your Mr English code will get you in.' He was at the door when he realized that he still had Matt's pen.

'Hey sorry Mr Marten – don't want to steal your pen just because you've taken nearly 4 million dollars away from us!'

J J lobbed the pen accurately to the side of Matt's left arm. Ignoring his instincts, Matt stretched across his body with his right hand to catch it. He fumbled it to the floor and Nigel picked it up and returned it to him.

'Thanks again,' said J J as he left the room, answering Nigel's wink with a hardly discernable nod.

Having agreed the transaction, Matt then suggested to Nigel that it was about time that they changed their procedures.

'Nigel, what I would like to do is to put our transactions on a more formal basis, and as now I have very few occasions when I need money to be transferred urgently, I suggest that everything should in future be done in writing. I will therefore keep the same account number if it suits you, but please will you accept no instructions related to this account unless the following procedure is adopted.

'Firstly, I think that we will reverse the roles and I will write to you as Mr Devon and perhaps you would be kind enough to refer to me as Mr English. I will give you the following permanent access code number – 123987654. This will be followed by another number, which will be the amount in my account as shown on my last statement in reverse. Once you have these two codes, then you can carry out the transaction requested in my letter.

'From time to time, however, I will need to know what is in my account, and I think to simplify matters, we will use the existing telephone system. It must be emphasized that should I telephone you or anyone on my behalf, that the only information that may be imparted by telephone using the existing code, is the amount of money in the account.

'As a further precaution, to protect my privacy it is essential that all documentation related to my account is destroyed, and that only the current balance is maintained on computer.'

Nigel agreed, and having made careful note of the figures and having repeated them to Matt, they shook hands and Matt left.

Matt returned to the sunshine in Fort Street and after the air-conditioning of the interior of the bank, he almost suffered a thermal shock. From what he had seen, the Cayman Islands looked beautiful and he resolved to return one day on holiday. He was sorry that he had no time to explore, but it was now nearly 3.00 p.m. and his flight was scheduled for 4.00 p.m. The taxi ride back to the airport was far more comfortable in a garish Ford Fairlane of unknown vintage, but he reflected that it hadn't been so interesting as his ride out.

Matt checked in and was slightly relieved to hear that the flight would be on time, scheduled to land at Orlando at 18.20. With luck, he would be back at the house by 7.00 p.m., which should be some time before the golfers returned. The flight back was uneventful apart from a visit to the toilet when he needed to reapply some glue to his moustache which was showing signs of becoming unstuck due to the humidity on Grand Cayman.

Matt collected his car, removed his moustache and glove and locked them away with his gun. He drove via the short cut that he had found on Boggy Creek Road and arrived back at Buena Vista just after seven.

'Shit,' he said to himself as he approached the house. The other car was on the driveway. Matt turned left into the crescent, and by-passing the house he drove back to the shops at the mall. He went into the pharmacy and purchased a bottle of 100 Paracetamol and a box of powders that guaranteed a cure for hangovers. He then returned to the house, and parking behind Tony's car he went in through the front door.

'Hi boys. You're home early.'

'Yes,' said Chris. 'As a three-ball we flew around. We've been back nearly an hour – we were getting worried about you. Where have you been?'

'Oh I was feeling slightly better, but I developed a real bastard of a headache – I went out for some fresh air and eventually had to buy some pills and a hangover cure – I'll take it now.'

'You look better than you did this morning,' said Richard. 'Want a gin and tonic?'

They all laughed and Matt went into his room. He would have to retrieve his document case, disguise and gun later. He had pushed his portfolio under the front seat of the car out of sight.

That evening, they decided to go out to dinner and as he was so much better but unlikely to face drink for a while, Matt drove. He had one nasty moment when Tony, who was sitting alongside him in the front seat, began fiddling with the buttons on the glove locker.

'Hey, why is this locked?' he said.

'I think they always lock them at the hire station – it has the car documents in it, I believe. Not many people need it I suppose. The ignition key opens it.'

Hoping that no one would take the matter further, Matt spent the rest of the short drive even more conscious of the document case below his seat containing all the bank details and Chris's passport.

They returned home after midnight after having a substantial Chinese meal at the north end of Orange Blossom Trail. Luckily for Matt, the glove locker wasn't mentioned again.

When everyone was sound asleep, Matt crept through the house and into the garage to recover the evidence of his trip to Cayman. The sound that the car door made when closing was only a click but to him it seemed like a loud slam. When he got back to his room, he replaced the document case in its hiding place under his shirts and put Chris's passport back into the safe. He removed the gun, and taking six bullets from the pack he loaded the chamber. He then took the remaining ammunition, and sealing the containers with Sellotape he crept quietly out onto the sun-deck. He used the gate to gain access to the side lawn and crept stealthily down to the water's edge.

There had been rumours of transient alligators in the lake and he had no intention of waiting too long to test the validity of these stories. Matt looked carefully around, but in the moonlight everything appeared quiet. Taking a deep breath, Matt hurled the boxes of ammunition with all his strength as far out into the lake as he could. Then he hurried back to the safety of the pool enclosure ignoring the loud splash. He crept past Chris's patio doors which were slightly open, and he could hear the puffs and snores as Chris slept.

Regaining the comparative safety of his room as quietly as possible, Matt closed the blinds and shut off all the lights except his bedside lamp. He then removed his golf clubs from the bag and laid them on the bed. Removing the divider strap from the top of the bag, he stretched his arm down inside but couldn't quite reach the lead container in the bottom.

He returned to the sun-deck and fetched the barbecue fork. With the additional length he was able to reach and lever off the lid of the secret compartment. Ensuring that the safety catch was on, Matt lowered his gun into the bottom with the fork and positioned it so that the trigger guard was over the drain-hole. He packed the foam rubber around the gun and when he was sure that it was secure, he replaced the lead lid, manoeuvred it into position and pressed it into place with his 3-iron. He replaced the clubs in the bag and realized that even in the air-conditioned room, his body was bathed in perspiration.

Matt showered, and as he was unable to sleep he lay on the bed reviewing his busy day. Sufficient pieces of the jigsaw were now in place to make the picture identifiable. At 3.00 a.m. Matt finally fell into an exhausted sleep.

*

The remainder of the week was spent playing at least 18 holes of golf each day, and generally they went out to dinner at a different restaurant each evening. Matt said he definitely had had enough of barbecues!

Due to the relaxed atmosphere, the warm climate and camaraderie of the party, and having done what he needed to do, Matt felt able to relax completely. Indeed he was surprised how much he enjoyed the remainder of the week. He was more surprised that he even took pleasure from Chris's company. He really did like him as a person and still found it hard to believe that he had cheated.

As the week progressed, the fine weather continued and all four men acquired healthy tans to their faces and arms. Chris's organization of the golf, tee-off times and general playing arrangements was first class and they didn't have one upset during the whole week. They were due to return on the Saturday afternoon flight. As they had no golf arranged for the Saturday morning, they all agreed on a good night out on the town on the Friday.

So that they could all have a drink, they arranged for a taxi to pick them up at half past seven in the evening. First they went to Rosie O'Grady's on Church Street Station in Orlando. The first Dixieland type burlesque show was just about to start and they had a few large beers each. They joined in the spirit of the audience participation show, singing the old popular jazz songs with great gusto. From there, they went into the Country and Western bar where a live group was playing Rhythm and Blues with considerable energy. They were also entertained by an Elvis Presley look-alike who Tony thought was more like Elvis Presley than Elvis Presley.

They ate steaks at their table and by half past ten they had consumed a considerable amount of alcohol which put them well into the swing of things. By now, Chris was jumping up and down and really excited about taking his mates to the 'stag' bar that he had found in downtown Orlando. He had been there on previous visits and it really was his type of entertainment. They were all in the right sort of mood and were delivered to the club by taxi just before midnight.

The nightclub was all that Chris had said it was, with buxom topless waitresses expecting tips to be slipped into their skimpy briefs, dim lighting and an air of sleazy iniquity about the whole place. A four-piece combo of saxophone, piano, bass and drums was playing on a tiny stage and girls were available for those wanting to dance. It was all very brash and quite coarse, but in their state of semi-drunkenness it was great.

Predictably, the cabaret was performed by a very dark striptease artist who took hardly any time at all to reduce herself to complete nakedness. The men had paid extra for a table right on the edge of the dance floor, and the 'Merry Widow', as the act was called, picked on Chris, probably due to his gloved hand. She had already pulled a bald man out of the audience and performed the crudest of feats with his glistening pate to the delight of the all-male audience. Catcalls from Tony, Matt and Richard followed Chris onto the floor but did nothing to embarrass him, and Tony remarked that she had almost certainly met her match with him!

The 'Widow', playing up to the audience and Matt's table in particular, slowly and sensually undressed Chris, tossing his clothes one by one behind the curtain alongside the stage. He was soon standing in front of her with only his underpants and his glove left on. She went through a great play of lifting up his hand, bending his arm at the elbow and feigning disappointment when it kept dropping to his side.

Then, acting as though it was his last chance, she pulled out the waist band of his underpants and peered down the front. Her face lit up with exaggerated pleasure and grabbing his other arm, she rushed him through the curtain to great guffaws of laughter and applause. When they were back stage, she spoke to him with a smile.

'Thanks for being a good sport.' Then she gave him a peck on the cheek. 'There's your reward.'

'If you think that's enough, you've got to be fucking joking! This is what I want!'

Chris pressed her back against the wall, pinning her small frame with the full length of his body.

'Do you want it now or later?'

She could feel his arousal through his pants, and although she had had many men, this one excited her somewhat.

'Later,' she said. 'When we can really enjoy it. I'll need a little present though.'

'Don't worry about that.' Chris picked up his trousers and took the remnants of their kitty from his back pocket. There were several 100 and 50 dollar bills. 'This should be enough. I'll dress and we'll go.'

Chris quickly slipped into his clothes while the widow took her final bow, and he joined her to the tumultuous applause of the thirty or so men in the club. Then Chris went back to the table.

'Okay boys, I've got lucky – I'll see you later back at the house.'

'For Christ's sake be careful,' said Tony. 'You could end up with a knife in your back – this area isn't exactly the nicest in the world.'

'Don't worry, I can look after myself and this bird's going to have the best screw she's ever had!'

Chris disappeared back through the curtains and the show continued. The second stripper seemed very young and she was a superb dancer. Matt remarked to Richard that if she had kept her clothes on and just danced, the performance would have been even better!

One of her props was a huge tiger-skin rug complete with the head and tail. They were amazed at the contortions that she performed with this threadbare piece of cloth. Then Tony caused a great guffaw.

'It's amazing. We're all sitting here getting horny over some bird flopping around on the floor with no clothes on – if I went home and found my wife doing that, I'd think she'd gone mad and I'd call the doctor!'

They finally left in the early hours of the morning, and arrived back at the house just as the sun was coming up. Chris wasn't home yet, but then he wasn't expected until much later.

*

When Chris and the 'merry widow' left the club by the rear door, he was pleased to see a cab already waiting.

'I called for it while you were making your goodbyes. We don't want to hang around here waiting for a cruiser.'

They got in the back and Chris immediately started to fondle her through her dress. She was quite naked under the skimpy garment.

'Don't rush honey! Wait until we get to my place.'

They pulled into traffic on the Beeline Expressway heading east and came off ten minutes later, eventually stopping at a small detached bungalow on a neat residential development to the north east of Orlando.

'Okay honey. We're here. Can I have my little present now?'

'Bollocks to that lady! – I don't pay until I know the goods are value for money!'

The driver swivelled in his seat and reached over the back. A huge black hand gripped Chris's shoulder and squeezed until he winced and involuntarily cried out in pain.

'Pay now, friend,' rumbled a deep gravelly voice. 'The alternative's to give me everything of value and walk home hurt. We don't mess with no clever Limeys – in our country you play by our rules. It's 100 dollars French, 200 straight, 500 all up or 1,000 for a stay over until ten in the morning. You got the menu, place your order!'

Chris knew at once that he was in trouble if he refused. This pimp was big, ugly and powerful and looked very mean. 'Shit, what the hell. I'll have the full works!' He passed over ten 100 dollar bills and was about to get out when the pimp called out.

'Don't forget the fare!'

Chris smiled at the cheek but passed over 20 dollars.

'Keep the change – you deserve it! Pick me up at ten o'clock and don't be late.'

The next few hours were spent in the most crudely exciting passion that Chris had ever experienced. He could not think of this as being lovemaking – it was pure, unadulterated and undiluted fucking. Even screwing was too simple a word.

The 'widow' used every orifice of her body to excite and re-excite Chris and although he thought he was was worldly wise, he had never experienced such ferocity and pure animal skill in his life. When he left at ten o'clock in the morning, he was totally sated, physically exhausted and in a complete mental whirl. He even gave the pimp an extra 20 dollar tip when he was dropped off at the house.

'That was magnificent. I'll look you up when I next come out.'
'Okay man. Spread the word – tell your friends!'
'That's the last thing I'll do,' thought Chris. 'I've just spent 1,200 dollars of their money!'

When he entered the house, the others were having coffee, having packed and readied themselves for the flight.

'Hi Chris. How was it? You look well and truly fucked – if you'll pardon the expression!' smiled Tony.

'Actually boys, it wasn't that good. Not for 100 dollars anyway. On top of that, the bastard stole my money, including the kitty I'm afraid. There must have been 900 to 1,000 dollars in it. I'm sorry, but I've been walking around for hours trying to find where she took me so that I could inform the police.'

Although they were obviously disappointed at losing their cash, they were genuinely pleased that Chris was unhurt and decided that it probably wasn't worth reporting it to the police or the night club. They would just be branded as another set of Limey tourists still wet behind the ears.

*

They packed up and left Orlando mid-afternoon on Saturday and landed back at Gatwick at 7.30 a.m. the next morning. They had all purchased presents for their families, and Matt had bought a large amethyst ring for Marie valued at 750 pounds. He elected for the red channel at the customs, along with Tony and Richard. Chris said he would take a chance, having only a few cigarettes over the limit and a not very valuable brooch for Jennifer. He enjoyed the bravado and laughed about it later.

When it came to Matt's turn, the officer charged him 68 pounds duty on the ring and asked him if the golf clubs were new. Matt explained that they were about six months old.

'Let's look shall we sir?' Matt opened his flight bag, and the customs officer lifted out the bag of clubs and laid them on the table. 'Would you take the head cover off please sir?'

Matt removed the top of the bag. The officer took out the 7-iron and inspected the head.

'Did you say you bought them in England?'

'Yes, I paid just under 1,000 pounds at the Purley Golf Shop.'

'Thought you had – see the registration numbers? They run vertically in England, but side to side if bought in the States.' He took out the clubs one by one and examined them. 'Anything else in the bag?'

Matt unzipped the side pockets and the customs officer examined the three packs of unused balls as well as those that were showing signs of use, then he lifted the bag to turn it over.

'Rather heavy, isn't it sir?'

Matt reached inside the large side pocket.

'It has my golf shoes in it for transportation and also my waterproof gear.'

The officer shone his torch inside the length of the bag and remarked that he could see through the drain-hole at the bottom.

'Okay sir, thank you very much. You can go through.'

9

Matt's welcome at his home-coming was as furious as his good-bye and any doubts over whether Marie had missed him were soon dispelled. It also convinced her that he had followed her forceful and specific instructions 'not to use it', while he was away!

They were sitting quietly by the pool that evening, after Matt had dozed for most of the afternoon to recover from his jet lag, and he told her all that he had done.

'We have the money secure now and I am wondering if we should leave it at that. The only trouble is, I could never trust that prick again, and if all the money is gone from the practice, it will fold up anyway. No, I think we'll proceed with the plan.' Marie felt the beginnings of a nagging doubt as to whether they should stop now, but was carried along by Matt's enthusiasm.

Matt then went to the garage, and using a sharp knife he disassembled his golf bag to retrieve the gun. Then he put the remnants of the bag together with the lead case, in a black rubbish sack for disposal with the rest of their refuse. He removed the bullets and brought them all through to show Marie. She handled the gun somewhat gingerly.

'I thought that with security checks and body searches it would be impossible to get it back here.'

'I knew I couldn't carry it on my person, or in hand luggage. Even if it had been packed in my suitcases they might have been x-rayed. The only option was to conceal it in with my golf clubs, but in such a way that if the bag was x-rayed, the lead case would just show up as a solid band. If it had been found, I would have denied everything and it would have been traced back to Chris. I know that it probably seems extreme to go to the trouble of buying a gun in the States and bringing it back here, but it was necessary.'

'I was going to ask you – why did you not get one here?'

'That's very important. I suppose I could have found someone in England who would sell me a gun illegally but that's not what I want. I need this particular gun to be used, then found and traced back. I have laid enough spores for the tracking to be made easy. Also, I knew I was going to the States, and guns are quite easily bought over there.'

*

The next day, Matt was at his desk at the normal time. Although he had been away for a week, the office had continued to function well in his absence and there had been no real panics.

Before any of the staff had arrived, Matt went down to the drawing office on the fourth floor. He knew that each group had an electric erasing machine. This was a low powered electric tool, useful for erasing ink lines on tracing paper drawings. It comprised a small hand-held electric motor with a metal tube projecting from the front. Rubber erasers in the shape of small quarter inch diameter cylinders were fixed in the tube and when it was switched on, the rubber rotated in a fast but gently abrasive way.

Matt took one of the rubbers back to his office. He had brought his Smith & Wesson into work that morning and he carefully removed it from its bag. The rubber was almost an exact fit and he pushed it into the barrel. Putting on his cotton gloves, he carefully wiped the whole of the outside of the gun with a duster, removing all traces of his fingerprints. He did the same with the six bullets. He laid the gun on his desk and the bullets stood on end like six little soldiers alongside it. He covered the gun and bullets with a sheet of paper, wanting only one person to handle them. After an hour or so, Chris poked his head around the door of Matt's office.

'Hi partner. Any panics while we were away?'

'No Chris. Come in and we'll have a chat. There have been four new major projects that could make up to 250,000 pounds in fees.' Matt had by now surreptitiously removed the piece of paper and he waited for Chris to notice the gun, which he did after a short while.

'Oh I see you've got another one. What's that called?'

'It's a Smith & Wesson 38. I've got a few shells for this one to lend authenticity to the display. What do you think?'

Chris picked up the gun and weighted it in his hand. 'I know nothing about them but it looks so real. It's even got a number stamped on the side.' He turned the gun so that he could squint down the barrel. 'I am pleased to see it's plugged – it could fool anyone. And look at these bullets!' Chris picked them up and bounced them in his hand. 'Are you sure they aren't real? They feel so heavy.'

'They are pure lead inside the brass jacket – no gunpowder or percussion cap, that's why they are so weighty.'

Chris lined them up one by one again and said he would like to see the display when it was mounted. They spent the next hour or so going over the things that had happened while they were away, and both agreed that as the office had run so smoothly, they could take more time off if required.

When Chris had left, Matt donned his white gloves once again and carefully reloaded the gun. Again, ensuring that the safety catch was on, he slipped the gun into a plastic bag and locked it away in his safe. He retrieved a further 1,000 pounds from his reserve.

*

Two weeks later, Matt left the office at four o'clock and was home in half an hour. He left his car on the driveway and Marie was ready and waiting in the Mercedes. They drove first to Sevenoaks and Matt went to the Thomas Cook Travel Centre to purchase 1,000 pounds in travellers' cheques in sterling. He signed them 'Alfredo Perez'. They then drove to Elmers End near Beckenham, where Marie dropped Matt at the station forecourt. He went into the Avis rent-a-car office located in the portakabin in the car park and donned a pair of plain glass spectacles.

'Good morning. I telephoned this morning to reserve a car for hire. My name is Alfredo Perez,' he said with a slight Spanish inflection.

'Yes sir. I have a Rover 216 ready for you. You said that you wanted to use it in France and Spain and leave it in Madrid in two weeks' time. That's perfectly okay. We have four offices in that city. I'll need your details of course, and the hire charges must be pre-paid. We also require a 500 pound damage deposit.'

Matt passed over his Spanish driving licence and said that he would need to pay with sterling travellers' cheques. Then, having completed the formalities, he took the keys and drove the red Rover back to his home, parking it out of sight in the garage.

Matt was now close to the end of his preparations, and for the umpteenth time he reviewed his plan. He was certain that Chris would be blamed for his impending disappearance, but feeling that everything was becoming too simple he decided to lay a few false and inexplicable clues as a possible distraction. He knew of just the person to give his unwitting help.

*

Michael McNean was an incurable drunk. He had taken his first drink followed by his first cigarette when he was 17. That was 25 years ago and he had hated the bitter and nauseous taste of them both. However, with the impetuous bravado of youth, he had persevered with the result that he was now totally addicted to both alcohol and nicotine.

Michael had long ago given up any hope of regaining his dignity surrendered at such an early age, and allowed each day, night, week and month to leak into the next. The vaguely distorted pictures of his memory only surfaced very rarely, and he now had no interest left in trying to recognize them.

His greatest motivation was Thursday morning when he would go to the Social Security office in Sevenoaks to collect his dole money. He changed his Giro at the off-licence next door, buying the first bottle of the week at the same time. He started with whisky and reverted to the volume provided by very strong lager through the week, finishing on the Tuesday or Wednesday with cheap wine or cider. By Thursday morning, if he hadn't judged it properly, he would be utterly desperate.

Michael was a well-known figure and a common sight in Sevenoaks and the surrounding area, although no one took much notice of him or paid him any attention. He expressed slight surprise with much delay when he heard his name being called late one night. He looked up from his resting place on the dwarf wall outside a smart office block. A very sleek white motor car was purring at the kerb, and a man was leaning over, talking to him through the open window.

'Michael! Here Michael! Do you want a drink?'

Michael looked down at the empty cider bottle by his feet. His biological gauge told him he had two days to go and that he had overspent already. He mumbled almost incoherently:

'What for? What do you want?'

Matt lifted a full bottle of malt whisky into view. 'Get in – I'll show you.' He opened the passenger door and Michael fell in, clutching greedily at the bottle.

'Not too much – just a sip now.' Although he knew that he wouldn't understand, Matt decided to explain anyway, just in case by the remotest of chances Michael might remember later.

'I'm researching the effect of alcohol on the ability to grasp or pick things up. I am going to take you to my home and then to my office where I want you to spend a little time going around touching things. Here – only a small sip.'

He passed over the bottle and Michael up-ended it, taking a long swallow. 'Enough! – You can have the rest when we finish.'

By the time Matt got home with Michael, Marie was in bed and he hushed him around the house as quietly as possible so as to not disturb her. He made Michael pick up a great number of articles throughout the house, open doors, and then he spent time touching objects in Matt's study. After a while, Matt then took him to his offices and repeated the procedure throughout his own office, at Cathy's desk and in the lift. He allowed Michael to sit behind the wheel of his car and play with all the buttons and knobs.

In just over an hour, Michael was delivered back to his wall in Sevenoaks where he fell into a deep sleep, cuddling his nearly empty bottle of malt. He would wonder in the morning where the 20 pound note in his pocket had come from.

10

The day had at last arrived when the final pieces would be placed into the jigsaw, thus completing the picture. Both Matt and Marie were jumpy and restless. Matt would be alright once he had got to the office; Marie would be on edge all day. In order that she could be occupied, Matt ran through their tasks for the day, and for the last time he reviewed the final part of the plan, re-examining every detail for possible flaws. He went through the contents of a Safeway plastic carrier bag once again before he departed for the office.

When he finally left home it was still early; Marie went back to bed but was far too wound up to sleep. She had a hollow feeling in the pit of her stomach and inexplicably felt that she had lost something very dear and important to her. Her foreboding almost seemed to be a premonition of some, as yet, unknown tragedy.

Matt arrived at the office at 4.15 a.m., and went directly to the keys cupboard behind the reception desk. Using his personal pass key, he unlocked the door and noted that all but a very few of the 100 hooks were occupied. Some were keys to lockable stationery stores, cupboards and other doors in the building, some to properties with which the architects and surveyors were dealing, and there were also spare keys for all of the company's car fleet, numbering 45 in all. The spares to Matt's car were on number 66, and the keys with the distinctive Aston Martin motif were on number 72. Although they only had one Aston, he double-checked the numbers with the schedule on the back of the door to ensure that these were Chris's, and locked up leaving the cupboard undisturbed.

Matt went through the door adjacent to the lift to the adjoining lobby. The carpeted staircase ran off to the right round the back of the lift shaft to the upper floors. A second locked door was to the left. Again, using his pass key, Matt went through this door and down the plain concrete finished staircase to the basement. Although it was only a service area for the boilers, air-conditioning plant and dead file storage, the floor was quarry-tiled and very clean. The pipework was neatly labelled and painted British Standard colour codes, and the large room had the appearance of a ship's engine room.

Matt took two black polythene refuse sacks from his carrier bag and unrolled them. He went to the rear of one of the boilers and located the safety pressure release valve on the side. Placing the plastic bag over the valve and holding the neck tightly round the outlet, he operated the lever below marked 'Pressure Release Test'.

He jumped involuntarily at the sound of air and a little steam escaping, and in about five seconds his bag was almost fully inflated. Satisfied, Matt closed the valve and deflated the bag. He refolded both bags together and putting them back in his carrier bag, he hid it behind one of the pumps in the corner.

Matt then went directly to his office, and wearing his cotton gloves he took his Smith & Wesson from the safe. Being careful to handle it as little as possible, Matt opened the loading chamber. Then, with a long cocktail stick he pushed the rubber plug out of the barrel and pulled a short length of cotton rag through it to clean the bore.

He then went to his window and checked that the first security shift had not yet arrived. Matt had examined the rota and knew that George Adams would be on the late shift today. Not only was this an essential part of his plan, but he knew that the early shift man was less conscientious and would not arrive before time.

Taking the gun, Matt stood in front of his desk and taking careful aim, he fired one shot into the back of his chair. He had never fired a gun before and was surprised, not only at the noise, but at the power of the recoil from what he thought to be a fairly small handgun. The bullet passed straight through the back of the chair and imbedded itself deep in one of the books on his bookshelf on the rear wall.

Having now some idea of the damage that could be caused, Matt moved to one of his plants and fired a second bullet into the hessian covered wall behind it. He moved the plant slightly to cover the fairly large hole that the bullet had made. Looking at his watch and noting that it was now 4.55 a.m., he knew that he just had time to carry out the next stage before security arrived. Going out through the lobby, Matt went up the stairs to the roof garden. Again, checking it was all clear, Matt fired two shots in quick succession into the air. In the still of the morning, the reports sounded deafening to him, but being seven storeys up he was fairly sure that they would not be recognized as gunshots.

Matt went back to the basement via the lift to the ground floor and the lower flight of stairs and concealed the gun in the bag at the back of the pump. Returning to the ground floor, Matt retrieved his front door key and opened up. He waved to the security man who had just arrived and who was going into his hut 50 yards away.

Throughout the day, Matt tried to act as normally as possible. He spent a little time writing on a plain sheet of paper in Chris's handwriting in purple ink.

'My computer code: 11–07–55
Safe code: 07 11 55.'

He signed it 'Chris' with a flourish.

He locked the sheet away in his safe, at the same time taking out the remaining 4,000 pounds in cash. He left a note of his own safe code in the top drawer of his desk, to which Cathy had a key.

As the day went on, Matt found it most difficult to concentrate on work, and he felt a stab of sorrow when he realized that after today he would almost certainly never see the likes of Cathy, Wendy, George, Tim and his partners and associates again. He was also jumpy about leaving his office, making sure that whenever anyone came into the room he was in his seat to hide the bullet damage. He realized that his whole lifestyle would change, and he would quite literally have to start again.

He needed a great deal of self-control when Cathy poked her head round the door just after 5.30 p.m. that evening to say goodnight. He had grown very fond of her over the past three years and knew she would be very upset when she heard the news. It came to him then that he would cause pain to many of his friends and relations, and he had a deep feeling of regret at the deception he was about to carry out on them. Matt told Cathy that he was going to stay on for a very private meeting with Chris to discuss some important issues that had come up.

At 7.30 p.m., Matt was still at his desk. Chris had already expressed some surprise, knowing Matt's working habits were somewhat different to his. When he remarked on this, Matt said that he had a dinner engagement with a client who would be picking him up at eight o'clock.

Matt quickly used the internal phone to check that the rest of the building was empty of staff. He also checked the main car park from his window. Only George's car was there.

Seeing that Chris was wearing a dark navy suit and a dark bow tie, Matt showered and changed into his dark suit before leaving. Matt poked his head round Chris's door, carrying his jacket so that his change of clothes would not be noticed and said goodnight. Then he called the lift and pressed the button for the fourth floor. When it stopped, Matt checked that no one was in the lobby at that level. He stepped out of the lift car and punched the button for the ground floor. The lift doors closed and it descended.

Matt quickly stepped into the staircase lobby and silently ran up the stairs two at a time, puffing slightly by the time he was at roof level. He quietly unlocked the door and let himself out onto the roof garden, relocking it from the outside. He sat in the shadow of the lift motor room against the clematis covered wall. The sun had long since gone down and the late autumn chill in the air caused Matt to shiver.

He knew that he had at least a couple of hours to wait and prepared his mind for the next phase. He crept quietly to the rooflight over the atrium lobby, and by craning his neck to one side he could just see into the corner of Chris's office. Chris was sitting in front of his computer with a stack of paper, transferring figures to his terminal. Knowing that Chris would be thus occupied for most of the evening, Matt sat down to wait.

Matt sat quite still, getting up only every fifteen minutes or so to ease his cramping muscles. On each occasion he peered down into Chris's office through the rooflight to check that he was still at his desk.

It was at 9.15 that he saw that Chris's seat was empty. Matt thought that he had probably gone to the toilet but moved quickly out of sight as he saw Chris walk across the lobby below and through the staircase doors. He was still in shirt sleeves so he was not going home.

Matt returned to his position by the lift motor room. He jumped, panic rising, as he heard a key being inserted in the lock of the door. He crawled behind the long planted trough next to the wall and lay flat, barely breathing. His heartbeat was echoing in his ears as he raised his head slightly to peer through the foliage.

Chris was strolling out onto the roof garden terrace with a glass in his hand. He placed this carefully on the parapet, took a cigarette from his shirt pocket, lit up and inhaled deeply as he looked out over the countryside. He spent the next few minutes puffing away and sipping from his drink as he leant against the wall, his eyes roaming the night sky.

So this was what Chris did when he worked late. Even though he was alone in his own office, he still observed the no smoking policy and came up here for a cigarette rather than going down to the smoking room on the first floor.

At last, Chris flicked the remnant of his cigarette over the parapet and watched the glowing ember arc away into the night. He swallowed the rest of his drink, locked up and returned to the staircase.

Matt breathed out slowly, and lay still for a full five minutes before carefully rising, wiping the drying perspiration from his forehead. He peered gingerly over the edge of the rooflight and was relieved to see Chris back at his desk once again. He forced himself to relax and decided to make his next move in half an hour.

At exactly 10.00 p.m. Matt checked on Chris again. From the diminished size of the pile of papers alongside the computer, he gauged that he had about 30 minutes. He left the roof garden, quietly closed the door and started to run down the staircase.

He skidded to a stop on the third floor when he heard a door open somewhere below him. Carefully edging his eyes over the balustrade, he saw a gnarled black hand in a dark blue overall sleeve sliding up the hand-rail two floors down. It was Joey, their janitor. He was humming a song gently from Porgy & Bess, and he was carrying a mop and bucket which clanked as he climbed.

Matt readied himself to slip through the lobby door, but was relieved when Joey left the staircase to go about his duties on the first floor.

'Damn,' though Matt. 'I forgot all about the cleaners.' However, he was too far down the road to change his plans, and having no contingency he had to continue. Matt ran down the remaining stairs to the ground floor lobby, being very careful to slip past the first floor door crouching below the vision panel.

Checking through the glass panel in the door at ground floor level and seeing that it was all clear, Matt stepped out into the entrance hall and went straight to the key cupboard. Taking the spare key from peg number 72, Matt returned to the staircase and the basement.

Matt went directly to his plastic bag and unpacked the contents one by one on to the workbench. He was about to carry out the part he had not been looking forward to. Removing his jacket and rolling up his left shirt sleeve, he placed an elastic belt over his biceps. Pulling it tight with his teeth, he pumped his hand, gripping and stretching his fingers until the veins in his arm stood out. He had practiced once at home, making Marie feel quite ill as she watched. He had performed with a fair measure of success, even if with some slight pain. He would have liked to have practised more, but Marie had bought only three sterile syringes and needles from the shop in the Edgware Road.

Matt took the needle and syringe from their sterile wrappers, and with careful aim he pierced his skin and the wall of the vein. Slowly pulling back the plunger the dark red liquid filled the barrel of the syringe. When it was full, he laid it on his forearm and quickly released the tourniquet. He then withdrew the needle, laid it on the table and pressed a small pad of cotton wool over the wound. Then, taking two pre-cut strips of Elastoplast, he stuck the pad in place. Next he took his false moustache, and with the help of a small mirror he applied it to his upper lip. He removed his tie and clipped on a bow tie to his collar. He was unworried by the fact that it was not an exact match to the one that Chris was wearing.

Taking his black plastic sacks, Matt inflated them one by one from the pressure release valve and tied them at the top with black sticky tape. He then tied them together with the same tape so as to produce a bulky, irregularly shaped cylinder about six feet long. Although they had little or no weight, he would rely on his acting abilities to add to the illusion. Matt pulled a black glove onto his left hand and now all was ready. He took his mobile phone from the table and punched in his home number. Marie answered after the first ring. He thought he sounded unnecessarily dramatic when he whispered the message.

'All okay. Telephone now!'

Marie hung up and immediately dialled the direct line telephone number of the security booth at the offices. In her haste, she misdialled and a mechanical recorded voice told her that 'the number you have dialled has not been recognised.' She took a deep breath to calm herself then started again. This time she was careful, but the stress she was feeling manifested itself in the form of sweaty palms. As she pressed the last digit, her relief caused her to relax her grip. The instrument dropped from her grasp. She snatched at it but only succeeded in helping it on its way to the tiled kitchen floor where the plastic handset shattered.

'Oh God!' She put her hand to her head knowing that she had let him down badly.

*

Matt waited behind the door to the reception area, counting off the digits that Marie would be dialling to get through to George. 'Right,' he thought, 'his phone will ring in about five seconds.' He left the shelter of the lobby and, stooping low, dragged his black plastic bags across the floor to the front entrance.

George looked up from his golfing magazine and saw Mr Chris limping slightly across the lobby 50 yards away. He appeared to be having a little trouble getting what looked to be a fairly heavy bundle across the floor and through the door, but he watched him successfully haul it to his car.

'For Christ's sake, Marie! Use the phone!' Matt was beginning to panic. He was looking covertly in the direction of the front gate when he realized that George was staring at him through the glass window.

George thought that Mr Chris looked as though he needed some help and so hoisted his not inconsiderable bulk from the stool in front of his counter. He left the kiosk and started across the car park.

Marie was desperate. The phone was obviously useless. She slammed her hand on the cradle to disconnect the line and rushed to the living room. Thank God! The handset there was still working. She dialled quickly and carefully.

'Oh fuck! It's all going wrong!' thought Matt, as he searched desperately around for an escape route. By now, although partly obscured by the car, George was only 40 yards away. Matt's eyes lit on the loading doors to the boiler room. Could he unlock them using his pass key, get through and close them before George covered the short distance?

Just then, both George and Matt heard the shrill bell of the telephone in the security hut.

George glanced back, then looked again towards Mr Chris. He seemed to be managing okay now, and had the boot open, so he went quickly back to the phone.

'Oh, hello, George. It's Marie du Bois here. I'm sorry to trouble you but I wondered if you'd seen my husband?' She sounded sightly breathless. 'I've tried his private line but there's no reply. His car phone is switched off and I was expecting him home early this evening. I just need to know if he wants to eat when he gets home.'

Matt breathed a sigh of relief. Keeping one eye on George through the windscreen, he looked down into the open boot of the Aston Martin and smiled to himself at the pristine neatness of the interior. Chris certainly was tidy!

'No, sorry, Mrs du Bois, I haven't seen Mr Matt. The lights are off in his office and only Mr Christopher is still here – apart from the cleaner that is.'

'Oh dear, I wonder where he is – it's just not like him. I'll try his Golf Club. Maybe he called in there on his way home for a drink. Anyway, how are you George?' She was making small talk while George continued to watch 'Mr Chris' at the back of his car. As he was now out of George's sight, Matt tore the sides of the black sacks to deflate them. He folded them roughly and stuffed them into his jacket. Then he allowed a few drops of blood from his syringe to drip onto the bumper before squirting a larger amount onto the carpet in the boot. The blood was already beginning to clot and he knew that a fresh supply would be needed later. He plucked a number of hairs from his own head and let them fall haphazardly into the boot, close to the blood stain.

Matt took the Smith & Wesson from his pocket, careful to hold it only in his gloved left hand, and lifting the back corner of the carpet he wedged it in position alongside the spare wheel.

'And how's your golf, George? Are you still playing off that inflated handicap?' Marie continued.

George was watching Mr Chris close the boot of the car and walk back to the office, arm across his chest and his limp only just discernible. By now, Mrs Du Bois seemed to have run out of chit-chat. After telling him she would let him know where Matt had been that evening, she hung up. George recorded the call in his security log. He also made a short note that Mr Chris had removed a large package of unknown contents. He noted the time at 10.29 p.m.

Matt went directly back to the basement, and as a precaution against Joey stumbling in on him he locked the door from the inside, leaving the key in the lock once again. He quickly removed his moustache, bow tie and glove, and dropped them together with the plastic sacks, carrier bag, tape, mirror and the needle and syringe into the incinerator. Matt then turned out the light and sat waiting. At 10.40 p.m. he heard someone leave. It was probably Joey, and five minutes later he heard Chris's car start up.

As Chris passed the security barrier and said goodnight, George asked if he knew where Mr Matt was. Chris was as gruff as usual.

'He left a few hours ago – said he was going out to dinner with a client. I'm surprised you didn't see him being picked up. Anyway, that's what we pay you for, to look after people's coming and goings'.

George reddened.

'No, there was only one time when I went in the back to spend a penny earlier – it must have been then. I see his car is still here. Anyway, Mrs Du Bois didn't know he was going out – if he gets home having already eaten she'll be cross if she's kept his dinner for him. Perhaps I should phone her to let her know where he is.'

George reached for the phone, operating the barrier at the same time. Only as Chris's tail lights disappeared round the corner did he realize that he had forgotten to ask what was in the bundle. He would probably have been told to mind his own bloody business anyway. When George got through to her, Marie seemed relieved that someone knew where Matt was, even though she did sound a little cross.

When he was sure that everyone had gone, Matt stayed in the boiler room for a full half hour. Only then, when it was approaching midnight, did he carefully let himself out to return the Aston Martin car key to its position in the key cupboard. He also switched off the alarm system at the reception desk, working by the light of his small torch.

Matt then climbed the stairs, for some inexplicable reason not trusting the lift, and went straight to his office. With his second syringe and needle, he repeated his blood letting exercise, this time with greater difficulty using the vein in his right arm. He spread some blood from the syringe onto his seat and a large patch on the carpet alongside his desk.

He then walked across to the door, dripping a little as he went and left a reasonably sized patch by the lift door. He went into his private shower room, and pulling off several sheets of toilet paper he went back to his office and mopped up as much of the blood as possible. He purposely missed a few drops and having cleared up, he flushed the paper down the toilet. He changed back into his grey suit.

Next he went back to his office and made an entry in his diary for the previous evening regarding an appointment with Chris and a certain Alfredo Perez. With one final look around the office, he felt a small lump grow in his throat, making it difficult to swallow. On an impulse, he took his bottle of Hennessey XO from his bar.

He saw from the lift indicator that the car was at the third floor so when he got to that level, he came off the staircase. He flicked the last of the blood from the syringe into the back corner and knew that he had now completed his final task at the office. He used his mobile phone again and established that Marie would be on her way in five minutes. He went back to the boiler room and disposed of the syringe and needle in the incinerator. He locked up and set the alarm once more as he left.

Matt checked that the car park was clear, and keeping to the shadow of the perimeter hedge he walked the short distance across the adjoining field to the by-pass. He arrived almost at the same time as Marie in the hired Rover, and they kissed briefly when he got into the car. Then she drove speedily away.

'It's done! And how did you get on?'

'Fine, your bag is in the back. I've done as you suggested and packed only essentials – four sets of underclothes and socks, some soft shoes, a pair of slacks, two short-sleeved shirts and some washing and shaving gear. Alfredo Perez's documents are in the carry bag I bought for you last year. There's also your ticket for the Dover–Boulogne ferry. I picked it up from the travel agents today and paid cash. It's for the seven o'clock in the morning boat so you've plenty of time.'

Marie drove to the edge of the woods by the common land backing onto their house, and they left the car in a lay-by, locked up and doused the lights. They walked through the woods hand in hand in silence; their path was lit by the dim glow from Matt's pen-light. They entered the garden through the gate in the rear fence, their arrival announced by Rambo's shrill barking. It was now well past midnight and Marie had prepared a light salad supper for Matt. They sat in the kitchen with blinds drawn, the only glow coming from the lights under the wall units.

Matt tried to eat but found the food turned to sawdust in his mouth. He went over Marie's role over the next few weeks, and they tried to guess at the sort of questions she would probably be asked.

Both Matt and Marie had expected to make love that night, but all they wanted to do was cling to each other in silence.

Once she started to weep, Marie became uncontrollable, the sobs racking her body. Although he was trying desperately to be strong, Matt could not help himself and they cried together well into the early hours.

At four o'clock, he gave Marie a last long hug with a lingering kiss full of love and compassion. He had changed into a light pair of trousers with soft grey shoes. His light grey suit was packed in a bag and would be taken with him. He left by the rear door, and skirting the pool he regained the safety of the woods without making a sound. He put on his clear glass spectacles and drove carefully within the speed limit on the motorway. He arrived early at Dover at 5.45 a.m. He produced his ticket and passport and boarded the ferry forty-five minutes later. He had just started his new life as Alfredo Perez Gandia, a millionaire semi-retired artist and architect, who had inherited his wealth from a recently deceased aunt.

On the boat, he changed his remaining sterling travellers' cheques into some French francs and a few pesetas. He would change the remaining sterling notes to local currency in Madrid. When he was about in mid-channel, Matt took the small plastic bag that contained his wallet together with his credit cards, English driving licence and office keys. He would never have use of these again and after weighting them down with a large bolt taken from his workshop, they made hardly a splash as they sank into the wake of the ferry. He was now well and truly Señor Perez.

When Matt had left, Marie sat quietly in the darkness of the kitchen, Rambo curled gratefully in her lap. She was subconsciously tickling his ears and her mind was in a whirl. Her husband, the man she loved dearly and the father of the child growing inside her had gone. She knew it was not for ever, but it was for at least six months. He had said at the outset that there would be some sacrifice, and although she had anticipated this moment she had not in her worst dreams thought it would be as bad as this.

In two months' time, her baby would be born without his father to help and encourage her at the birth. Neither would he be there afterwards to comfort her. Matt had warned her of this and underlined the strain that she would have to bear single-handed, and she now knew that it was out of loyalty to him that she had agreed to his plan.

'Don't panic!' she told herself over and over again. 'It's the early hours of the first day of his absence. You've had very little sleep after a stressful day and you're tired and frightened. Go to bed, try to relax. Just think beautiful thoughts,' as an old friend had once told her.

She went back to bed, and after a few minutes she was once more sobbing uncontrollably into her pillow.

11

The next morning, Marie anxiously telephoned the office at nine o'clock to speak to Cathy.

'No, I don't know where Matt is. There is nothing in his diary for the early part of the day, only a meeting with Group Three later on. He had nothing in his diary for a dinner meeting with a client last night – he was still at the office when I left at the normal time. Have you tried Chris?'

Marie knew that Chris was not an early riser but telephoned him at home anyway. Jennifer answered the phone and said that Chris was just out of the shower. Then he came to the phone.

'Yes, Matt told me he was going to see a client last night. He was being picked up at 8 o'clock at the office. He left at that time. His car was still in the car park when I left – I guessed he was going home by cab. You say he hasn't been home all night? Leave it with me, I'll check if his car's still at the office.'

With an amazing display of insensitivity he continued. 'If his car's not there and he tried to drive home after a boozy dinner, he may have been arrested for drink driving. Look, don't be alarmed – there's probably a simple explanation.'

He put the phone down and turned to Jennifer, 'Sounds like Matt's had a night out on the tiles – well, she is seven months pregnant!' He sniggered, because Jennie was always singing Matt's praises and holding him up as a paragon of excellence and an example of how Chris should behave.

Chris was told by the office that Matt's car had been in the car park all night, so he phoned the local police. He was told that no

Mr Du Bois had been arrested and that as far as they knew, there had been no serious road traffic accidents in the area last night. Chris didn't know where Matt had gone to dinner. It could have been anywhere. He telephoned Cathy and explained what was wrong. He asked her to telephone all of the hospitals inside a ten mile radius. Anything could have happened, he thought.

Throughout the day, Marie telephoned the office every half an hour or so and it was obvious that she was becoming more and more distraught. Eventually, at two o'clock Cathy asked Chris's permission for her to go and sit with Marie to give her some moral support. Marie was delighted to see Cathy and it was plain that she had been crying. Her eyes were red and puffy and she looked terrible.

Two hours later, they still had no news. Cathy said that to be on the safe side, they should report Matt as suspected missing.

Detective Inspector Roger Webb had not been on duty for long when Cathy's call was put through to him. After taking down some details, he suggested that as Mr Du Bois had been missing for less than 24 hours, he really didn't think that there was a major problem.

'If we jumped every time a wife phoned up to say that her husband had been out all night, we'd have no time left for real policing. Phone back tomorrow if he stays out again tonight.'

Cathy became more forceful. 'Look, you don't know the man you're dealing with. He doesn't just go off without saying where he's going. There's not even the name of the man he was meeting in his diary. He certainly doesn't stay away from his wife all night, and even if he had, he would surely be back by now.'

'Look Miss, how do you know "the client" was a man? It could have been a lady, and if it was he would hardly put her name in his diary, would he? Anyway, it might be that she's so good that he doesn't want to leave her yet. It's my bet that he's having a fling; it does happen you know! You phone tomorrow if he doesn't come home tonight.'

Cathy was furious. As Marie was there, she couldn't tell the inspector that what he was saying was absolute rubbish. If Matt had wanted a substitute wife for a short while, she was sure he would have come to her. She slammed down the phone, and turning to Marie she put her arms around her.

'It's easy to say, but please don't worry. If you like, I'll stay the night.

Detective Inspector Webb put the phone down and turned to his sergeant, Graham Walker. 'Another bloke feeling deprived. Why do all these women think their men are angels?'

Although his manner with Cathy had been somewhat brusque, the inspector was thought by his colleagues to be a good, if somewhat plodding, copper. At 40 years of age he had been married, divorced, re-married, and he was now separated. He admitted that he was probably too much in love with his job to give sufficient attention to a wife.

Inspector Webb enjoyed and often sought out female company, but he found excuses to be away from home too easy. He had had the occasional affair over the past seven years, but nothing had lasted more than a few months. He now visited a still young-looking prostitute in Catford two or three times a month for free favours, but even this was now out of habit rather than need. He was now living in a neat and always tidy one-bedroomed flat in South Croydon and worked at Orpington Police Station.

*

The next morning at 9.00 a.m. sharp, Detective Inspector Webb received an unexpected call from Cathy.

'Very well Miss, can you come down to the Station?'

'We can, but wouldn't you like to see where he lives?'

'Okay, I'll be there in 30 minutes.'

Still not wholly convinced he was not wasting his time, Inspector Webb and Sergeant Walker drove the short distance to Marie's home. Both were suitably impressed by the opulence and quiet wealth of the house.

Although Cathy had collected a few overnight things from her flat and was beautifully presented, Marie, once again, looked awful. She had made no attempt to hide the facial evidence of her grief and worry, and she had not bothered to dress with her usual care. After a few preliminary queries regarding his job, status and home relationship, it became clear to the inspector that Matt was definitely not the type to run off, even for a few days. He asked for a recent photograph of Matt, so Marie brought his passport from the study, and another one taken in Cyprus last year when Webb asked for a larger one. It was not really a very good likeness, but only Marie knew this. It would distort even more if reproduced in newsprint.

After an hour of questions, Inspector Webb said that he needed to talk to Matt's office staff and telephoned Chris to make an appointment for that afternoon.

As they left, Inspector Webb turned to his sergeant. 'There's no doubt about the worry that woman is feeling. If he is just out on the tiles he's a real bastard, but somehow I don't get that impression. If not, he's either had an accident, or it's foul play. If it's foul play, if could be kidnapping as he's well off, or mugging but they don't normally get hurt that bad, or it could even be murder.

'You know the golden rule, if a man disappears, check the wife first and his business associates second. If they check out, look for any enemies he might have made. This guy looks pretty straight, so I don't think he's made too many enemies – if his wife and secretary are to be believed that is.'

Sergeant Walker interjected 'I must say, I think the wife's genuine as well – if she's faking, she's brilliant at it. What about the secretary? She's very tasty – I wouldn't mind giving her one! Do you think they are at it?'

'No, she was with Mrs Du Bois last night. That's far too clever! I think she's just loyal to her boss.'

When they arrived at the office, they were met at the security kiosk by George Adams. He had heard of Matt's disappearance and had asked Wendy to let him know if and when the police were visiting the offices. Her phone call had George at his post earlier than normal and he introduced himself to the detectives. Inspector Webb shook his hand warmly, he had heard of George Adams on the grapevine and was always happy to meet 'good' coppers. George would be pleased to help in any way he could.

'Mr Matt is a real gent and if anyone's hurt him they'll have me to answer to.'

The inspector was shown Matt's car and George confirmed that it had been in the car park for the past two days. As far as he knew, Matt had left the office some time around eight o'clock and hadn't been seen since. He confirmed that he had been on duty but didn't actually see him go. It must have been when he went for a pee. Mr Christopher had told him that Matt had left at that time. The two policemen were then escorted to the top floor by the receptionist and met at the lift by Wendy.

'Please come this way, Inspector,' she said and took them to Chris's office.

'This place smells of affluence and success,' whispered the inspector as they crossed the lobby.

As always, Chris's door was open and he came round his desk to greet them. He was charm itself, and after only a very short time he had explained the reasons for his gloved hand. Sergeant Walker took notes as the inspector asked a number of background questions which Chris answered frankly and honestly. They had a good successful practice, and both he and Matt had contributed equally to that success.

Chris was obviously quite astounded at Matt's disappearance, but at first he had thought he was just out on the tiles. He was now getting more and more concerned. Inspector Webb asked to see Matt's office, which Chris confirmed had not been touched for the past day, since it had been cleaned. That was the evening of Matt's disappearance.

The inspector walked around the office looking at the prints and diplomas on the wall, remarking on Matt's academic achievements. When he reached Matt's desk, he paused by the *Ficus Benjamina* in the corner.

'Did you say the room was cleaned? In which case you might want to give your cleaner a rollocking – there's dust all over the floor here.'

He pointed at the chips of plaster around the base of the pot, and when he moved a branch aside he glanced quickly and pointedly at Walker.

'What's this then?'

The sergeant joined him at his side. 'That's a bullet hole,' he said and reached in his pocket for his pen-knife.

Inspector Webb literally slapped his wrist. 'Don't touch anything please – anybody!' he said looking at Chris.

'Jesus, what's a bullet doing here?' Chris almost shouted.

'I think we'd all like to know the answer to that sir.' The inspector's voice had taken on an icy tone.

He continued his cursory inspection of the office, taking care to touch nothing and watching where he trod. When he reached Matt's desk, he stooped to inspect the back of the seat.

'There's another hole here,' he said, and turning the swivel seat with his elbow he saw the ragged leather around the exit hole. Returning the seat to its earlier position and eyeing the trajectory through, it was a simple matter to see the line of the bullet into the books and bookshelf behind.

'Did Mr Du Bois have any guns, or contact with them?' asked Sergeant Walker.

'Not as far as I know,' said Chris, 'Oh, except he had started a collection of replicas. He kept them at home I believe. I've only seem them twice.'

'How about you, sir?'

'No – never had one or fired a proper gun in my life. Went on a clay pigeon shoot last Christmas, and that's all.'

Inspector Webb stooped to inspect a stain on the carpet by the desk.

'What do you make of this, Sergeant?'

Sergeant Walker bent down and looking at his superior, he nodded in agreement.

'I'm going to have to seal this office, Mr Marten. Will you please ensure that your staff are all available for questioning. Graham, would you please phone for a forensic team? Get them here as quickly as possible – if not sooner. I'm logging this as a murder or an attempted murder investigation.

'Please can you set aside an office for me to use for interviewing, Mr Marten? I'll start with you, if I may, and then Mr Du Bois' secretary, then yours and then Mr Adams, the security man.'

'Of course,' said Chris, 'You can have the boardroom just across the lobby. Please make yourself at home and use any of the facilities that you need. I'll just get my secretary to cancel any appointments I have left today and I will be right with you.'

Chris could not put his finger on the slight nagging feeling he had at the edge of his mind.

In the ten minutes or so that it took Wendy to organize the meeting room for the policemen's use, Chris had time to ponder on the latest events. What had happened to Matt? He was fairly sure that he had no enemies through work. To his knowledge, Matt had always been scrupulously fair in the handling of his projects and he could not think that any of the parties to the contracts, clients or builders, could be so upset by his decisions to have killed him.

He thought Matt must have returned to the office after he had left and security had gone home. That was after 11.00 p.m. He remembered Joey had poked his head into his office at about 7.30 p.m. This was a common occurrence as Chris was quite often there late and had no problem with Joey clearing his waste bin and dusting around while he worked.

He thought that Joey had gone into Matt's office afterwards and he certainly would not have missed the mess on the floor. That meant that the bullets must have been fired later. Supposing Matt had brought whoever he went out to dinner with back late, that they had an argument and he had pulled a gun on Matt. Surely Matt would have told him if he was associating with dubious people.

Although there were some bloodstains about, Matt's body wasn't there so maybe it was kidnapping. No – they would have had a demand for money by now. If they had killed him or hurt him badly, why take him away? To dump his body or finish him off if he wasn't quite dead.

Chris's mind was racing and uncharacteristically jumping from point to point in a haphazard manner.

'God!' – it suddenly struck him that if Matt had been killed, it would solve a multitude of problems! He had his back covered with Matt's having signed away his profits – no one knew of the deception, except him and Bullock. He had Bullock by the balls. He wouldn't talk – not with the photos he had of him!

Also, if Matt had been killed, Marie would get two million pounds and the practice would get a further million from the new insurance which would be useful, and he was sure he could negotiate a good deal in purchasing Matt's assets in the practice. Ignoring the problems of replacing Matt, all in all it could be the solution to all his worries.

Chris found it difficult not to smile when he strolled into the boardroom to be interviewed by Inspector Webb. The look of concern that he had forced onto his face was not, he felt, too convincing.

*

Inspector Webb had considered what he had so far and discussed this briefly with Sergeant Walker.

'Let's assume at this stage that it is foul play – I think there's little doubt of that. The only alternative is an accident with a firearm, and as far as we know Du Bois didn't have one.

'So, it was either murder, attempted murder, robbery with violence or kidnapping. I don't think it's either of the last two – nothing appears to have been taken. Make a note to check that with his secretary please, Graham. And we haven't had any demands yet. A kidnapper usually makes contact in the first twelve hours, so that he can demand that the victim's family and friends do not inform the police.

'So – murder or attempted murder? What do we have? Two bullets, bloodstains on the floor. Last seen at eight o'clock by his partner. Check that the building was empty and if he was seen leaving at that time, or if anyone saw who picked him up. Unless their timing was spot on, either Du Bois or his lift must have been hanging around for a few minutes outside.

'It's not a heavily populated area but check locally – someone may have been passing in a car or walking a dog – they may have noticed something. Ah, good! Forensic's here.'

Wendy ushered the team of four detectives and their equipment into the board room. Inspector Webb left the rest of them with a cup of coffee poured by Sergeant Walker and took the senior man, Detective Inspector Maine into Matt's office, moving the 'Do not enter – sealed by police' sign taped across the door. He explained briefly the details of the case, and pointed out the two bullet holes and the stains on the floor.

Inspector Maine quickly assessed the situation and his trained eye had picked up the thin trail of droplets across the door and followed them into the lobby.

'I think we should clear the whole of this floor level. Look!' Inspector Webb also saw the stain in the lobby by the lift door, so he called Walker to clear the floor of people.

'Before they go, please can you take fingerprints from everyone for elimination purposes. Also, if they know them, get their blood groups.'

Chris, Wendy, Cathy and the other partners and their secretaries were ushered to the floor below. The fingerprint man took impressions from each of them before they left. They all knew their blood groups except Tim and Wendy. Cathy was able to confirm that Matt's was A Rhesus Negative. She knew this because as it was a rare group, he carried a card to that effect.

Because he had been on the top floor on the evening of Matt's disappearance, Inspector Webb asked for Joey to be fingerprinted as well. Old Joey was visibly frightened by the presence of the police, because once in his younger days he had been persecuted and badly beaten by a rogue policeman in Brixton. Inspector Webb skilfully put him at his ease and after a short while, Joey had almost relaxed completely, even though his hands still shook slightly when he was fingerprinted.

The inspector questioned him about his visit to Matt's office two nights ago. Joey remembered that it was quite normal for Mr Christopher to be in but rare for Mr Matt to be there so late. It was around 7.30 p.m. when he did Mr Chris's room. He had only emptied the trash can and dusted around. He didn't use the Hoover when Mr Christopher was in his office – that was done at weekends. He had cleaned his toilet and kitchen area and washed up the few cups that had been used. He had also put a fresh pot of coffee on for him.

He was going to see if he could do Mr Matt's room, but when he knocked on the door he got no reply. He poked his head round and could hear Mr Matt in the shower. He didn't want to disturb him, so as the office looked fairly tidy from where he was standing, he thought he would leave it until later.

Inspector Webb took Joey to Matt's office and they stood in the doorway.

'Does anything look different, Joey?'

'No, sah – it all looks 'xactly the same.'

The inspector took him to the plant in the corner. 'What about that?' he asked, pointing to the plaster dust around the pot. Joey grew indignant.

'You sayin' I ain't doin' my job proper? I wouldn't leave the floor laike that. It def'nitely weren't thar when I came in. I'd a swept it up.'

'Okay Joey. Where did you go from here?'

Joey explained that he had gone down to the floor below at about 7.45 p.m. and worked his way down to the ground floor by about 10.00 p.m. He had emptied the waste bins and cleared cups and saucers into the kitchen stations on each floor. His last job that evening had been to mop up the floor of the first floor kitchen where a bottle of milk had been broken. He finally left at about 10.45 p.m., turning off the lights as he went. Mr Adams, the security officer, clocked him out and told him that Mr Christopher was still working.

*

Chris entered the boardroom just as Joey was leaving, and he was able to confirm the same times that had been given by Joey. Once again Chris expressed his concern about Matt and asked for Inspector Webb's first thoughts.

'One thing I've learned in this business is not to jump to conclusions. Now, you quite often work late – was that night any different?'

'No, not really. However, it was fairly rare for Matt to be here. He was the early man and normally left by half past five to six o'clock. I think he had been getting in extra early over the past several months – he does his best work he says, before the phones start ringing. As it was so unusual for him to still be here that late, I asked him why and he said he had a dinner appointment with a client. That's not unusual, we quite often entertain clients to lunch and dinner. No, he didn't say who it was and quite frankly, I didn't think to ask. It must have been someone pretty important – he showered and changed his shirt before he went out.

'Yes, I can remember – he was wearing a light grey suit that day and a white shirt. Can't recollect the tie but it wasn't anything startling. He said he was being picked up at eight o'clock. He said goodnight at just about that time. The last I heard of him was when he went into the lift.

'When I left at about eleven o'clock, Adams of security said he hadn't seen Matt go – said he was probably having a pee out the back. Lazy bastard was probably asleep!'

'What financial arrangements do you have as far as the practice is concerned? And how would his disappearance affect you, particularly if it was permanent?'

'Of course I would be devastated. Matt was – is – my partner. He is also a mate. I would find it impossible to replace him. As far as money is concerned, we recently increased our insurances to three million pounds each. In the unlikely event of death, the practice gets one million and the deceased's estate two.' He paused. 'Hold on! I know what you're thinking! The suggestion to do this came from Matt, not me!'

Chris went on quickly, 'I don't know of course whether his wife put the idea into his head. She's the main beneficiary, of course.'

Inspector Webb made a note to get a copy of their partnership agreement.

By now, the forensic team had thoroughly examined Matt's office and the lobby. They had several sets of fingerprints and had established that there were two unidentified sets, one of which they thought would be Matt's. The other could be the killer's. They would later check that they matched with nobody else. They took samples of the blood taken from the carpet, the chair and the lobby, and they had recovered two bullets. On a preliminary inspection, neither of the bullets seemed to have passed through a human body – there was no sign of blood, tissue or bone splinters which would have been normal.

If the blood was as a result of a gunshot wound, the bullet was still in the body.

In Matt's private shower room, the detectives had found samples of his whiskers in his electric razor and hair from his head in his hair brush. Body hair was removed from the shower tray. They also removed a large used bath towel that might reveal skin tissue under careful laboratory examination. As they cleared the room, Inspector Webb was handed it back by the forensic team and Cathy was asked to join him there.

He was impressed with this attractive and efficient young woman. However, she was showing signs of strain and was visibly worried at her boss's possible fate. She explained that she had left the office as normal that evening, at around 5.30 p.m., and she confirmed Matt was wearing a light grey suit. She had no knowledge of his dinner appointment with a client. He would normally have put the name and venue in his diary and asked Cathy to book the table at one of a number of good restaurants that he knew. Cathy fetched his diary and pointed to other such appointments earlier in the year where entries were made, sometimes in her hand and sometimes in Matt's. Cathy recalled that Matt had seemed a little tense during the day, and when she left he had said he was staying on to discuss a number of very important issues with Chris. He had said he needed absolute privacy for these discussions.

At that point, Inspector Maine interrupted with an apology to Cathy. Taking his colleague to one side, he told him in a lowered tone that they had just found more blood in the lift. Most of it had been mopped up from the floor and the cleaner had confirmed that the lift car was swabbed out each morning. However, there were traces on the wall right down in the corner. He had found nothing on the ground floor reception area. He thought it was far too late to seal that area off. It had had two days of traffic over it. Inspector Webb went back to Cathy.

'You are Mr Du Bois's private secretary. Apart from his wife and Mr Marten, you probably know more about him than anyone else. How much detail of his personal life are you aware of?'

Cathy explained that she knew Matt and Marie fairly well. She said they didn't socialize much, but that she saw Marie about once a month. They weren't bosom buddies but were friends more than acquaintances. Marie never came on as 'the boss's wife' and was a very nice friendly girl.

Matt, in her view, was wonderful! He was fair-minded and a completely scrupulous and honest man. He didn't suffer fools gladly but was always able to give someone a roasting in a pleasant but forceful way. She had seen senior men leave his office after a necessary dressing down, determined not to repeat the same mistake because they didn't want to go through that again! However, if they discussed it later, they couldn't recall what had made them so uncomfortable. There had been no raising of voices or thumping of the table – only quiet, persuasive and authoritative discussion. Matt had an amazing knack of being able to get the very best from his staff by help and encouragement and enthusiastic leadership. As far as she knew, all of his employees would do anything for him and his reputation in the profession was unrivalled.

'You obviously have the greatest of respect for him. Forgive me for asking, but I need to check all the angles. Are you, or have you ever been romantically involved with him?'

The slightest suggestion of a smile touched Cathy's mouth.

'As it happens, no. I should make it absolutely clear. He is a very attractive man – in all senses of the word. In the past, although he has never said as much, I don't think he has exactly been an angel. Neither have I, and although at the moment I'm unattached, I have had a few quite serious romances. In different circumstances, I am absolutely certain that Matt and I could have a great relationship – but not I am sorry to say at this moment. He is deeply in love with his wife and she with him. They are a wonderful couple, soon to be a "three", and I wouldn't dream of trying to wreck that.'

Webb recognized the sincerity of her little speech and was now even more convinced that Du Bois's disappearance was not as a result of having made enemies. He was returning again and again to his wife or partner as the main suspects.

'Thanks for that,' Inspector Webb said. 'Now I'd like to look at some of his personal papers. Do you have access to his more private files?'

'Yes of course,' replied Cathy. 'I'll get my keys to his personal and confidential cabinets.'

Cathy fetched a substantial bunch of keys from her desk and asked if Mr Webb minded if she stayed while they were going through them. She was, after all, still Matt's personal secretary. The inspector's attempt at a friendly smile in agreement looked, to Cathy, to be somewhat patronizing.

First, he looked through the four filing cabinets concealed behind the doors. Not many of the files were of great initial interest to him; clients, prospective clients, marketing, minutes of meetings and the like, but he stopped when his eye fell on a Partnership Agreement file.

He removed it and glanced through the bound and sealed official document in the front. Although it was over thirty pages long, he flicked through the headings fairly quickly and found nothing unusual in the 'In The Event of Death' clauses. It went through a complicated procedure of valuation by lawyers and accountants, and there was no obvious advantage to the surviving partner deriving from the death of the other.

Inspector Webb then asked Cathy if she would let him have a copy, so she set up Matt's photocopier to do it there and then. He returned to the file and flicked through a few memos and notes. His eye lit on a memo dated nearly four months earlier that stood out because it was in a different type-face. It was from Mr Marten to Mr Du Bois and it suggested an increase in insurance. He went through his notebook and confirmed that his memory was accurate. Marten had said that the suggestion to reinsure had come from Du Bois. The inspector had thought at the time that the reaction had been a bit too fast. Calling Cathy over, he asked if she could explain the memo.

'Yes, it's from Chris to Matt. That's Chris's signature and it's come from his own computer – he has a Pinwriter not a laser like the rest of us. I can't understand why it was done on his machine though, unless Wendy's had gone down for any reason and she used his. Wait though! It hasn't got her reference on it – only Chris's. I can only think that he typed it himself for some reason – maybe it was late at night and he wanted Matt to have it straight away. Sorry, I just don't know – you'll have to ask Chris.'

'I'll certainly do that,' said the inspector. 'I'll certainly do that!'

Cathy made him a copy of the memo, and at his request she showed him the insurance file that confirmed that the increase in insurance had been effected very quickly.

During Inspector Webb's questioning of Cathy, Sergeant Walker had been talking briefly to some of the staff, but as yet he had drawn a blank. The latest that anyone had been at the office that evening was just after 7.00 p.m. The sergeant had been directed to security who kept a log of the comings and goings of staff during the day. This was an essential feature of their 'health and safety at work policy' which enabled a check to be made on the whereabouts of staff if they didn't return to the office from site. Sometimes, they needed to survey old and empty houses, and once a few years ago, a surveyor had fallen through a rotten floor. He was not found for two days.

George Adams was waiting expectantly for Sergeant Walker. He was immediately able to confirm from his log that the last to leave, apart from the cleaner and Mr Chris had been one of the junior surveyors at 7.08 p.m.

The sergeant scanned the log for that evening, making notes in his jotter, and asked George what the reference was to Mr Christopher's 'package of unknown contents'.

'Well, I saw Mr Christopher dragging a fairly large and what looked like a heavy bundle across the floor of the lobby. No, I didn't see whether he came out of the lift with it or not – that's out of my line of sight. He struggled with it to get it through the doors and dragged it over to his car and put it in the boot. I assume he managed to get it in on his own, even with only one hand. I would have helped him but I was on the telephone. You can see the exact time – 10.29 p.m. Afterwards he just went back inside and I guess back to his office. He left about quarter of an hour later at exactly 10.45 p.m. – there it is in my log again.'

George confirmed that Mr Marten usually left before him if he worked late, but if it got to past 11.00 p.m. and he was still at it, George would sometimes go up and let Mr Chris know he was leaving, so he could lock the front door.

'Is Mr Marten's car always in that space?'

'Yes. Mr Chris and Mr Matt have reserved spaces for their own cars, as do the other partners and associates. The rest of the staff have a free-for-all but there are plenty of spaces to go round.'

'What about Matt's visitor? – you saw or heard nothing of him?'

'No. As I have already said, it must have been when I went for a pee about eight o'clock. I've got a loo and a sink at the back of my kiosk. I can have a brew up or have a pee without having to leave the barrier unattended. On odd occasions, if I'm in the back, people usually just toot their hooters and I can be back at the barrier in ten seconds. Nothing happened that evening, and I can only think Mr Matt and his visitor must have arrived at exactly the same time. Matt would certainly have called out goodnight as he passed if he had had time.'

Sergeant Walker left George to his own thoughts about the strange package and strolled over to look at the senior partners' cars. He glanced at the white XJS, looking at it enviously, knowing that he would never be able to afford such a magnificent car. Then he walked around the dark green Aston Martin with the CDM 1 number plate. He noticed the strange knob on the steering wheel, and although he knew that one-handed steering was not illegal, he wondered if Mr Marten would be breaking the law in having to reach across his body to select which automatic gear he needed with his right hand.

He strolled slowly around the car, and when he got to the boot he tried the handle but found it locked. His eyes lit on a brownish stain on top of the chrome bumper and he examined it carefully without touching it. He went back inside the building and asked the receptionist to locate Inspector Maine. The forensics inspector was having a cup of coffee with one of the architects' group secretaries and was slightly miffed at the interruption. He had been fairly close to organizing a date for later in the week. Sergeant Walker also spoke by telephone to Inspector Webb in the board room and asked him to join him in the car park, if possible bringing Mr Marten's car keys with him. Detective Inspectors Maine and Webb both arrived at the same time.

The sergeant pointed out the stain on the bumper, and Inspector Maine at once confirmed that in his view it was blood.

After he had carefully scraped the hardened blot into a specimen jar, Inspector Webb unlocked and opened the boot, taking care to touch surfaces as little as possible. All three men looked purposefully at each other at the sight which greeted them. On one side of the light grey carpet was a large stain, measuring some four inches across. Inspector Maine again took a sample, labelled it and continued his search of the boot with the aid of a magnifying glass combined with a powerful lamp. He picked up a number of dark hairs and a few traces of mud, but that was all.

'I need this back at the lab,' he said and spent the next ten minutes making a cursory inspection of the seats and carpets inside the car.

'Okay Mike. Arrange for it to be picked up. I need another little chat with Mr Christopher Marten.'

On the way up in the lift, Sergeant Walker updated Inspector Webb on his interview with George Adams. He was now quite sure in his own mind what had happened. All that he needed was a confession to sew it up.

It was now approaching 6.00 p.m. and most of the staff had gone home for the day. Not much real work had been done as everyone was obviously preoccupied with Matt's mysterious disappearance and this had of course been the main topic of conversation throughout the day.

The police presence had had a somewhat disruptive effect, and to this was added the arrival of the reporters from a national and two local newspapers at the gate. George Adams kept them outside the car park and warned the staff about not talking to them. He told the reporters that there were would be a press statement from the police and a senior partner of the firm later.

12

At about the same time that Detective Sergeant Walker found the bloodstain on Chris's car, Matt was crossing the border between France and Spain at Pau. He had driven slowly and leisurely through France over the previous two days, avoiding the autoroutes but keeping to the arterial roads through Amiens, to the west of Paris and Versailles. He had stayed the first night at a small hotel on the fringes of Tours. Matt was purposely taking his time over the journey, firstly because he had to avoid any chance of an accident at all costs, and also because he needed to time his arrival in Madrid for the Monday morning.

He had gone to the railway station in Tours and used a public telephone in the forecourt that evening to telephone his home at exactly eight o'clock. He had let the phone ring once, hung up and then dialled again, letting it ring twice before replacing the receiver. This was his signal that everything was running to plan. By the number of the rings on the second call, Marie would know where he was from his pre-planned route.

The second day had taken Matt through Poitiers, Angoulême and Bordeaux, and he reached the French-Spanish frontier at Pau just after 7.00 p.m. local time.

He found a motel off the main road to Pamplona on the Spanish side where he ordered sandwiches and a jug of coffee from the small cafeteria which he brought to his room. His excellent Spanish was only just about understood by the waiter. Matt had learned and spoke Catalan, the most popular dialect, but it was used mainly in the north-western and southern parts of Spain. Classical Castillian was the language spoken in this region.

As the room was equipped with an IDD telephone, he decided to take a chance, and at nine o'clock local time he again telephoned Marie. On this occasion he let the phone ring three times on the second call. She would know that he was now in Spain.

The next morning, Matt rose and left early, aiming to travel the 450 miles or so to Madrid across the plains via Pamplona and Guadalajara, and then to arrive to take up his reservation at the *Hotel Soto Grande* which overlooked one of the many squares of Madrid that evening. He arrived late in the afternoon, and as pre-arranged he did not telephone Marie that night.

Early the next morning, after a fitful night, Matt sat alone in the dining room, hardly able to touch the hot sweet chocolate croissants on his plate. He was sure that this was a reaction after the intense pressure of the past few months, and he was totally unable to wind down.

The hotel had a small gift and sports shop in the lobby, and on impulse Matt purchased a pair of shorts, a T-shirt, some sports socks and trainers and set off on a punishing run around the streets of Madrid in the early morning October mist of the city. He returned after three quarters of an hour, having covered about six miles, dripping in perspiration but feeling much better. He had neglected his physical fitness of late, and he resolved to work out at least once a day in the future. He knew that it would be very easy, if he was not careful, to lapse into indolence and lethargy through enforced inactivity. He determined to find tasks to keep his body and mind fully exercised and alert over the next several months.

Having showered and changed into his freshly pressed suit, Matt spoke to the hall porter.

'*Donde està Banco Centrale de España, por favor?*'

'*Si señor. Cami Prats de Moló. Cerca Estasción de Autobus. No es posible aparca. Tiene taxi, señor.*'

'*Muchas gracias, hay parada de taxis aqui?*'

Matt decided to take the porter's advice as there was no parking at the bank and went straight to the taxi rank. Matt took a cab with a very talkative driver to the *Banco Centrale*. When he arrived, he asked to see one of the manager's clerks and explained to him that he wished to purchase a motor car in Madrid and needed a telegraphic transfer of approximately five million pesetas from his bank in Menorca. He would then need *Banco Centrale* to prepare a banker's draft for the exact value of the car once he had selected and arranged the purchase. The clerk took all of his details and said that arrangements could be made for the transfer of the money later in the day.

Before leaving England, Matt had given instructions for his bank in Jersey to transfer $100,000 to his Mahon account and a further $5,000 per month on a regular basis. He was keen to keep his Spanish account only just in credit, because he knew that at the end of each year an assessment would be made by the Inland Revenue for a 'Wealth Tax' based on a percentage of the average balance in his bank account. Although he had no objection to paying this, Matt did not want to draw attention to himself or his finances. He had previously been assured by José Maldoras that Alfredo Perez Gandia's tax affairs and records were entirely in order.

Once he had completed his arrangements with the bank, Matt asked for directions and then walked the short distance to the large Mitsubishi showrooms in the *Cami Del Carmen* nearby.

There were a number of vehicles that would have been suitable for Matt but he finally decided, because it was immediately available for delivery, on a Shogun 4x4 Jeep, fully equipped with air-conditioning, electric roof, windows and mirrors and a full range of audio equipment. The salesman was delighted with Matt's quick decision to take it and agreed to a five per cent discount. The total purchase price which included registration and an extended warranty was 4,780,000 pesetas which equated to about 24,000 pounds.

Matt telephoned the clerk at the *Banco Centrale* and arranged for the exact sum to be prepared on a banker's draft to *Coches Madrid SA* which would be sent round that afternoon at four o'clock. This slight delay would give the salesman time to register the vehicle in Señor Perez' name and also to arrange for insurance.

Matt returned to his hotel by taxi and established the location of the nearest Avis rent-a-car office. It was some thirty minutes drive away, and after lunch he took the Rover and parked it in the return vehicle compound at the front of the office. A bored looking young clerk inspected the vehicle, made some remark about it being very dusty and completed the paperwork. With some apparent regret, almost as though he were passing over his own money, he wrote out a cheque for Matt for the return of the damage deposit.

Matt returned to the car showroom and collected his *Permiso de circulación* and his *seguro*. These registration book and insurance documents were all that were needed for Matt to take the car away, and five minutes later the banker's draft arrived by messenger. Matt signed it Alfredo Perez with a flourish and drove the car away after instructions on how to engage the four-wheel drive.

Matt returned to the hotel where at last he seemed to relax. That evening he enjoyed a very good *conejo cocido en cazuela*, baked rabbit, with an excellent bottle of *Rioja Faustino No. 2*. He had collected a copy of the *Independent*, the only English newspaper available at the kiosk in reception. It was dated yesterday and although he scanned it from cover to cover, there was no mention of the disappearance of an English architect in suspicious circumstances.

*

While Matt was now at last beginning to relax, by contrast Christopher Marten was feeling exactly the opposite. When Inspector Webb and Sergeant Walker arrived back at the seventh floor, Chris was obviously a very worried man.

'Why did you need my car keys, sergeant?'

Inspector Webb spoke, ignoring the question.

'Can we go into Mr Du Bois's office please, sir?'

The inspector was quite polite but very firm and it was clear to Chris that his former friendly attitude had cooled. However, the sergeant was reassuring and still amicable.

'Don't worry sir, I'm quite sure it will all work out okay.'

The two policemen had worked together long enough to have perfected this 'Bill and Ben', act as they called it. At times like this, a bullying stature by one would be countered by a friendly, confiding approach by the other, and it was the latter who would usually extract the confession.

'Sit down,' said Inspector Webb brusquely. 'I'd like to clarify a number of things. Firstly, you pointed out that Mrs Du Bois is named as the main beneficiary in her husband's insurance. It's just incidental,' he spoke the word sarcastically, 'that you benefit to the tune of one million pounds.'

Chris was feeling uncomfortable. 'Now just a minute. Not me – the practice!'

'With Du Bois gone, you would be the practice.' Consulting his notes, Inspector Webb continued, 'I also recall that you said it was Du Bois's idea to increase your insurances. I have that recorded here, quite clearly. Can you explain this, please sir?' He emphasised 'sir' in an aggressive and sneering manner.

Sergeant Walker took the sheet of paper proffered by Webb and passed it on to Chris with a sympathetic frown. Chris scanned the photocopy of a memo from him to Matt.

'I've never seen this before! It's an obvious forgery!'

'It would be helpful to you if it was, wouldn't it? Do you never send memos or letters out typed by yourself and printed on your own machine?'

'Very rarely,' said Chris. 'I would like to see the original – it looks like my signature but it can't be. I've never written a memo like that. Matt suggested the insurances increase, not me.'

Just then the phone rang and Sergeant Walker answered it. He turned to Chris.

'I'm very sorry to be a nuisance Mr Marten, but I wonder if you might agree to your car being taken away for a thorough forensic examination. I know it's an absolute pain but it would be of tremendous help to us. We just want to check out some stains found on the bumper and in the boot. We'll give you a lift home of course, and pick you up again in the morning.'

Chris was furious. 'What stains? What do you mean? I really am getting tired of being pushed around by you arseholes. I'm going home – we'll speak again tomorrow – that is, of course, if you're still on the case. I have contacts you know. Far higher in rank than you!'

Chris started to rise, his face red with anger and his mouth working from side to side.

'Sit down!' Webb hadn't raised his voice, but the effect was so authoritative that Chris felt compelled to flop back in his seat.

'On the face of it, you could be in deep, deep trouble. I suggest that you co-operate. By doing so, you might, you just might get some help from me.

'Now, why do you say this isn't your memo. Is it the typeface from your machine?'

Chris looked at the copy again. He had calmed down a bit, knowing that he was in the right. He would let these two prats dig themselves into a deep hole by running with them.

'Actually, any of our machines could produce this typeface. You just have to insert a different font into the printer. It's the style of printing that's different. Mine's a Pinwriter which works on a dot matrix system – the others are laser printers. We can solve this straight away. If I had sent that memo, I would have a copy on my files. Shall we check?'

Chris led the way back to his office and opened the doors to his filing cabinet cupboards.

'Now, Wendy would have filed a copy either under 'Insurances' or 'Matthew Du Bois, Personal File.' He selected a yellow and red tabbed key from his bunch and unlocked two cabinets.

'There – help yourself!'

Walker located the two files mentioned by Chris and leafed through them, looking at the papers filed around the date of the memo. He glanced at his senior colleague, shaking his head. The gesture was not lost on Chris who allowed himself a smug smile.

'Hmm, try the Partnership Agreement file. That's where the top copy was filed in Mr Du Bois's system,' suggested the inspector.

The sergeant located the file in the second drawer of the green cabinet, and placing the file on the open drawer leafed through it. He stopped about five pages from the top.

He looked first at Chris with a blank face, and then brought the whole file over to Webb, open at the page.

'I think you've helped our argument, sir. You did say that if you had written it, there would be a copy on your file? Well, well – here it is! Does anyone but you have keys?'

'Yes – that must be it! Wendy has a set. She must have loaned it to someone – the fucking bitch is trying to stitch me up!'

'Why should she do that, sir? I thought she was your loyal secretary.'

His mind screamed at the inspector in silence. 'I've got the proof but I can't tell you why, you stupid bastard!'

Chris took several deep breaths and then stood quite still. His mind was in a whirl. The copy was there and it looked just like his initialling done in the special colour of his pen. Jesus! Was he going mad? Had he written it without remembering? He really couldn't believe it. He decided that the best thing for the moment was to stay silent. He knew that he had nothing to do with Matt's disappearance – let them prove otherwise! His morale felt boosted by the thought.

'I'm sorry. I just can't explain any of this. You seem to have a pre-conceived notion of what's happened. Of course, if it's absolutely necessary, you have my permission to take my car and please can you explain what you have found?'

Sergeant Walker made a very short call on the internal phone, informing forensic that they could take the car away. Inspector Webb pondered for several seconds, his eyes holding Chris with an intense stare over his hands, his fingers steepled in front of his face.

'I don't normally tell anyone my thoughts at this stage, not even my sergeant. However, I think it may clear up this little mess somewhat more quickly if I run over to you what we have to-date.' He consulted his notebook.

'Fact one: Your partner has disappeared under very suspicious circumstances. Fact two: You were the last person to see him, after, I believe, having a meeting to discuss "a very serious matter". Fact three: We have found evidence of guns being fired in Mr Du Bois's room. Fact four: We have evidence of bloodshed – probably your partner's – this will soon be checked out of course. Fact five: We know that two people will gain considerable financial benefit from Mr Du Bois's death. Fact six: We know that one of those beneficiaries only a short time ago suggested the process whereby that benefit would accrue. Fact seven: We have found –' and here Webb paused and placed his palms flat down on the table – 'stains remarkably similar to those on the floor in this office in the boot of your car!'

'I don't believe this is happening! I very rarely use the boot of the car – I haven't opened it in weeks.'

Sergeant Walker, who had been scribbling furiously in his notebook, leaned forward.

'What did you take home that night, sir? Something large, heavy, bulky…?' He let his voice trail off.

Chris put his right hand to his temple and ran his fingers back through his hair.

'I took nothing home that night except a cashflow forecast that I had just printed out. It was only three pieces of paper and I didn't even take my briefcase.'

The sergeant flipped back through his notebook. 'What would you say then if I told you that you were seen at precisely 10.29 p.m. on the night before last, dragging a heavy, bulky bundle from this building, which you proceeded to put in the boot of your car? I have an extremely reliable witness to this fact.'

Chris's frown deepened. This was getting crazier by the minute. He was trying desperately to keep calm but his voice was rising involuntarily to almost a screech.

'I've told you – I was in my office all evening, working until about a quarter to eleven. I left then and locked up. The fucking security man was still there – ask him – he'll tell you. I had nothing with me. God! This is so stupid. What's happening here?'

A knowing look flickered between Inspector Webb and Sergeant Walker. The inspector rose and went round the desk to Chris, perching on the corner. He patted Chris's shoulder gently.

'Come on sir, don't get fraught. Let me get you a glass of water. We can talk about it all when you have calmed down.' He patted him again and went across to the bar area to fetch a drink. The 'Bill and Ben' role had reversed.

Walker was just about to press his attack further when the phone rang. He picked it up and listened for a few minutes. He turned back to Christopher.

'You have never, I believe you said, sir, fired any firearm except a shotgun,' he asked quietly. Chris nodded.

'In which case, sir, can you please explain how a Smith & Wesson 38 calibre pistol has just been found under the carpet in the boot of your car?'

Chris stared at Sergeant Walker and then looked across at Inspector Webb, and he tried to stand up. His legs wouldn't take his weight and the sergeant just caught him before he crashed to the floor.

*

Over the past two days, Marie had kept up the pretence of extreme and profound worry about her husband's disappearance. It was not at all difficult to present the distressed exterior to the world. However, it was not so much concern about what might have happened in the recent past, but genuine fear of the immediate future that made her performance more authentic.

She had, of course, spoken to her mother and her brothers and to Matt's family. His brother, James, was particularly concerned and offered Marie a room in their house until things got sorted out. On advice from Detective Inspector Webb, who had called her twice very briefly for a chat, she avoided the press, and the security arrangements at the house kept them at bay. She had not been out, saying that she needed to stay by the phone for any news.

Cathy had stayed over for a second night, but Marie insisted that she go back to her flat. After a while, their conversation dried up and they just sat and stared at each other, or into space. Although she was a little worried about her, Cathy left Marie alone.

The second night that Matt had been away had been terrible. At exactly 8.00 p.m. the phone rang once, and then after a pause, a further two times. She had been close to snatching it on the first ring of the second time to beg Matt to come home or let her join him somewhere. They had partly anticipated this dilemma and knew that they would need extra strength of will in the early days.

Marie had desperately wanted to phone Stephen Murray. He would, she knew, offer his shoulder to cry on, but she couldn't trust herself to not tell him the truth. She hated herself, and sometimes Matt, for this loathsome deception that they were thrusting upon their friends and relations.

To keep herself occupied, Marie had collected together from Matt's list all of the documents that she would need. He was so organized. He had prepared a schedule of his credit card numbers and the emergency line for reporting their loss, his driving licence and passport numbers, bank account numbers, savings bonds, share certificates, car key numbers and so on. In addition, he had a schedule of insurances for the house, contents, cars, his and her life and pension plans. A copy of his will was also in the wall safe in his study.

Matt had calculated that once he was accepted by the insurance company as dead, the total payout would be in the region of three million pounds and his share of the practice, including the property, would be about two and a half million. Though the value of the practice would be somewhat damaged by his disappearance and Chris's tarnished reputation, Matt had felt fairly sure that the remaining partners would pull through. He had the quarter of a million pound mortgage on his house linked to further insurances, and this would be unencumbered once his death was accepted. Marie would therefore be a very, very wealthy widow.

Marie would inherit his estate in its entirety, and in his will he had nominated the family lawyer and his personal accountant as executors.

*

It was now past 8.30 p.m., and Inspector Webb and Sergeant Walker had been working solidly for twelve hours. Christopher had recovered, and he was slumped in the easy chair in his office, his head bowed. He was confused and scared. The only explanation that he could think of was that someone had killed Matt and used him to set him up to be 'the patsy', he thought it was called.

So much didn't check out. If Matt's body had been put in his car at 10.30 p.m. that night, when had he been killed? They said that four chambers of the gun had been fired, guessing that two had missed and two were in the body. But he would have heard the shots and Matt would have said 'hello' when he came back. He would have seen him – his office door was open all the time for Christ's sake! No, no, no, no – this is a bad dream! He literally pinched himself, hoping he would wake up.

Inspector Webb and Sergeant Walker had debated arresting Chris on suspicion of murder due to the evidence that they had, but they knew that if they did this they would have another four or five hours of work that night. If they had him watched instead, he might just lead them to the body. The combined weight of these two considerations made them decide on calling it a day.

Inspector Webb went across to Chris's office.

'Come on sir. I think it's time we took you home. Get a decent night's sleep and we'll continue in the morning.' He was 'Bill' again – the nice one.

Chris, still in a daze, allowed himself to be helped up and they left the building. While Sergeant Walker was getting the car and settling Chris in the back, the inspector went across to the security kiosk. George Adams was still there and the strain of the inactivity was showing on his face. Inspector Webb talked to the reporters for a few minutes and confirmed that Mr Du Bois had disappeared and they were investigating the matter, fearing foul play. He gave them a copy of Matt's photograph together with a description of the clothes in which he was last seen. He said there were no suspects at the moment but that they were continuing their line of enquiry.

Afterwards, Inspector Webb asked George Adams to ensure that the building was locked up and the alarms set, and said he would have a constable on duty all night. Knowing how cold and boring a job this could be, George offered the use of the security kiosk overnight and the inspector was too good a 'guv'nor' to refuse. He used George's phone to contact his station to arrange for a bobby to come to the offices, and also for an unmarked surveillance car to be stationed outside Chris's house that night.

Inspector Webb finally got home at about eleven o'clock. He reflected as he lay in his bed that it was all coming together extremely well, and he wondered if, maybe, it had not all been just a little too easy? The next day would tell.

13

Matt woke up early the next morning and was pleased to be on the road by half past eight, after a simple breakfast of orange juice, croissants and coffee. He had only about 450 miles to travel to Barcelona, which he calculated, on the not too good Spanish roads would take about ten hours. He had reserved a place on the *Compañia Transmeditaranea* ferry which would leave at 9.00 p.m., so he had plenty of time.

He arrived at Barcelona with an hour and a half to spare having lunched on bread and cheese and a little coarse red wine at a small farmhouse just east of Zaragosa. He found the shipping office and was settled into a first class cabin before the ship sailed at 9.15 p.m. The anticipated journey time was 13 hours.

Matt settled back with the four English newspapers that he had bought on the pier side, all carrying pictures of him on the inner pages. The headlines ran along the lines of 'Well-Known Architect Missing', with minor variations, and they gave brief details of the timing of his disappearance. His description was accurate, but he was pleased to see that the photograph was very poor and bore little resemblance to Alfredo Perez. One of the articles had a picture of Christopher Marten being driven away by the police. Another gave a list of some of his better known architectural achievements and the third, for some reason, gave emphasis to his wife's seven months pregnancy.

Not for the first time, Matt felt a twinge of remorse and sat alone in his cabin. In the middle of the ocean, he felt very isolated.

The ferry docked at exactly 10.00 a.m. the next morning in Mahon. As there were very few cars and passengers, Matt was on the quayside within 30 minutes.

Matt knew that he would need the services of a lawyer. He had met José Maldoras's lawyer once before in Mahon, but could not take the chance that he would be recognized by him, particularly as Tim, one of his partners in the practice would almost certainly be taking on the Es Grau project.

In view of this, he drove the length of the island through Alayor and Mercadel to Ciutadella and asked at the *Correos* for the addresses of lawyers in the town. As he would only require their help for the simple tasks related to the purchase of a parcel of land, he didn't need to be too choosy.

Matt was directed to a small first floor office in the *Avenida del Consquistador*, where he met a young and energetic freshly qualified lawyer by the name of Nicolás Brechia. Before going to see him, Matt established that the site that he had seen last year was still on the market, and that as yet it was still unsold.

*

During the few visits that he had made to the island for his marina project, Matt had explored, finding those beaches on the south west much prettier and in the main less spoilt. Many could be reached only by boat and others had a poor track only suitable for jeeps and such vehicles. They were used by those intrepid holiday makers who found the tortuous walk worthwhile. There were no beach bars or other tourists' facilities, and even in the summer these beaches did not get too crowded.

Matt had found two such unspoilt spots suitable for his purposes at Cala Mitjaña and Cala en Turqueta. Mitjaña had a large deep beach enclosed by high rocky promontories to the sides and a pine forest at the rear. A tiny cove called Mitjañeta adjoined the main beach and the whole setting was idyllic. From Matt's viewpoint, however, there appeared to be no land available for sale there, so he decided on Turqueta.

This beach was equally beautiful and it was split into two by a small rocky outcrop. Again, the pine trees grew right down to the back of the pinky white sand of the beach. A berth for mooring boats had been cut into the natural rocks to the west side of the bay.

An old stone watchtower could just be seen from the beach, perched up on the rocky pine covered ground to the west. It had long since been disused and in fact, would be of no use in its original function, due to the growth of the trees around it. On his last visit, Matt had found that it had been on the market for a few years. No one apparently was interested in purchasing or developing this difficult site.

However, with his architect's vision, Matt had been able to establish that with careful, selective tree removal, the watchtower could form the nucleus of a villa that would command a magnificent view. The agent confirmed that the landing jetty was part of the property, and that he could, if he wanted to protect his privacy even more, refuse to grant a licence for pleasure boats from Ciutadella to land there. This would make the beach even less crowded, though Matt knew that if he took this action, he would feel somewhat selfish.

*

Matt introduced himself to Señor Brechia and explained that he was now semi-retired and wanted to build himself a home in Menorca. He passed over a faded sheet of details of the site at Cala en Turqueta which he had been given by the agents and instructed Nicolás to make an offer on the asking price of 20 million pesetas for the 30,000 square metres site. This converted to about £100,000 for 7½ acres, most of which was natural pine and olive tree forest. Nicolás Brechia said that he was sure that he could secure the site for less – if Señor Perez allowed him to negotiate.

Matt told him that he could keep any saving that he made, but only if the whole deal was signed, sealed and settled within 21 days. He also needed confirmation that the building permission for a 600 square metre villa granted seven years ago was still valid.

Matt handwrote a letter to his bank in Mahon asking them to confirm to Nicolás that his account contained sufficient funds to allow him to pay cash for the site. He left Nicolás with the name of the hotel at which he would be staying in Ciutadella until he could arrange the winter rental of a small villa.

Pleased with everything he had done so far, Matt set about preparing sketch designs of his first ideas for his new home. At exactly 9.00 p.m. local time, Matt made a telephone call to England. He let the phone ring three times the first time and four the second. Marie would know that he had selected the Turqueta location for their new home.

*

Meanwhile, Inspector Webb had discussed the Marten–Du Bois case with his Superintendent who was quite clear in his own mind that Christopher Marten should be arrested and charged with murder. He felt that Marten's reaction, as described by Inspector Webb, was sufficient indication that he would break if arrested and that he would confess. The inspector had persuaded him to wait until they had more forensic evidence which he felt sure would put the final nail in the coffin. He confirmed the surveillance team had reported that Marten had stayed at home all night.

Detective Inspector Maine had promised that his team would have some initial results that morning, so hopefully it could all be tied up later on in the day.

Inspector Webb then phoned Chris's home. When Jennifer answered, he asked her to tell Chris to stay at home until he heard from the police. He told her that no, there were no further developments. She sounded very tearful and relieved to end the conversation.

Just before 10.00 a.m., Inspector Maine called Inspector Webb.

'I have some findings for you. Firstly, all of the blood samples show up to be Group A Rhesus Negative. As you know, only 0.3 per cent of the population, that's 3 in 1000 are in that group, and the missing person was Group A Rhesus Negative.

'Secondly, hair taken from the Aston Martin boot carpet matches those taken from Mr Du Bois's hair brush in his shower room. Thirdly, the only set of fingerprints on the Smith and Wesson are Mr Marten's. There are a few smudges, but no other prints. Fourthly, the bullets in the wall and in the bookcase come from that gun. So I think that probably gives you enough, but we've established from the gun manufacturers that the gun registration number indicates that it was issued in Florida, USA. They are checking at which retail outlet and will let us know later on today. I'll have my full report by tomorrow evening. As you know, we have identified everyone's fingerprints except Mr Du Bois's. We found a considerable number of two identical sets in his office and in his car, and we have found that they are also present at his home. We haven't yet been able to establish which is Mr Du Bois's but it is definitely one of those two sets.'

'Thanks, Mike. That's great. Can I borrow the gun for a while? I'll pick it up when I pass the lab if that's alright.'

When Inspector Webb told his Superintendent of the forensic evidence, he arranged for a warrant for Marten's arrest immediately. He picked up Sergeant Walker and they drove to Chris's house in Beckenham.

Jennifer answered the door to their ring and the redness of her eyes betrayed her emotional state. She showed them into the lounge and called Chris, saying she would bring in some coffee.

'Please wait, Mrs Marten, I think you should hear what I have to say.'

Chris came into the room, and although he was freshly shaven and smartly dressed he had dark swollen bags underneath heavily bloodshot eyes. He looked as though he had spent the night drinking rather than sleeping.

'Good morning, gentlemen. Any news?'

'Yes, sir. We have had what we think is a breakthrough.'

'Good – have you found the body?' Jennifer had brightened to ask the question.

'No, Mrs Marten. Perhaps I should explain to you sir,' he said, turning to Chris. 'The bloodstains in the office, the lift, and indeed in the boot of your car are the same rare group as Mr Du Bois's.' He paused, and then went on, 'There is other strong forensic evidence to indicate that his body was placed in the boot of your car at some time.' He looked intently at Chris.

'The bullets which were recovered from the office were fired by the gun found in the boot of your car.' His stare was now quite intense. 'And lastly sir, the gun and the cartridges in the gun are covered in your fingerprints!' His words had increased in volume perceptibly with this last sentence.

'Mary, Mother of Jesus!' said Jennifer, crossing herself and forcing her forefinger between her teeth to stop crying out further.

Chris just sat silently, even paler than yesterday evening, and Walker thought he was going to pass out once again.

Inspector Webb continued, 'Christopher David Marten, I have a warrant here for your arrest for the murder of Matthew Ronald Du Bois. You are not obliged to say anything, but anything you do say will be taken down and may be used in evidence. Will you come with us please, sir?'

Chris was just staring into space. He was quite numb and didn't even hear Jennifer sobbing into his shoulder. He slowly rose and spoke quite calmly.

'Okay, let's go. Will you telephone Peter Nash, Jennie. He'll know what to do.'

Walker fetched a glass of water for Jennifer and sat her down.

'I'm very sorry Mrs Marten. Is there anyone who can stay with you, or would you like a WPC?'

Jennifer recovered. 'No thank you. I'm okay. I'll get my sister to come over. Oh god, what will I tell the boys?'

Her face collapsed again and she covered it with her hands, sobs raking her body. Walker hated this part of the job even more than the hate he felt for Marten at this particular time. His crime would touch the lives of many people before the affair was over.

As Christopher Marten was being driven away in the back of Sergeant Walker's car, a free-lance photographer managed a lucky shot through the window, capturing the dismay on Chris's face.

*

Marie was sitting in the kitchen idly sipping her third cup of coffee in as many hours, staring into space, her thoughts drifting elsewhere. She felt absolutely lost and desperately in need of the comfort that only Matt could give her.

She was overwhelmed by the attention and compassion of her family and friends, and even the reporters seemed to have no desire to impose on her privacy. All of this care was, however, second best. She knew that it was bad for her and the baby to be in this constant state of dull depression, but found it impossible to shake off the mood.

Marie jumped, spilling a little of her almost cold coffee as the telephone rang at her elbow. She felt her heart jolt as she recognized Stephen Murray's voice. He was obviously concerned for her welfare and asked for the latest developments. Marie told him that there was no news of Matt but that the police had told her they were fairly close to making an arrest. She felt terrible, not only for saying it, but also because she was saying it to Stephen. She told him that she feared the worst and was steeling herself to face the unthinkable – that Matt was dead.

Even saying that to Stephen, her voice broke and she felt as though she might be tempting fate. She was describing to Stephen the policeman in charge of the investigation and almost on cue, the buzzer from the front gate sounded. Marie said a hurried goodbye, with a promise that she would let him know of any developments and pressed the intercom to the gate.

'Good afternoon, Mrs Du Bois. Detective Inspector Webb here. May I see you for a few moments?'

Marie pushed the button on the entryphone and the inspector returned to his car and drove through the gate, followed by a young and pretty WPC in a Mini Metro. He parked in front of the house and Marie was standing with the door open by the time he climbed wearily from his car. Rambo scampered out to greet him, barking and jumping up to be petted.

Marie took Inspector Webb and his WPC into the dining room and poured them both a cup of instant coffee. When they were settled, she asked, almost with trepidation, whether they had any news for her.

'Yes, Mrs Du Bois. We are fairly sure who was responsible for your husband's disappearance. We don't have a full confession yet, but the evidence we have is so strong that it won't be long in coming.

'This will probably come as a shock to you, Mrs Du Bois, but we have arrested Mr Christopher Marten.'

Marie put her hand to her mouth. Even though she had anticipated this moment over the past week or so, she had no need to feign genuine shock. Her face was quite pale, accentuated by the puffiness of the bags under her red-rimmed eyes.

'God,' thought the inspector, 'I hate this!'

'I also have some very bad news. We have charged him with the murder of your husband.'

Marie dropped her cup, Rambo just avoiding the scalding liquid. The WPC was by her side immediately, putting her arm around Marie's shoulders, dabbing at the few spots of coffee on her slacks as she did so. Marie was sufficiently aware to ask a well-rehearsed question.

'Have you found Matt's body, then? What was his motive – was it money?'

'No, Mrs Du Bois. We haven't found him yet, but we expect Marten to come up with that sort of information once he has confessed. He is at the station now undergoing further interrogation. I will, of course, keep you fully informed. I am deeply sorry to have to put you through this ordeal. We are still carrying out the questioning of people in the vicinity of the offices.'

Then, almost as an afterthought, Inspector Webb said, 'Oh, just one thing. I believe Mr Du Bois collected replica handguns. May I see his collection?'

Marie frowned. 'I don't know where you got that idea from. He's never had any interest at all in guns – he hated the things!'

With this, the inspector rose and left, leaving the WPC to look after Marie. He stopped at the wooden post 30 yards short of the gate and pressed the weatherproof button mounted on the back to open the gates.

When Inspector Webb left Marie, he had a nagging doubt at the back of his mind regarding the motive that Marten could have had for killing Du Bois. Marie had touched on it when she asked if it was about money. He decided to go back to the offices to see if anything there would give him a lead.

He asked Cathy if she would open Mr Du Bois's private filing cabinets again and this she did.

'You mentioned that on the last night, Mr Du Bois seemed drawn and tense and said he needed to discuss something very serious with Mr Marten. Have you any idea what that was?' he asked.

'No,' she said, 'but it must have been very serious and confidential. He would normally confide everything in me.'

He spent the next two hours leafing through files and could find nothing to prick his imagination into life apart from the insurance payout, but that would not be enough to kill for, particularly as the business was so strong. They had, according to the accounts in Du Bois's cabinet, in excess of a million pounds each in the business, plus the property and the goodwill. No, it had to be something they had argued over and Marten had killed him in the heat of the row.

He also questioned Wendy again. She denied, quite forcefully that she had ever loaned Chris's keys to anyone else at any time. She knew that Matt had never given her away, and now of course it looked as though he never could.

When Inspector Webb got back to the station, Sergeant Walker had told him that he had run up against denial after denial from Marten.

'I think he's in shock. His lawyer, Peter Nash, is with him at the moment – oh and forensic has traced the gun. It was sold by a licensed dealer in Kissimmee just south of Orlando back in September. He has all the details and the registration document. It was sold to a Christopher Marten who has a house on the Buena Vista Estate in Greater Orlando, six miles from the shop.

'I've checked with Marten. He's admitted that he went to Orlando with Du Bois and two friends for a week's golf at about that time. He denies any knowledge of the gun. I haven't confronted him with this fresh information yet.'

'Well,' said Inspector Webb, 'that's it, then. The final piece. Okay, let's see him again.'

Peter Nash was a tall, dark, middle-aged lawyer who had looked after Chris's legal affairs for the past 16 years. During all of that time, he had not known Chris do anything remotely dishonest and he was convinced of his innocence. It was just too out of character for Christopher Marten to have contemplated murder. What could the motive have been?

He rose when the two detectives came into the room. Sergeant Walker dismissed the police constable who had been keeping watch just outside the door. After introductions, Inspector Webb asked if Peter Nash had any objections to their continuing to question Chris.

'With the usual reservations and as long as the questions are reasonable. Of course, go ahead.' He turned to Chris. 'Don't answer any questions until I give you the nod, and don't speak at all if I tell you not to.' Chris nodded meekly.

The inspector started. With a not inconsiderable sense of drama, he pulled a labelled plastic bag from his jacket pocket and dropped it with a thud on the table. The Smith & Wesson 38 shone in the bright overhead lights. 'Have you see this before, sir?'

Chris looked at Nash who nodded. 'No, never – Wait a minute – maybe I have. Can I touch it?'

'Yes, it's been through a thorough forensic investigation and it has been unloaded. I would rather you leave it in the bag though.'

Chris picked up the plastic bag and examined the gun. 'I thought I'd seen this one, but I haven't. The one I saw was a replica and had a solid barrel. I told you before, Matt was starting a collection. He had one just like this. He showed it to me not long ago.'

'I think you said, sir, that you had never handled a gun. Can you tell me then how your fingerprints appear on this, and also on each of the bullets?'

Nash interjected. 'He told you, Inspector. He has never seen this gun before. He obviously cannot therefore explain his fingerprints!'

'Very well, Mr Nash. We'll draw our own conclusions. To continue, do you play golf Mr Marten?' Chris nodded.

'Yes, thought you did. Do you play abroad at all?' The nod this time was hardly perceptible. 'I believe you went to Florida recently with Mr Du Bois and two friends, Messrs Richard and Anthony Grace.'

What was he getting at? Chris didn't look for Nash's approval and said 'Yes, yes, yes! That was weeks ago! What is this to do with Matt's disappearance?'

'Do you know that it is fairly easy to purchase firearms in the USA, as they have no stringent laws and regulations relating to sales?'

'I did know that, but it is of no interest to me.'

'Do you know of a shop on Vine Street, Kissimmee, that sells guns?'

'No, of course not!'

'Have you ever considered buying a handgun to bring back to England?'

'No, never! I'd never get it through customs!'

'It could be well hidden.'

Peter Nash interrupted the inspector's flow once again. 'Look, Inspector, where is all this leading?'

'It's leading to, I hope, a full explanation of the truth. Perhaps you should advise your client about the sense of coming clean. You already know that this pistol was fired in Mr Du Bois's office on the night of his disappearance. You also know that samples of Mr Du Bois's rare blood group have been found in your client's car. You also know that your client's fingerprints were on this gun and on the bullets and spent shell-cases in the gun. What you don't know, but I will tell you now, is that your client purchased this gun at Mitchell's Hunting Store on Vine Street, Kissimmee, Florida, the USA on Saturday 19 September!'

Nash's control was amazing. He turned to Chris and said, 'We'll say nothing more until we've had a chance to talk in private.'

'Yes, sir. We'll leave you alone. We shall be taking Mr Marten to Bromley Magistrates' Court tomorrow morning to have him committed to trial and seek to remand him in custody. We will not be granting police bail.'

Inspector Webb stood up, and without a further glance at Chris or his lawyer, he strode out. Sergeant Walker followed, gathering up the gun in its bag as he left.

Chris sat quite still, his hands on the table. His left hand remained quite motionless in its glove. The fingers of his right hand were quietly drumming on the table, the tempo and volume increasing until he smashed his fist down causing Nash to visibly flinch.

'Easy, Chris! Do you want to tell me what happened?'

'Oh, Jesus! Even you, Peter. Even you. Matt has been killed, that's obvious, but I had nothing to do with any of this! It's an elaborate plan to get me screwed and I don't know why! This latest thing with the gun in Florida – I've never been near the place they are talking about. What I don't understand is why and who!'

'Look,' said Nash, 'I think I have an idea. The Florida thing narrows the issues. If only four of you were there, you say you are innocent and Matt is dead, then it could only be one of the other two framing you.'

'Brilliant!' Chris almost screamed. 'Now you have to find out which one of those bastards and why!' He knew that he was clutching at straws but his mood had brightened noticeably.

*

Inspector Webb went straight to his Superintendent and requested permission to fly to Florida to interview the owner of Mitchell's Store in Kissimmee. His boss just laughed. 'Do I look as if I've just fallen out of a tree? No, of course, you can't go buzzing off to Disneyworld at the tax payers' expense. You can get Interpol to help and the local police to take statements and collect the evidence. With what we already have, we'll get a conviction anyway. I'd like to know how he got the gun back here – security at the airport must really be shit! It doesn't give you much confidence to fly, does it?'

While Inspector Webb was trying to persuade his boss to finance a trip to the sunshine, Sergeant Walker had made an appointment to interview Tony and Richard Grace. He had been lucky to get them in their office at the same time. They were both most concerned about Matt's disappearance, and for the umpteenth time he had to say that they had no news and that they were pursuing their enquiries.

He then asked about the recent trip to Florida. Both Tony and Richard enthused about the whole holiday having been superb – the best that they had ever had. When he asked them if all four of them had been together all of the time, Richard replied.

'Yes, we played golf together every day and went out to dinner in the evenings – Oh, except once. That was when Matt cooked a barbecue for us. He got so pissed out of his brains that he couldn't play golf with us the next day. He stayed at the villa the whole day with a real beauty of a hangover. He'd drunk a whole litre of gin the night before, but we all went out to dinner together that night.'

Tony interjected, 'The only other time we weren't all together was on our last night. We did the town that night and Chris got lucky with one of the strippers from a girlie club. He spent the night with her. He came back about lunchtime the next day, which was in fact when we left. We were slightly concerned in case he didn't get back in time to pack and catch the plane. The stripper had rolled him over for about 1,000 dollars out of our kitty! He wasn't very happy.'

'You said your last night there, sir. If he was missing for a few hours the next morning, when would that have been?'

'Oh, let me see.' Tony consulted his diary. 'We travelled on the Saturday, getting back on the Sunday morning. That would be Saturday 19 September.'

Walker smiled and underlined the date in his notebook.

Just after Sergeant Walker left, Tony's secretary said that there was a Mr Nash at reception who would like to see him, if he could spare a few minutes. He was Mr Marten's lawyer.

An hour later, Peter Nash left the building, convinced that he should persuade Chris to plead guilty in an effort to get the whole sorry mess sorted out quickly. He would have to find out from Chris exactly why he had done it, and try to formulate a defence that would mitigate the inevitable prison sentence that would follow.

14

The next morning, Chris was woken up early by a large but surprisingly gentle constable with a steaming mug of tea. To say that he awoke would be untrue. He had hardly slept at all that night. Peter Nash's idea of one of the brothers framing him had buzzed around his head all night, and it was not until just before his jailer had opened his cell door that he regretfully abandoned the idea as not being even remotely possible. There were too many things, too many clues too remote from their involvement to make it possible, that is even if they had a motive to bump off Matt and frame him. No, it had to be someone else.

He kept coming back to Marie. With Matt gone, she would be very wealthy. Had she hired someone to lay all these red herrings? It would have meant being really well in the know and he would have had to follow them to Florida as well. She was Chris's number one suspect.

Yes, if she had the right accomplice, she could have arranged most of those things that pointed the finger at him. She knew all about Matt and him and the business. The more he thought about it, the clearer it became. He would get Nash onto it as soon as he came in. The fucking bitch! Fancy killing her own husband! Revenge was going to be enormously sweet!

Nash arrived at the police cells at half past nine in the morning. He was amazed at how brightly Chris greeted him.

'I want to tell you something. Can we have some privacy?'

The policeman withdrew to the far end of the room.

'Look Peter,' Chris was trying hard to keep his voice down, but the excitement in him was bubbling over. 'I think I know who did it. You've got to get an investigator on to that cow Marie – she did it and she's trying to frame me!'

Nash sat back with a long, sympathetic look on his face at Chris's ebullient enthusiasm. 'Chris,' he said, 'Chris, Chris.' At his tone, the look of glee on Chris's face slowly faded. 'Don't you understand, Chris, it's over! You can't possibly dig yourself out of this. I don't know why, perhaps you had a brain aberration and can't remember a thing that has happened.

'The trouble is, you've obviously done something that is so abhorrent to you that you have pushed it deep down into your subconscious. We have to plead guilty this morning and try desperately hard to get medical help. It is going to be of enormous benefit that you haven't had a blemish on your character, and ... '

'Bollocks!! You prick! What are you saying?' Chris was screaming and standing over a dejected Nash looking as though he was about to strike him. 'I'm innocent – I'm fucking innocent! Can't you understand that? If you don't believe me I'll get another lawyer who will!'

By now the police constable had bounded down the room and forced Chris back into his chair. His mouth was working and spittle dribbled down his chin. Nash tried to placate him.

'Okay, Chris, it's okay. Of course I believe you. We'll go in and plead not guilty. I'll get you the best defence I can.'

Nash knew that it was no use arguing. Chris had obviously flipped. He hoped that he could persuade the court to rely on medical evidence before passing sentence. Until then he would have to humour Chris for his own good.

Just before 10.00 a.m., Chris was taken by the police to a car waiting in the yard at the rear of the station. He was handcuffed to a young constable and suffered the ignominy of having a blanket over his head as they sped past photographers waiting in the side road.

By the time they got to Bromley Magistrates' Court, Peter Nash had already arrived. The bench was made up of three magistrates, two men and a woman. The lady chairman of the bench was a very tall and slightly overweight spinster with iron grey hair, rimless spectacles and the suggestion of a moustache.

During the few minutes that she listened to the facts delivered briefly by Junior Counsel for the Crown Prosecution Service, she played with two long black hairs that protruded from a mole on the side of her jaw.

The hearing lasted barely four minutes and Chris was committed for trial. Peter Nash, sitting alongside him was extremely nervous that Chris would jump up to defend himself there and then. He need have no worries however, for Chris had already decided that he would have to investigate this matter himself and would do nothing to endanger his bail. At the appropriate time, Peter Nash made a courteous application for bail on the basis that his client would need his freedom to properly prepare his defence.

The young counsel, at a nod from Inspector Webb who was sitting behind him opposed bail as forcefully as his inexperienced style would allow, arguing that the crime of which Chris was accused was for murder. As such, and taking into account the gravity and nature of the offence, he should be locked away to protect the public. The magistrate fixed him with a stony stare and at last left the mole alone.

'You may know, or you should, that is the prosecution's duty to persuade me why I should not grant bail. In my opinion the accused has an exemplary record without blemish and I see no reason why he should be held in custody pending his trial. There is no reason to expect that he will commit any further crime, and I would remind you that he has not yet been proven guilty of this crime.

'I therefore grant bail in the accused's own surety of 5,000 pounds. I do not think that a figure any higher than this is appropriate. This is not a case of monetary fraud, and apart from his freedom he has no reason to abscond. I will, however, rule that he reports to the police at Orpington Police Station each Monday and Thursday morning, and that he is ordered to surrender his passport.'

With a final glare at the young barrister, the magistrate dismissed the court.

After completing the formalities with the clerk, Chris and Peter Nash left the court. Strangely, Chris was quite unprepared for the number of press reporters and photographers outside, and the video recorders gathering material for the lunchtime and early evening television news. Chris pushed his way through the throng and both he and Nash forced their way into the first taxi in the rank.

'Drive away!' they ordered the cabbie. 'We'll give you our destination as you go.'

Chris did not see, or even notice, a tall fair man who had sat through the short hearing in the public gallery. There was no reason for him to do so as he had never even met Stephen Murray.

That evening, Chris sat at home behind locked doors and curtained windows and removed the telephones from their sockets. He ignored all of Jennifer's and the boys' attempts to get him to talk or spend a 'normal' evening at home. He was deep in thought and knew that he had to plan carefully. The next few days would be critical.

*

Inspector Webb was the type of copper who, once the crime had been solved, wanted to get onto the next job and as long as the 't's had been crossed twice and all of the 'i's dotted, he felt no need to cross and dot them again.

He therefore put the wheels in motion for an inquest to be held, and as their evidence was all available, the coroner set his court for the next day at 10.00 a.m. Inspector Webb delivered the police evidence, but ever mindful of the quicksands and pitfalls of the law, he confined his facts to those related to Matt's disappearance and made no reference to anyone having been arrested for his murder.

He was conscious that Marten's case was *sub judice*, and it would be quite wrong for him to bring out any evidence that might prejudice Marten's defence. In any case, it was not the coroner's duty to apportion blame or to sit in judgement, but merely to record the cause of death. The inspector noticed that Peter Nash predictably, was seated in the public gallery.

In the event, the coroner made the only decision that he could, and in the absence of an identified corpse he recorded an open verdict.

*

Chris spent the whole of the next day in his study plotting. He had spoken to the office briefly, telling his partners to deal with all important matters and to continue as though nothing had happened. Tim was taking over Matt's workload, and they had all agreed that they would have a brain-storming meeting later in the week, to establish the best way forward.

A few of their private clients had expressed concern at the loss of one of the key players in the practice and the possible absence of the other in a very short time. Chris felt his anger rising at this pre-judgement of the case and felt sure that he would make them eat their words once he had established who was the real guilty party.

He knew in his mind what had happened. Marie had taken a lover, and probably the baby was his! He was sure that between them they had plotted Matt's death. She had access to keys to the office and had him killed there later that night when everyone had gone home. Somehow, they had managed to plant the gun in his boot the next morning and put some of Matt's blood there as well. Bloody Security! They hadn't even noticed anyone tinkering with his car!

The night before, he decided, they had dragged a big bundle over the car park and put it in the boot of the car, pretending it was Matt. They probably took it out the next day when they planted the gun. He'd sack Adams and his lot when this was all sorted out. Marie's lover had gone to Florida when they were all there and bought the gun from a store just down the road from their house. Marie must have sussed that out when she and Jennifer were out there buying furnishings. God – this must have been planned over three years ago!

That was it, the frame up was complete. The only problem was the memo. Somehow Marie had got into his computer and – wait! He knew what she had done. She had bought a small laptop computer compatible with his printer, typed the memo and when the office was empty, linked her computer to his printer and run off the copies! 'Chris, you are brilliant!' he thought.

Of course! It was the printer that was unique, not the computer. He would check in the morning if the memo was on the memory – that would be proof enough for Webb and his lot!

Chris was getting more and more excited about his discovery of the real truth. 'I wonder if I can sue her privately as well as getting her convicted of murder – I'll take her for everything!'

Now that he knew the truth, Chris had to prove it. He needed this proof to clear his own name, and after all, he owed it to Matt.

The first thing was to establish the name of her accomplice. He racked his brains, searching for a foolproof method but could think of no way apart from direct interrogation and forcing it out of her. None of these namby-pamby police methods! There was no such thing as the Marquis of Queensbury in this fight – anything goes! However, he knew that Marie would not let him into her house if he just turned up, so he decided on a simple plan to gain access. He also had to give the reporters the slip. The bastards were still outside his house and would follow him everywhere.

That afternoon, when Jennifer left to pick up the boys from school, Chris asked her to leave her car in a side street about a quarter of a mile away so that he could use it to go to the office that evening without the reporters following. He would sneak out through the back garden when it was dark. Although it meant Jennie and the children running the media gauntlet, she was a tough lady and could handle them with no trouble at all.

When it was quite dark, Chris slipped out of the dining room door, and keeping to the shadows he crept silently across the rear garden to the fence. With a little difficulty, partly due to the three large vodkas he had had before leaving, he climbed into the adjoining owner's garden and then, through their side gate into a small tree-lined cul de sac.

Taking a slightly circuitous route, Chris found Jennie's Toyota Supra automatic at just after half past eight, and set off for Marie's house. He found it only slightly difficult to steer the car one-handed, but the power assisted steering was so responsive that it didn't present much of a problem.

He arrived at the tall electric gates just after nine o'clock, and was pleased to see that the reporters had left her alone. He was relieved, although slightly surprised, that the police had not left a constable on duty. Chris pressed the intercom set in the brick gate pier.

'Hello Marie. It's Chris. Now please don't hang up, I have Jennifer and the boys with me. They need to talk to you. Please may we come in?'

Marie cursed herself that she had never had a video camera installed at the gate, but knowing that she didn't have to open the front door if she didn't want to, she operated the gate-opening switch. She stood by the front door, relieved when she saw it was Jennie's distinctive white Toyota coming up the driveway. Rambo scampered out of the door at the approach of the car and ran to the edge of the drive, tail wagging in expectation of the visitors. Marie knew that he was quite stupid when it came to cars and hurried to pick him up, just as Chris brought the car to a halt.

Chris quickly jumped out and was at Marie's side before she could run to the safety of the house.

'Where's Jennie?' she said, with a slight panic in her voice.

'We have no need for Jennifer yet. We need a little private chat on our own first.'

Taking her elbow firmly, Chris hustled her into the house. Marie knew that to scream would be useless, as the nearest house was over a quarter of a mile away. She could smell alcohol on Chris's breath. Rambo sensed Chris's aggression and managed quite a deep growl for such a little dog.

'Easy, Rambo.' Marie stroked his ears to quieten him down.

Chris slammed the door, and still holding Marie's arm, he forced her into the lounge.

'Okay,' he said. 'Sit down and listen!' He half pushed her roughly into an armchair, ignoring her seven months pregnancy.

'Now – I've got everything worked out! I know all about your plot and how you did it!' His voice was rising in excitement.

Chris went to the table in the corner and helped himself to half a tumbler full of vodka. He raised his eyebrows at Marie who shook her head; she had gone quite cold.

'Now we're comfortable, tell me. Who is it?'

'What do you mean?'

'Come on you bitch. Who's your accomplice! Who's your lover?' He was shouting now. 'Who killed Matt for you?'

She almost laughed out loud, partly in relief – he didn't know the truth after all. 'You must be crazy. You have been charged with his murder – you must be quite mad!'

Marie was now back in control and Chris sensed that her fear that had been so evident a few moments ago, had dissipated. He stood over her menacingly and they both jumped when the phone rang shrilly on the coffee table. It rang only once. Marie glanced at the clock over the fireplace. Exactly nine o'clock. Matt had changed his call time and it would go back to eight o'clock next week. They both looked at the phone and Chris was about to continue when it rang again. 'Answer the fucking thing, but don't say I'm here!' He moved and put his hand on her throat when the ringing stopped again.

'Jesus!' he said. He stormed over to the outlet in the wall in the corner and stamped angrily on the plastic box, shattering it and tearing out the wires. 'We won't have any more interruptions!' he shouted, and returning to Marie again stood menacingly over her.

'Now, bitch, I want some answers!' He raised his hand as if to strike her, while Rambo, his courage belying his size, leapt from Marie's lap and sank his teeth deep into Chris's left hand. His sharp canines pierced the black glove and his weight dragged Chris's hand to his waist. Shaking his arm with his other hand, Chris couldn't dislodge the little dog and although he felt no pain at all, the sight of his own blood on the dog's white fur incensed him. He grabbed Rambo by the scruff of his neck, and with an enormous jerk he tore him free, breaking two of the dog's teeth as he did so.

'You little bastard!' he screamed, and with all his might he threw Rambo as hard as he could from him. Rambo was still growling as his small body smashed into the large full-length framed mirror by the door. Marie heard the stomach-churning crunch as his small bones were smashed. Almost in slow motion, Rambo slid to the floor, panting, his legs jerking slightly. Marie screamed as she waddled as fast as she could. She dropped to her knees by Rambo's side. She gently lifted his head, and he whimpered quietly just once before the light went out of his eyes.

'Oh no!' Marie cried. 'Oh, no! No!' Still on her knees, she gently lifted the lifeless body and cradled it to her breast, tears streaming down her face, quickly to be absorbed by Rambo's fur. She turned on Chris, who had removed his glove and was examining his torn and bleeding hand.

'You bastard!' she screamed. 'You absolute, indescribable fucking bastard!' Marie had never used that word in her life before but repeated it over and over and over again. At last her voice trailed off as her head sank into Rambo's fur. Chris was quite unrepentant.

'Tell me! Who is it?' He was now screaming, and in a strange way this seemed to calm Marie. She looked at him coldly with hatred in her eyes.

'You think you have all the answers, but you know nothing! You are so wrong. I'll tell you the answers! You are a crook of the worst kind, but not clever enough. You will be put in prison for murder and I'm glad. You'll be ruined! and I'm glad! And, you bastard, you will die penniless! And I'm glad! Don't think you are rich, your Caribbean bank has given all your money away and you'll never get it back! And I'm glad, I am really glad!'

Chris frowned. 'What do you mean, bitch? What do you mean?' Marie sat staring at him defiantly, her tears still wet on her face and a sneering smile touching the corners of her mouth.

Chris bounded across the room. 'I said, what do you mean? Explain yourself!' He slapped her as hard as he could across the mouth, knocking her onto her side, Rambo's body falling to the floor. 'Get up!' he screamed. 'Get up and answer me!' By now he was completely out of control and grabbing Marie by the hair, he dragged her into a sitting position. She stared at him, her teeth still rattling from the blow. He half dragged her to her feet, and when she started to slump again, he released her hair and punched her very hard on the side of the face. As she fell, she caught her head on the corner of the coffee table with a terrible crack and lay on the floor quite still.

Chris stared at her prone body and then at Rambo's. 'Jesus Christ Almighty! I've killed her. Oh God, how did this happen?' Chris ran to the phone but it was quite dead of course. Yes, he could just remember having smashed the plug. He ran into the kitchen and lifted the extension but that was also dead. 'Oh, shit. It was the main incoming line I smashed!'

Chris slumped onto a stool by the breakfast bar. 'What shall I do?' he moaned to himself. 'What shall I do?' He then remembered with a jerk what Marie had said about his numbered account. 'Jesus, if that's gone, I've really had it!'

He charged through the hallway, and smashing the front door back on its hinges he ran to the car. He sprayed gravel all over the lawn as he careered down the driveway. Forgetting about the electronic opener, he skidded to a halt just in front of the gate and then reversed furiously back to the post. He pressed the button and he rocketed through the gate which was still opening, smashing both wing mirrors as the gap was too narrow. He was sweating and drove erratically and far too fast to the offices. He was running scared!

*

When Chris screeched to a halt at the office car park barrier, it was just approaching ten o'clock. He knew that the bank in the Cayman Islands closed at six o'clock in the evening, so with the time difference, he would be okay. He sounded the horn impatiently when the barrier was not raised immediately, glaring at the security man as he shot through the gap. He skidded to a halt in his car parking space and leapt out, running to the door.

'Is everything all right, sir?' The security man was trotting across, intercepting Chris as he went in.

'Yes! Get back to your post! I'll lock up. You can go home early. I'll be here for a little while!'

The security man was pleased to get an early night – just time for a quickie before the pubs closed. He filled out his log, including Chris's permission to leave early and closed up at 10.07 p.m. precisely.

Chris dashed from the lift to his office and in his haste misdialled the code to his safe. At the second attempt it opened and he grabbed the 'Access' envelope. He feverishly dialled his number, drumming on his desk while he waited for the connection to be made. A sing-song voice merely answered, 'Good afternoon. How may we help you?'

'Good afternoon. Mr English please?' After a short pause, a voice said, 'Good afternoon, sir.'

'Good,' said Chris, and then went on: 'Account number 3870018472/07. CDM. 11.07.55. British.'

'Go ahead Mr Devon.'

Chris read from his last statement, 'Access code 13722471.'

'Could you please repeat it, sir?' Chris did so.

'I'm sorry, sir. The Access code doesn't match. Access is denied.'

'What!' screamed Chris. 'What do you mean? It doesn't match!' Chris stared at the handset. The line was quite dead.

He checked his statement again. This was the last transaction back in June when he had transferred 250,000 dollars to the Sevenoaks Branch. On impulse, he telephoned his mother's home in Petts Wood. He was very short with her when she answered and took no time to ask how her rheumatism was. 'Is there one of my private letters for me from America?'

'Yes, dear, it came through last Thursday. I was going to phone you to let you know, but with all your other problems, I didn't want to worry you.'

Chris took several deep breaths and controlled his irritation with some difficulty.

'Okay, Ma. Can you open it for me now?'

After a short pause, during which he could hear her struggling with the envelope, she said 'I've got it now – shall I read it out?'

'No, Ma. Just give me the number right at the bottom.'

He wrote it down and repeated it back to her. '28428369. Good, now what's the figure in the last column?'

'Oh, let me see. It looks like 10,263. Would that be right?'

'No. It can't be! There's another figure, about three million and something.'

'Oh, I can't see that, dear. Where would it be?' He could hear her turning the statement over and looking at the back.

'Don't worry, Ma. I'll check it out. Oh, and don't worry about me, I'm okay!'

He replaced the phone, and before redialling Cayman he poured himself another large vodka from his private bar. There was not much left in the bottle. Incongruously, he made a note to replenish his bar the next day.

Once again, he got through in very quick time and went through the procedure with Mr English. When he reached the access code, he read out the figures just given to him by his mother.

'Thank you, Mr Devon. I can confirm that your account stands at 10,263 dollars. That includes interest as at close of business this evening.'

'What!?' Chris screamed. 'That's wrong! There's nearly four million dollars in that account. What was the last transaction?'

'I'm sorry, Mr Devon, I can only give the balance of the account on this code. I repeat 10,263 dollars. Thank you, sir.' The line went dead.

Chris slowly replaced his receiver. 'Jesus, what a mess!' He really was going mad. He poured the last of his vodka into his glass, and not bothering with a mixer he threw it down his throat in one. He gagged as the liquid burned his throat and he felt tears sting the back of his eyes.

He slumped at his desk and tried hard to think. After a short while, a mixture of vodka and shock caused him to abandon the idea of unravelling this unholy mess. All he knew was that he stood accused of murdering his partner and that he could find no defence. He had probably killed Marie and her dog too, and now he was utterly broke. He reached again for the bottle and sobbed when he remembered that he had just drunk the last drop. 'How long ago was that?' he thought. He was now crying quite uncontrollably as he packed up his 'Access' envelope, and tidy as ever, he locked it away in his safe. He turned out his lights and staggered across the lobby to Matt's office. He went to the bar and took a full bottle of Stolichnaya from the shelf.

Chris had taken two full swigs from the bottle by the time the lift reached the ground floor, and he stood in the lift, trying to regain his balance before lurching across the reception lobby. He tripped over a coffee table half way across and was lucky to land on a soft, low chair, spilling only a little of his drink. As he lay there, he felt sorry for himself again, knowing what a pathetic picture he must make.

After a short while, he wobbled to the front door and collapsed into the front seat of Jennifer's car. 'God!' he thought. 'I could end it all. Drive this bastard into a brick wall!'

He knew that he didn't have the courage for that, so he took another swig, only managing with some effort to keep down the bile rising into his mouth. He turned on the radio cassette player and barely heard the tape that Jennifer had left in the deck. Frank Sinatra was singing *One More for the Road*, from his album *Only The Lonely*. This did nothing to cheer Chris as he took another swig from his bottle. 'That's it,' he said out loud. 'I'll do it.'

He almost fell out of the car when he opened the door and just about managed to open the front door of the offices without falling. Using the reception desk for support, he staggered to the staircase door, and at the third attempt he managed to open the door to the basement. Nearly falling down the stairs, he finally got to the boiler room. He rummaged around in one of the cupboards and found a Stanley knife and some wide masking tape. He went to the hose used for draining down the boilers, and he cut off about a 12 foot length. Strangely, now his decision had been taken, he seemed less drunk, although he found it difficult to climb the stairs and get back to the car park. Chris did not bother to close or lock any of the doors behind him, and he started to giggle. 'Who cares? Makes no diff'rence now!'

Chris knelt at the back of the Toyota and poked the hose into the exhaust pipe. When it was in about six inches, he tore a length of masking tape with his teeth and stuck the hose in position. He got angry when he couldn't find the loose end of the roll again, and he smashed his hand against the exhaust pipe. He didn't even feel it as his middle two fingers snapped.

At last he had the hose in position and the gap around it largely sealed. He felt his way back down the side of the car and fell into the front seat, with the open end of the hose gripped tightly in his broken hand. He switched on the ignition and opened the window slightly, passing the hose over the top as he slammed the door. He then wound up the window to trap the hose. Chris tore the tape and stuck it over the half inch gap over the top of the door, sealing it roughly but not completely.

He took a further swig from his bottle and settled back in the comfortable seat and started the engine. He felt nothing more, no guilt, no remorse, not even sorrow. He slowly slipped into unconsciousness to the mournful strains of Frank Sinatra's *Willow, Weep for Me*.

*

The next morning at 5.00 a.m., George Adams arrived at the offices. His first impression was that Mrs Marten was at the offices, as her car was in the car park and the lights were on in the reception area. It was only when he had switched off the engine to his car and was walking across to the entrance that he noticed the engine of the Toyota was running. He dashed the last 30 yards and tried to wrench open the locked door when he saw the body on the front seat through the misted windows. He dragged the hosepipe out, and gripping the top of the door through the gap he pulled with all his might. The glass broke off cleanly and with his hand over his mouth, George reached in and switched off the engine. He dragged Chris out onto the ground.

He knew that resuscitation would be useless. Christopher Marten was quite, quite dead.

15

Marie regained consciousness to the sound of terrible, terrified screaming. She realized with a start that the horrific sounds were coming from her own throat. She tried to raise herself, but her arms were so weak that she collapsed again. Waves of pain and nausea were sweeping through her body.

She lay still for only a moment, trying to remember. The sharp pains on both sides of her head and her face jogged her memory. 'Oh, God,' she felt terrible. Just then, the pain in her head was overridden by the agonizing pain coming from her abdomen. She rolled over again and screamed.

The pain subsided momentarily and she put her hand down to her legs. It came away sticky, and this time her screams were of terror. She knew that she must get help quickly or die. And her baby! Her fears grew worse. Her eyes lit on the still, now quite cold form of Rambo, and her recollection of what had happened was complete.

How long had she been out? She stared at the clock over the fireplace, and after a struggle she brought it into focus. It showed ten minutes past midnight – she had been unconscious for over three hours.

Marie dragged herself to the coffee table and tried to kneel but the pain was too much. She found the telephone on the floor but it was quite dead. She remembered that Chris had smashed the socket.

In agony, Marie hauled herself into the hallway and through the doorway to Matt's study. She scrabbled at the desk and pulled his phone into her lap by the cord. 'Damn!' It was dead as well. 'Matt, oh Matt, I need you! Why aren't you here?'

Where could she get help? She knew that if she waited until the morning she would die, and her instincts told her that her baby required immediate and expert attention.

She could still not stand and she was leaking blood and mucus down her legs. She managed to get to the front door, which was letting an icy blast of October air into the house. She reached an umbrella from the stand by the door and managed to press the button that opened the garage door.

Crying with the pain in her head and abdomen and opening new grazes from the gravelled driveway, she hauled herself over to the garage and stretched up to open the Mercedes. Thank God! It wasn't locked. Marie reached in, and dragging the phone from its cradle she switched on and dialled 999.

She got an immediate response and ignoring the request for her number, which she couldn't remember anyway, she cried, 'Send an ambulance at once – I'm dying.' She gave the address in a very weak voice and mumbled 'Yes, yes,' when the operator repeated it. With great presence of mind, she managed to reach the hazard warning lights switch before collapsing in a heap on the cold garage floor alongside the car.

Her last thoughts were of Matt, then Stephen Murray, then of them both merged into one grotesque two-headed figure.

Ten minutes later, an ambulance from Orpington skidded to a halt at the gates. The driver's mate jumped out and pressed the entryphone buzzer.

There was no reply and after several attempts, he called to his driver, and with a great show of athleticism he climbed the gate. There had to be a lever or a handle somewhere. With the aid of his torch he searched on the back of the brick piers, then he shone his torch up the driveway. He sprinted to the post. 'Thank God!' he said, pressing the button. The ambulance driver reversed quickly as the gate opened towards him, and as soon as it was clear he accelerated through. His mate jumped in while it was still in motion, and by now they could see the lights of the house and the flashing orange lights in the garage.

They picked out Marie in the headlights, and the driver left the ambulance facing the garage. His mate was already bending over Marie, both of them casting weird shadows on the rear wall of the garage.

Luckily for Marie, the medics knew their job and she was being rushed to hospital within five minutes, wrapped in thermal blankets and with a saline drip in her arm. Her legs were elevated and the driver's mate applied an oxygen mask to her nose and mouth. She was aware of the drive to the hospital only vaguely, and the pain and distress she was feeling would mark her mentally for the rest of her life. Only once did she speak. 'Stephen!' she screamed, 'Stephen, I need you!!'

*

It was expected that Marie would stay in hospital for four weeks. On arrival, the doctors' immediate concern was for her, and they ensured that her condition was stable before turning to the baby. When she was checked in they had just been able to detect very faint heart beats, and the gynaecological surgeon was summoned to prepare for an emergency caesarean delivery. Marie was sedated and she had no knowledge of what was happening. In the emergency, the surgeon ignored the consent procedure and the operation was performed at 1.35 a.m.

It was recorded that a baby boy of 4 lb 3 oz at about 30 weeks term, was dead when delivered at 1.45 a.m. Marie did not wake until 9.00 a.m. the next day when she was told by her mother, who had been at her bedside since the police collected her at 4.00 a.m.

'You poor girl,' her mother wept. 'You've lost your husband and your baby in the same week. I know how you feel. I really do know how you feel!'

*

Over the next few weeks Marie was distraught and quite inconsolable. The news of Christopher's suicide had upset her more than she thought it would. Even though he had directly caused the death of her baby due to his ferocious and violent physical attack, she found that perversely, she was blaming Matt. He had left her to cope on her own and had devised this intricate and devious scheme as an act of vengeance.

If only he had just taken the money, he could have shamed Christopher into resigning from the firm and they would all still be happy. Damn him! Why did he go? Why was she left alone? Why was he not here now? She knew now that she would never forgive Matt.

Marie was silently crying almost continually, and her deep depression was a cause of concern among the medical staff. She only seemed to brighten for a short time when she had visits from Stephen Murray. His many and regular gifts of flowers when he visited brought a splash of colour to her very comfortable but rather plainly decorated private room.

Every third day, Marie received a beautiful bouquet of Sonia roses which had always been her favourite. When the first bouquet was delivered via a Teleflorist agency without a message, she was only told that the order had been placed in Spain. She demanded that the nurse take them away and refused to accept every delivery after that.

*

Matt had been very busy over his first two weeks in Menorca. With the help of Nicholás Brechia, he had settled into a two-bedroomed villa in Santandria just south of Ciutadella.

Although the small inlet was bustling and quite crowded in the season, it was secluded and almost deserted at this time of year. He thought the isolation and quiet would suit him through the winter months. He hoped to only spend a little time at this villa to eat and sleep. His time would be spent at Turqueta with organizing, supervising and helping with the construction of his new home. His design had been finalized and lodged for planning approval with the help of a freshly qualified Spanish architect in San Clemente. Matt had made funds available to grease palms and smooth the passage of the application through officialdom. He had been assured that work could commence on site and that the approval would follow on in due course.

Matt spent many hours in the lawyer's office and had, as a result, become very friendly with Claudia, Señor Brechia's secretary. They had dined out once and Matt found her Spanish charm and slightly prudish nature strangely attractive. She was 23 years old and very dark; her eyes were such a deep black colour that they seemed to flash in the light.

Matt collected his English newspaper, as usual, from a small stall in Ciutadella. His normal routine, which he had established early on, was to leave the Santandria villa after only taking a cup of coffee, pick up his newspaper and any mail from Ciutadella and have breakfast at the hotel overlooking the square in *Cami del Caballeros*. He would then get to Turqueta at about half past nine in the morning and the work would have already been under way on site for a couple of hours.

This morning, Matt did not get as far as the hotel. He glanced at the headlines of yesterday's *Daily Telegraph* and stopped in his tracks. The bold print screamed at him, PARTNER OF MISSING ARCHITECT FOUND DEAD. Below, in only slightly smaller print, SUCCESSFUL BUSINESS MAN BEATS UP DEAD PARTNER'S WIFE AND THEN COMMITS SUICIDE.

He felt quite weak as he read a graphic report of how Christopher Marten, a successful and respected architect and businessman, had apparently forced his way into Mrs Marie Du Bois's house and severely beaten her, killing her dog and leaving her badly injured. He had then returned to his office and was found the next morning by a security guard in a car full of exhaust fumes. He had been dead for some hours.

The article continued with a brief statement from the officer in charge, Detective Inspector Webb from Orpington Police Station, saying that Mrs Du Bois was in a private hospital near Sevenoaks and her condition was said to be satisfactory. She had been seven and a half months pregnant, but her baby had been born dead. The article then went over old ground, giving details of Chris's earlier arrest for the murder of his partner. A photograph of Chris headed the article, with a rather poor reproduction of Matt's likeness at the end. He felt only a moment's remorse for Christopher.

Matt's heart was racing to provide a blood supply to his brain; his face had drained of colour. His immediate thought, stimulated by panic, was to rush to the airport and arrange a flight to England straight away. He forced himself to calm down, and after several deep breaths he knew that he must plan; he couldn't allow blind panic to drive his actions.

He had to know how Marie was and where she was. They had private medical insurance, but she could be in any one of a number of hospitals. The article only said the hospital was in the Sevenoaks area. Matt knew that anyone who knew Marie well enough to pass on information to him over the phone would surely recognize his voice, no matter how well he disguised it. No, he couldn't speak. He would need help.

Claudia was already at her desk when Matt burst into her room. Her ready smile at seeing Matt unexpectedly died when she saw the worry in his eyes and replaced it with a look of concern.

'*Alfredo, que pasa?*' Their conversation continued in Spanish.

'Claudia, I've had some very bad news. The wife of a friend of mine has had an accident in England. I want to know how she is, but I can't phone her husband. She and I had a little … ,' he searched for the most appropriate Spanish word ' … "involvement" some time ago, and he will refuse to talk to me. Please would you telephone England for me – I'll give you the numbers and the questions I want to ask.'

'Of course, Alfredo. Give me the details.'

Matt scribbled a telephone number and a name on her notepad.

'You will have to wait until ten o'clock – that's an office number. She won't be at her desk until nine o'clock English time. While we are waiting, I'd love a cup of your delicious coffee.'

Matt felt strangely at ease in Claudia's company and although Marie was foremost in his mind, his immediate concern diminished. He told himself, partly to assuage his feeling of guilt, that this was because he could do nothing more anyway for the next half hour.

At just after 10 o'clock, Claudia made her call. She was connected at once and asked for Cathy Steiner, Mr Du Bois's secretary. The telephonist asked who she was, and Claudia, on Matt's direction, said in passable but not totally fluent English she was an old friend of Mrs Du Bois. After a short pause, Cathy came on the line.

'Good morning, Miss Steiner, I am very sorry to worry you. I know Marie Du Bois from a holiday she had in my country last year with Matt. I heard of his problem and have read of her accident. I wish to send "get well quickly" card. Do you have address of hospital, please?'

She had read the names from her notebook without hesitation, and to Matt she sounded very convincing. Cathy obviously felt the same because she gave Claudia the name, address and telephone number of the hospital in Sevenoaks straight away. She also answered Claudia's question, saying that Marie was as well as could be expected, adding that they were all devastated by what had happened over the past few weeks. The conversation finished and Claudia tore off the page on which she had scribbled, and passed it over to Matt.

'Of course, you can use the phone here. I'll go next door to leave you in private.'

'Gracias, Claudia. Eres una amiga de uerdad.'

Although Matt was sure that he could not be overheard, he affected a slight Spanish accent to his English when he called the hospital. He got through to a young auxiliary nurse who was just going off duty after a ten-hour stint, during which she had spent every spare minute studying for the exam she was due to take in a week's time. She was certain that she would fail. There was so much to learn.

'Maternity Wing – Nurse Greene speaking. How may I help you?'

The hospital was insistent on a good 'front of house' image for their high-fee paying private patients. She recognized the slight accent in the voice, Spanish or Italian, but was suspicious of the pidgin being spoken – it sounded slightly false.

'Another of those nosey-parker bloody reporters,' she thought.

'Yes, Mrs Du Bois is here. She is quite stable and she had a satisfactory night. Yes, I can give her a message – Mr Perez you say, from Spain? Yes, I'll tell her you called and pass on your best wishes. Goodbye.'

God, she thought, the tricks they get up to. Tomorrow he'd be on the doorstep saying Mrs Du Bois knew him and could he see her. If they weren't so vigilant, their patients would get no peace at all.

Nurse Greene screwed up the page on which she had written 'Mr Perez from Spain', and dropped it into the waste bin overflowing with her notes from the night's study. Her relief came on duty looking clean and freshly starched and Nurse Greene left for a few hours of sleep before the next round of anatomical reading.

*

When Matt left Claudia, he drove straight to the florist in the main square to order a dozen roses to be delivered anonymously to a hospital in Kent, England, every third day. As the order originated from Spain and only he knew that her favourite rose was Sonia, she would know that they were from him. She would understand that he could not get to her in person, and he hoped that the knowledge that he was with her in thought would be enough.

He also telephoned on each of the successive ten days and was rewarded every time with the news that Mrs Du Bois was getting slowly stronger each day and they hoped she would soon be sufficiently recovered to think about convalescence. On the eleventh day, Matt was worried to hear that she had discharged herself that morning.

He immediately telephoned his home number, but only got the 'unobtainable' signal. In near panic he telephoned International Directory Enquiries to be told, after a long search, that the number had been changed and the new entry was ex-directory.

16

Detective Inspector Webb wanted to close his files on the case. Christopher Marten's suicide had effectively tied his hands as far as further investigation was concerned, and his superiors were satisfied that the case was solved. However, he still had some nagging doubts.

Firstly, why did Marten not dispose of the gun when he got rid of the body? Possibly, he thought he might need to use the gun again. Certainly, some men, particularly hitherto mild men, enlisted a great sense of power from owning a weapon. Also, he had bought two boxes of ammunition – a hundred rounds in each, so he obviously hadn't bought it just for Du Bois's murder. In his own mind, he thought that the killing had been in the heat of the moment, not pre-planned.

The second thing that was slightly incongruous, was his getting rid of the body almost straight away after the killing, as he supposed. Why did he not wait until security had gone home before taking it to his car?

It could have been just through blind panic, or Marten had forgotten all about being seen from the security hut. More likely, he had thought he wouldn't be seen at all. After some reflection, Inspector Webb recalled that on occasions that Marten had apparently worked on after eleven o'clock when security left, George Adams had said that he sometimes went up to Marten's office to tell him he was leaving so that Marten could lock up. Maybe he had been afraid that Adams would stumble on something that would trigger suspicion in his mind, particularly as he hadn't seen Du Bois leave the offices that evening.

Additionally, if the murder hadn't been planned, he probably wouldn't have checked for the bullets that missed the target, he would have just wanted to get rid of the evidence. Would they ever know where he had disposed of the body, he wondered.

Inspector Webb had attended the short inquest on Marten's death that morning, and the expected verdict of 'his having killed himself while the balance of his mind was disturbed' was recorded by the coroner. He remarked that the quantity of alcohol in his blood indicated that he had drunk nearly one and a half litres of spirit, and this had probably added to the loss of the equilibrium of his mind.

Apart from his reservations, the inspector was happy to close his files. He had again asked his Superintendent if he could go to Florida to interview the owner of the gun store, but the best that he had achieved was a number of faxes between his office and the Sheriff of Osceola County who had spoken to the owner of Mitchells.

There was confirmation of the signature on the registration document and Mitchell had given an accurate description of Marten, right down to the gloved left hand, the moustache and the unusually coloured ink which he used in his pen.

However, the final piece in the jigsaw had been provided the day before in the afternoon. A rather tearful Cathy Steiner had telephoned him. She was cleaning out Matt's desk and private files when she came across a couple of items that he might find of interest. He called round to the offices at once. Cathy firstly told him that she had found the code to Matt's safe in his desk. Thinking that there might be something of importance addressed to Matt's lawyers, she went to the safe. She found that Chris had given Matt a note of his own safe code and also the access number to his computer. Cathy was upset.

'I don't want to appear disloyal to Matt, but this means he knew how to get into Chris's computer and could have typed the memo. I hope you can prove me wrong. I really do.'

'Don't upset yourself, Miss. It doesn't look too serious – Look, the signature was Mr Marten's and the copy was filed in his private system with the only keys being his and Wendy's. Wendy has already said quite forcefully that she would never let anyone have her set – Chris expressly forbade it. No, I really don't think this incriminates Mr Du Bois. After all, he was the one who was killed.

'I do think though, that as we have now got the code to Mr Marten's safe, we ought to take a look. Would you accompany me please?'

As they walked across the lobby, Webb asked what was the second thing she had found.

'Well, not found, really – rather remembered. Chris had asked Matt to go to Nigeria on business and the travel arrangements he had suggested were so incredibly dangerous as to be stupid. I've located Chris's memo on the subject. Matt didn't go, of course.'

'There you are then. Further evidence incriminating Mr Marten. I don't think you need have any fears about the credibility of your old boss – but thanks for raising it anyway.'

By now, the inspector knew the location of Chris's safe and went directly to the rosewood panelled doors behind his desk. They opened at a touch and reading from the handwritten note in Chris's impeccable script, he punched in the code in the panel on the door. It opened slowly towards him and he reached in, taking out a number of A4 manilla envelopes.

'Well, the accountants will want these,' he said, spreading the contents of the first two on the desk. They were insurance policies and a few share certificates. He replaced them in their envelopes and frowned as the photographs from the third envelope spilled onto the desk. Standing behind him, Cathy gasped.

'I think Wendy should see this,' she said.

Inspector Webb nodded. 'Yes, give me a few minutes to think, please.'

He steepled his fingers in front of his face. Hmm. Could she be involved? No, it looked at though she had been stupid enough to allow some sordid pictures to be taken, but that was all. He could see no connection with the crime, viewed from any angle..

He replaced the polaroids and re-sealed the envelope which he took out to Wendy in the lobby, sitting melancholically at her desk, looking completely and utterly lost.

'You may like to destroy these, Miss – they're of no use to anyone and I would hate to think of them falling into the wrong hands.'

He nodded to Cathy to rejoin him, and as he closed Chris's door, he heard a loud sob escape from Wendy's throat. Going back to Chris's desk, he selected the next envelope entitled 'Access'.

He read with considerable interest the complicated procedure for gaining entry into Chris's numbered account in the Cayman Islands. He had to be either wealthy or crooked to need one of those. He scanned the remaining envelopes, selecting the one he was looking for, labelled 'First National'.

His eyebrows raised when he saw the balance at the bottom of the last statement – over 3,600,000 dollars – God, this would have to be reported to the Inland Revenue – he was fiddling something somewhere. Where had all that money come from?

At the bottom of the last statement, above the figure that he knew from the previous 'Access' envelope to be the final code needed to get into the account, there was another handwritten figure. On impulse, he telephoned the number shown on the procedural notes. When he got through, he followed the directions implicitly and giving the final handwritten access code was rewarded with 'Your account, Mr Devon, stands at 10,312 dollars as at opening of business this morning. Thank you, sir.'

He replaced the handset. 'Well, Marten must have pre-planned this,' he thought aloud. He had even moved all of his money – three and a half million in cash was gone. It would never be seen or heard of again. The secret of its whereabouts, like Du Bois's body, had gone to the grave with him.

Marten had accrued an enormous wealth, but where from? He would need to get Inland Revenue to check this out with the firm's accountants. The inspector turned to the final envelope and was even more surprised than before when he saw the photographs of Adrian Bullock.

'Not again!' he sighed. 'I'd better speak to him. Can you get him up please, Cathy?'

Adrian Bullock was something of a enigma in the practice. He was given the status of a partner, without being one, and attended all partnership meetings, taking minutes and giving advice on staffing and welfare matters. Most of the partners thought him a pain in the neck but tolerated him knowing him to be of immense help to Chris.

He had a considerable chip on his shoulder, having never attained the status of really being an employer and he acted, though he did not want to be treated, like an employee.

In the past, Chris had been very close to sacking him, largely due to Bullock's lack of respect and consideration for the technical staff. However, he realized Bullock's use to him and held his sometimes obvious dislike in check, not feeling that this in itself was a sufficient, or indeed valid, reason for his dismissal.

Bullock was approaching 60 years of age and was still strikingly handsome and fairly fit, although he had in the past had operations on abdominal glands. He still took medication on a four hourly basis, and he would use this as an excuse for his shortcomings on the many occasions that Chris picked him up on a mistake committed or an instruction not executed.

He looked quite concerned when he knocked on Christopher's door and entered, seeing Cathy and Inspector Webb. His eyes at once took in the open safe and the envelope on Chris's desk. He had seen it only once before, but he recognized it and its contents at once.

'Good afternoon, Inspector. I can see you have found those pictures taken by Christopher. I'm sure you want an explanation, but please can it be in private? I really don't think this is anything to do with secretaries.'

Inspector Webb had taken something of a dislike to Bullock at previous interviews, and in view of his condescending manner, reversed his decision to let him off lightly.

'I'll decide, Mr Bullock, who stays or goes at my interviews – not you! However, on this occasion, I think it is in Cathy's best interest to be protected from the filth I have uncovered.' He glared at length at Bullock, forcing him to lower his eyes, and then turned to Cathy with a smile. 'Perhaps you would like to leave us for a while, and again, I am sincerely grateful for your help.'

Cathy smiled and quietly left the room. Bullock spoke:

'I've been expecting this for some time. Ever since Matt's disappearance, in fact. As far as the photographs are concerned, I had a night out with Christopher not long after I joined the practice. We went to the annual dinner at my lodge and I took Christopher as a guest. We ended up at a sleazy bar in Swallow

Street in the West End and were picked up by a couple of girls. It was all good clean fun and we finally arrived at a small bedsit in Croydon that Chris rented on the quiet. He said it was useful for taking his girlfriends to if he wanted what he described as "a bit of illicit fun". I don't know who he was carrying on with at the time but he boasted about his sexual activities.

'Anyway, by the time we got there, we were all quite merry, and well, you know how it is, Inspector. One thing led to another and to the obvious conclusion.

'Although I have been happily married for nearly 40 years, my wife has little interest in sex any more. Unfortunately, I still rather like that sort of thing and that evening with Chris was quite memorable.

'As you can see, Chris had one of those Polaroid cameras at the flat and took a couple of pictures of the girls. They were good fun and joined in; then we all got involved, and rather stupidly I see now, took pictures of each other.

'I thought that Chris had destroyed them – he told me he had – until one day a few years ago. I think I'd better tell you the whole story, you'll find it out eventually anyway, when the executors to Chris and Matt's wills start digging.

'Over the past six years, Christopher has been rooking Matt out of his share of the practice profits. He had devised a scheme of changing a couple of pages of the accounts and then getting Matt to sign them without his knowing. This signed Matt's share of the profit over to Chris almost in its entirety.'

Bullock explained how Chris had given Matt the true top copy of the balance sheet and altered the remainder. He was most surprised that it had worked for six years, and at the end of each fiscal year when the accounts were prepared he expected an explosion when the scheme was discovered. However, Chris had got away with it, right to the end.

'I suppose that Matt's estate will sue for recovery of the funds. I don't know where Chris salted them away, but there must be a considerable amount of money by now.'

Inspector Webb blessed his good luck. Had he just given the photos to Bullock as he had with Wendy, none of this information would have been imparted. He could have had egg on his face when these facts came to light, as they obviously would later. Webb warmed slightly to Bullock.

'I actually know where he put the money, Mr Bullock. He had it in a numbered account in the Caribbean island of Grand Cayman. That was until a few weeks ago, just before Mr Du Bois's death. He moved it on then, and with the protection that numbered accounts give I doubt if we'll ever know where. This is a job for the Inland Revenue investigation branch. I'll give them a full report, though frankly, I don't think they'll be that interested. From what you've said, taxes were fully paid on the profits and it's of no consequence to them that the net profit was "given away" by one partner to the other. It's of obvious interest, of course, to Matt's estate, but that's all. At least, we can now guess what their argument was about! Now, what shall I do with you?

'Blackmail is no defence to committing a crime, although it does mitigate the sentences passed by some judges. What is your crime? It really is one of non-disclosure of another's fraud, of which you were aware. In the circumstances, I don't think you would even be convicted. However, I must put a full report in to the Director of Public Prosecutions, and it will be up to him to decide if he wants to proceed. In any case, I think these pictures paradoxically will be of some help to you – they will be evidence of the fact that you were blackmailed.

'Personally, I don't think the matter will go any further and there is no reason to worry that these pictures will remain anything other than totally private.'

With a grateful nod, Bullock left the office and Cathy came back in.

'Well Cathy, I think that just about wraps this up, although there will almost certainly be further investigations regarding the profits of the practice. That's for others though and I think now my work is just about done.'

Webb wavered, on the brink of asking Cathy out for a drink, but decided against it. She wasn't his type really, but then, not many women were. Instead, he set his course for Catford in South East London.

*

When Marie decided that she had had enough of hospital, she telephoned Stephen Murray to ask him to collect her and take her home.

Her doctors and surgeons tried desperately hard to persuade her to stay for a few more days. It was essential that her body fully recovered from the shock of the beating and her miscarriage. Additionally, she would need very careful counselling as a result of the mental trauma that she had suffered. The doctors feared a permanent scarring of her personality; her friends and family had already noticed a change and a hardening of her attitude. She smiled only rarely, as was to be expected, and most of the time her lips were compressed, giving her mouth a straight and rather austere look.

Stephen collected Marie from the hospital in a somewhat battered Ford Sierra, and although he attempted light conversation Marie was perfectly still and quiet all the way home. Marie's daily help was at the house, and Marie sent her home once she had placed a light salad lunch in front of them.

Marie just played with her fork and not a morsel passed her lips. She was staring into space, her thoughts obviously miles away. Respecting her mood, Stephen quietly cleared the table and sat opposite her, waiting for her to speak. They sat like this for over an hour until at last Marie turned her gaze slowly onto Stephen's face.

'Let's start again,' she said, and coming round the table she placed her hands on Stephen's shoulders. 'Let's start again.' She kissed him long and gently on the mouth, then he rose and held her close to his chest. His eyes were stinging. He knew that for him, life really was going to begin at 40. He had no way of knowing that he might well be used in a calculated and unforgivable way.

*

The next day, Marie made an appointment to see her family lawyer. He was also a good friend and had visited Marie several times over the past few weeks, not only to see that she was recovering, but also to underline his availability should any new problems arise.

Marie was polite and friendly but Michael Burford was conscious of a subtle change in her demeanour. She told him quite firmly that she wanted the whole question of Matt's estate tied up as quickly as possible.

Michael agreed to get on to it at once and had already made a start. Matt's will was simple – as Marie had not died before him, she would inherit everything. As far as his estate was concerned, this was in the main, fairly straightforward. The house, insurances and property would produce in excess of four million pounds. The only complication was related to the practice.

Michael had received a call from someone in the office of the DPP. It appeared that over the past six years, Christopher Marten had been taking Matt's share of the profits and hiding it away. It was doubtful if it could ever be recovered, but Marie could, of course, sue Chris's estate for the sum involved which was about a million pounds.

Michael had already spoken to Chris's lawyer, Peter Nash, who he knew quite well, in an attempt to get things moving. Nash had confirmed that the suicide clause in Chris's insurance would limit the payout to Jennifer to a few thousand.

Marie had already considered this matter and her mind was made up.

'I feel extremely sorry for Jennifer and the boys. Her husband was a crook and a thief and he has left them all to fend for themselves. I know exactly how she is feeling. I want Jenny to live comfortably for the rest of her life. Presumably most of Chris's insurances will be affected by the fact that he killed himself. I am now very wealthy and need very little from the practice. Please will you speak to Jennifer's lawyer, and set it up so that she gets as high an income as possible from the practice for the rest of her life. I want nothing, and as far as I am concerned, the other partners can take over the whole firm, lock, stock and barrel, absolutely gratis.'

Michael Burford considered her proposal for a few seconds.

'I can see, and fully understand your thinking, but I have only one suggestion to make. Please will you allow me to transfer the office building into your and Jennifer's names. The mortgages will be cleared by insurances and it will therefore be totally unencumbered, and worth about two and a half million pounds. I really can't let you give that away.'

'Once it is in your name, you can let the offices to the practice on a long lease, and it will give you and Jennifer an income, at today's rate of about 300,000 pounds a year. You can both live on that without touching your capital. I am sure that the partners will find this most acceptable, particularly as they will be getting the existing practice for nothing. Remember that they will get about a million pounds from Matt's insurance, and I am sure that I can tie them into a good lease for you. Although it has been damaged by the events of the past few months, the practice is still viable and running with a good client base. Tim and the others will be pleased, I am sure, to accept such a proposal.'

'Very well,' Marie said wearily. 'Please get on with it. Now how long will this take?'

Michael sighed, 'Normally, this sort of thing is quite straightforward when the deceased has left a will. However, although everyone is quite sure that Matt is dead, we only have an open verdict from the coroner and therefore no death certificate from the registrar of deaths.

'This slightly complicates the matter, because due to the large sums involved, the insurers may insist upon a death certificate before releasing any money. However, you have no need to get involved – I'll do all the work.

'Firstly, I'll have to make an application to the Probate Registry. As executor of the will, I will have to prepare an affidavit and apply for an order giving me leave to swear death, as the court's permission for me to say that Matt is dead. The court should grant permission and I can then apply for probate and execute Matt's will in the usual way.

'Once we have permission, I can further apply to the court to order the coroner to grant a death certificate.

'In view of what's happened and the police files on the case, I don't think we'll have any problems. It's just that the system is a little long-winded and time-consuming. It will probably be over in about four months.'

Marie got up to leave, giving Michael a card with her new ex-directory phone number printed upon it.

17

Matt was extremely worried about Marie through not being able to make any sort of contact, but the compressed programme that he had set for the construction of the villa kept him very busy. His thoughts only turned back to Marie when he had brief moments of solitude.

The winter in Menorca had been unusually dry and he was now well ahead of schedule. The days had lengthened into the month of April, and the construction work was nearing completion. Matt had spent a great deal of time selecting furniture and accessories from the large furniture stores in Ciutadella, Mahon and Alayor.

He had been accompanied on several occasions by Claudia; their friendship had blossomed to the point where he knew that with a little nudge from him, it would become deeper and more physically intimate. She had no knowledge that he belonged to someone else, and she was slightly unsure as to why he made no moves of that type towards her.

She knew he found her attractive and sensed his arousal on the odd occasion that they brushed past each other, or even when he gave her a brotherly twin-cheeked goodnight kiss. However, she was patient and wouldn't force the issue, but she did hope that the delay would not last too long.

Matt was fully aware of Claudia's feelings, but he held himself in check; his life had become complicated enough over the past seven or eight months – God, had it happened in that short space of time?

Matt spent nearly every hour of daylight at the new villa, and his body was now honed to a hard and muscular form; the exposure to the wind and sun had darkened his skin to an even and healthy looking tan. He felt in the picture of health and was looking forward to Marie's first short visit with some anticipation.

They had arranged that once the villa was complete, Matt would send a letter from Señor Perez to her, as an old acquaintance of Matt's on his Spanish project. Marie would visit for a couple of weeks, and then again in a few months' time.

She would tell her family and friends that she had met a charming Spaniard, and after the second visit she would confess that she had fallen hopelessly in love. She would try to paint a picture of Perez as being a 'gold digger', and hope to turn her family against him. This would make their elopement more plausible and she could hide Perez away from them.

She could later effect a reconciliation with the family and friends for herself, but they both accepted that Matt could never meet his 'new' in-laws or family and friends. 'There will be sacrifices,' he had said, and this would be a further one.

After a while, Matt and Marie would plan their future together. They might spend the rest of their lives exploring the world, or live on some exotic but remote south sea island, doing whatever they wanted, whenever they wanted. Their income from the investment of their capital would be in the region of 600,000 pounds per annum – they thought that they might just 'get by' on about 1,700 pounds a day!

Matt had already composed his letter and had sent it a few weeks ago. His lack of contact with Marie had concerned him more when he first read the news of the loss of the baby and Chris's death, but he knew that she was resilient, and that after a cooling-off time she would be back to normal. She had no way of getting in touch, and she could not let him know of her new telephone number.

*

Matt had just finished a hard day on site and was returning to Santandria, with paint splashes on his shorts, legs, arms and head as evidence of his day's labours. The carpenter had only to replace the oak doors, removed during the decoration process, to make the villa complete. He would spend the next day removing protective tape and film from the fittings and plumbing. The light American oak furniture with its soft-coloured fabrics would be delivered the day after. The pool had now been filled and was operational, and he checked the chemical balance before he left. It had been heated to a very comfortable 28°C which would be maintained by the sun in the summer months.

On impulse, Matt stopped off at Brechia's office in Ciutadella and asked Claudia if she would like to see the finished product the next day. Claudia readily agreed, thrilled that he had thought to ask her. She said she would be happy to help with the cleaning tasks, so he agreed to pick her up at eight o'clock the next morning.

*

That evening, after showering and eating the light salad he had prepared, he re-read the copy of his letter to Marie.

> Dear Señora Du Bois,
>
> May I please introduce myself. I am a retired architect and first met your husband while he was working on the hotel project in Calpe in my country. You may recall that you and I met briefly when I visited your husband in England last year.
>
> I have just returned after a long vacation in Brazil to my new home in Menorca, which you may know is in the Balearic Islands.
>
> I actually stopped over in London on my return and I saw Matthew on the evening before he disappeared. I spent several hours with Matt and his partner having a few drinks in his office and talking over old times. He even let me clean up in his shower and loaned me one of his clean shirts.
>
> You can understand the shock that I felt when only two days later I was told of your husband's tragic death and I was devastated to hear this very sad news.
>
> I was very fond of Matthew and I would really like to meet you again – he spoke of you all the time. We met when he made

site visits – he always said that he missed you immensely when you were apart and could not wait to be reunited with you. I wonder if it would be possible for you to join me in the very near future for a short holiday. Having secured a large investment recently, I have just completed a brand new villa on a lovely location at Cala En Turqueta. I know that you would love it and I hope that you can join me on the tenth of May. I believe that there are two flights from Gatwick on that day and if you would please telephone me on the above number, I will meet you at the airport.

With sincere best wishes,

He had signed it 'Alfredo Perez.'

Matt had addressed the envelope and had dropped it into the post office the next morning. Hopefully, Marie would receive it in a few days and he would hear from her by the end of the week. He wondered if he would be able to control his emotions and voice when he spoke to her on the telephone.

*

The next morning, Matt collected Claudia from her small apartment in Ciutadella. She looked very attractive in a pair of oversized dungarees and a floppy yellow T-shirt with 'Gordon's Gin' emblazoned across the front. Matt could see that she had no bra underneath it and felt his excitement grow as she trotted down the staircase towards him, her full breasts bouncing with the movement. Claudia was carrying a small basket which she said had their lunch in it, and when they arrived at Turqueta at half past eight, the carpenter was already half-way through his task of replacing the doors.

Matt and Claudia started cleaning and sweeping and by midday, the villa looked sparkling. All of the tiled walls and floors had been washed, and the contractor's window cleaner had polished the glazed units to a brilliant finish.

Matt and Claudia strolled through the villa, taking in each room, and Matt explained how the furnishings would enhance and act as a foil and soften the fairly stark white walls.

The contrast of the original stonework of the tower worked even better than Matt had envisaged. The shafts of sunlight, through the partly glazed roof surrounding the tower in an elliptical shape, gave a stunningly dramatic effect and Matt kept this view until last. They stood together, comparing the old with the new, Matt with his arm lying gently across Claudia's shoulders.

'This is brilliant!' she said quite breathlessly, and not just because of the beauty of the architecture. The nearness of Matt contributed.

Matt noticed the catch in her voice, and quite naturally and without thought, he turned her to him and bent to kiss her gently on the mouth.

'Thank you for all your help – as I've said before, you are a very good and a dear friend.' He kissed her again, but this time her arms were reaching up around his neck and her tongue probed his mouth as she pressed her body firmly against his. Matt knew he should stop now. He had managed so well over the last five months – would he let it all go now?

His conscience strived to persuade him that purely physical enjoyment of this girl was not worth it, but the closeness of her body and her moving urgently against the swelling in his groin quickly ground any resistance to nothing.

Matt reached down and fumbled with the old black leather belt that was securing her dungarees at the waist and slipped the straps from her shoulders. They dropped to the ground and she stepped out of them, pulling his shirt over his head as she did so. He quickly stepped out of his shorts and ran his hands outside her T-shirt over her firm and erect breasts. Claudia's hands were working insistently at the waistband of his underpants, and she gasped through her kiss as she pulled them down to his thighs releasing the restriction holding back his manhood.

She grasped him in both hands and gently massaged his full length, groans and small whimpers escaping from her throat between kisses. Matt had slipped his hand down the back of Claudia's tiny panties and was gently kneading her tight buttocks, his fingers searching urgently for the source of the moistness that guided him.

Matt quickly broke their embrace and kicking off his pants stood quite naked in front of this beautiful and sexually aroused girl. 'God,' he thought, 'I had no chance at all – none at all!'

Matt slid Claudia's panties down the length of her legs, kissing her body as he went. He then stood upright and gathering her up in his arms almost ran with her to the terrace. Claudia clung to him, her arms around his neck; she buried her head deep into the crook of his neck, kissing, licking and biting gently.

Matt turned Claudia to him, and holding her under her arms he gently lowered her body, kissing first her breasts then her neck and mouth as he let her down. She spread her legs and Matt transferred his hold to the back of her thighs, her moistness guiding him into her to his full length. They were now both grunting and making animal noises in their throats, lost to everything except this deep and irresistible moment of pure, brutal, overpowering sex.

Claudia was now quite uncontrollable and her climax coincided with Matt's, in a release of six months' unrequited desire and lack of sexual relief. The world exploded around them.

Matt held Claudia close to him for several minutes and then gently lifted her off and led her to the pool. They walked, exhausted, down the wide mosaic steps into the cool, gin-clear water. She discarded her T-shirt as she went and whispered half to herself, '*Te amo, cariño, te amo.*'

*

Both Matt and Claudia were so absorbed in each other that neither of them had seen the glint of sunlight from a lens trained on them from the rocky outcrop across the bay.

18

November and December had been a nightmare for Marie. She later recalled those days and even Christmas through a haze; the only brightness in her life was the constant attention paid to her by Stephen. He had asked several times if he could move in with her, not for his benefit, but because he was fearful for her safety. It also seemed unnatural for her to be floating around in such a large house still full of Matt's memories and belongings.

In January, Michael Burford reported that he was making good progress with the Probate Registry, although it was not until five weeks later that Matt was officially declared dead.

The family pressed Marie to mark his death and a memorial service was held in the small village church. Even in her new state of emotional lethargy, Marie could not help but be impressed by the huge number of people who attended to pay their respects. The small church which held only 400 was over-flowing and the service was relayed to those outside by loudspeakers.

Marie either shook hands or embraced those present, but later she could not recall any names and very few faces. The only time that she reacted with any emotion was when she saw Jennifer standing in front of her with the two boys. She felt her cheeks wet with tears as she hugged them all tightly, no words being necessary.

It was on 24 March that Michael Burford asked Marie to go to his office. He had resolved all matters related to probate and was now in a position to execute Matt's will. He had collected all insurance monies together and finalised the leasing arrangements with the practice. Out of respect to its previous senior partners, Tim and his co-partners would continue to practice under the same name.

'So, Marie, this is the bottom line. Firstly, I have negotiated, along with Peter Nash, that Jennifer shall receive 100,000 pounds per annum, paid to her by the practice on a monthly pro-rata basis for the rest of her natural life. This is index-linked and the agreement is irrevocable. She will get her money in advance of payments to anyone else.

'Secondly, the new partners have entered into a new 99-year lease for MDB House, with yourself and Jennifer as the beneficial owners. This will give an immediate income to you and Jennifer of 150,000 pounds each per annum, paid quarterly in advance. I have a cheque of 37,500 pounds in your completion statement for the first payment of rent. The lease allows for upward only rent reviews every three years. This alone will allow you to live comfortably, and in accordance with your wishes, Jennifer will have a total of 250,000 pounds per annum from now on. I believe that Peter Nash will have told Jennifer of your generosity.

'Now to the main item. As you know, Matt had several Life Insurance policies and others linked to his property mortgages and pension plans. I have had several heated discussions with the investigations departments of the insurance companies. I have, however, managed to convince their senior man, a Mr Masters, that they must honour their obligations.

'I won't go into all the detail just now – the full amounts are on the completion statement, but suffice it to say that you are now a very wealthy young woman. I know that money could never replace Matt, but I hope that the knowledge that he provided for you so well helps you to bear the pain. I have a cheque for you netted down after my costs and charges for 4,384,842 pounds.'

Michael slid the cheque, drawn on his clients' account across the desk to Marie. She read it carefully before folding it and slipping it into her handbag with a simple and soft 'Thank you.'

'Now, with all that wealth you have absolutely no financial worries for the rest of your life, but please do nothing without consulting your accountant – he will advise on the best and safest investments to protect your capital and income.'

'Thank you, Michael, that is already in hand. I intend to do absolutely nothing at all for at least six months. This money will stay in my account, and no decisions will be taken until I feel 100 per cent fit and well again. I shall miss Matt and can't even consider any major steps until I'm over him. Thank you again for all of your help.' Marie rose and left to be met outside the offices by Stephen who was driving Matt's XJS V12.

*

Now that everything had been resolved, Marie knew that she must make her choice. She had been considering the options as coldly as possible over the past three weeks.

On the one hand she had Matt who had been brilliant, lovable and loving; totally her man. She wasn't sure now if he was the same person. His deviousness and cunning in setting up the plot was, she had thought, entirely against his nature.

On the other hand, there was Stephen. He was kind, attractive and completely faithful. However, he was not a strong character, and Marie wondered if her domination over him might eventually break him. The last thing she wanted was a human lap-dog.

Her concern was that if she went through with the plan to join Matt, would their relationship ever regain its previous level of love and trust? He had taken this whole thing too far, with disastrous results, and she hated him for that, although she still had a notion that deep down she loved him. Surely they could recover all that was lost, and in time build on their love to construct a new and meaningful life together.

The other option was even more perverse. If she chose Stephen, he would have to do things that were so hostile to his nature that it could well change him. If that happened, would his virtues still override his irritating and bad points? She really did not know.

Marie's real doubts stemmed from her not knowing how she would react when she saw Matt again. Would she fly at him to scratch out his eyes or would she fall into his arms and melt as she had before? She really did have to know before she made a decision. She had to see him, covertly, in the flesh.

She had received a letter from Matt that morning that stimulated her course of action.

That afternoon, Marie drove to Thomas Cook's in Sevenoaks and arranged for an open return first class ticket to Mahon with Iberia Airways. She would leave at 07.05 a.m. the following Tuesday from Gatwick.

Later, Marie telephoned her mother to say that she was having a few days holiday in Spain and that she would telephone as soon as she knew where she would be staying. She told Stephen that he could use the XJ12 if he took her to the airport. He was so used to it now that to give it up for his old Ford would be a considerable wrench.

As she had a first class ticket, Marie only had to check in 30 minutes before take-off. Stephen drove her to the airport, and she insisted that she didn't need help to carry her small weekend bag. She kissed him hurriedly on the cheek and crossed over to the terminal building without a backward glance. Stephen watched her in her casual lightweight green jumpsuit and trainers until she was out of sight.

The 757 scheduled service took off on time, and after a short stop in Barcelona to pick up passengers it landed in Mahon at half past ten local time. Having only her small bag as hand luggage, Marie passed quickly through immigration and customs, and by eleven o'clock she was driving her white Renault Clio hired from Hertz down the main road between Mahon and Ciutadella that divided the island horizontally from east to west.

Matt had always told Marie about Menorca, particularly its beauty in the spring and early summer. It was true. The landscape was surprisingly green, and cows, goats and pigs dotted the dry-stone walled fields.

The road, which had a very good surface, was lined with the deep vermilion of wild poppies providing a smoky red carpet border. Pine trees, with lime green new growth and the deeper almost black-green of the olive trees hung over the road, in some places their tips touching, thus forming a tunnel of dappled shade.

The temperature was well in the seventies, and Marie felt more relaxed than she could remember having been over the past year. Perhaps she should abandon her plan, just find Matt and stay out here with him – why go through all that complicated reply to his letter stuff?

No! She thought she still loved Matt, but had to know for sure. She thought she'd be certain by the end of the day and if she was, she would stay. She pressed her white and green-flashed trainers a little harder on the accelerator, feeling the urgency of seeing Matt again, even from a distance. The sparkle in her eyes was rekindled.

Marie had very little knowledge of the geography of Menorca, but Matt had told her that the two sites he had investigated were on the south of the island. One was approached by the Cala Galdana road, and the other via Ciutadella. The basic map which she got with the car showed Cala En Turqueta quite clearly. It indicated a reasonable road most of the way except for the last mile or so to the beach, which was just a track.

She felt relieved at the first roundabout on the outskirts of Ciutadella when she saw a signpost with *Playas Sud* indicated to the left. Thereafter, through a few side roads on the edge of the town, Turqueta was signed all the way. Marie eventually found herself driving down a fairly narrow but reasonably surfaced country lane with dry-stone walls on either side. It was still quite early in the holiday season and she encountered very little traffic at all.

At last, she came to a metal double gate spanning the road. There, an official looking man wearing navy blue trousers and a navy blue army type jumper with denim shoulder pads, stopped her. He pointed to a sign stapled to the gate saying that it would be open between ten in the morning and six o'clock at night. The tariff below told her that she must pay 200 pesetas. '*Gracias, Señora,*' he said, opening the gate and tapping the '18.00' on the sign as she passed through.

Marie proceeded carefully up the level but unsurfaced track towards the large rendered maroon and white painted house. A high, non-climbable stone wall surrounded the house and the heavy wooden gates were closed; they had the appearance of being barred from the inside.

At this point the track split, the right fork being gated with a large sign hanging from it, '*Privato – Prohibito El Paso.*' There were deep dried ruts in the soft ground beyond the gate, indicating that heavy vehicles had used the track in the fairly recent past.

The left fork was signed '*Playa*' painted free-hand in faded white paint on a cracked board and nailed to an olive tree. The surface really deteriorated now as Marie guided the small car over the humps and bumps. The track descended through a pine, olive and eucalyptus forest, the quiet and solitude broken only by the squeaks from the car's suspension. After about half a mile, Marie followed the sign and swung left into a large enclosed, unsurfaced car park, where the spaces were defined by young English plane trees.

She parked in the shade, and taking her small beach bag with her she left the car and strolled towards the beach. The view of the beach and the sea that greeted her was everything that Matt had said it was. As she strolled through the trees, the colour of the sea and the sand, and the rugged limestone rocks with small saplings clinging onto every crevice was breathtaking. Looking over to the right from this position, Marie could just see the top of the stone tower that Matt had described.

'Well, at least I've got the right place!' she said to herself, and again she felt an excitement rise in her chest that slightly constricted her breathing. She had guessed that with his love of the water, Matt would come down to the beach at least once during the day and she intended to watch him unnoticed from a distance. She would know how she would live for the rest of her life according to her reaction at seeing him.

Marie panicked momentarily when she saw that the beach was almost deserted. There was only one family with two young children with their beach paraphernalia in the far corner. She could hardly sit unnoticed on the beach if Matt came down for a swim.

Looking around, she saw a well-worn track climbing up into the rocky outcrop to the left of the beach, with a number of trees rooted to the sparse earth in its fissures. She walked across the beach, nodding to the Spanish family, and climbed the steep path between the rocks. This was perfect – she had a commanding view of the whole of the beach from this elevated position, and she could see the roof of the new structure of the villa surrounding the stone tower.

She searched around her and saw that the pathway climbed even higher, and although the beach would be somewhat obscured, she would be able to see the entire villa. She climbed away, and in a few minutes she found a vantage point that gave a commanding view of the whole of the coastline. She was above the level of the villa, looking down slightly onto its roof about 800 yards away. She blessed her forethought, and getting herself comfortably wedged in the lowest fork of the fir tree, she took her 8 x 50 Permafocus binoculars from her bag.

The villa looked beautiful, evidently the result of Matt's style of design and detailing. Although she couldn't see the water in the pool, she could see its dappled reflection on the walls. She ran her glasses over the terrace and picked out the barbecue and the seating area alongside it. She could see the frames of white plastic garden chairs, and loungers which hadn't yet been upholstered. The large patio doors were partly open and she could just detect movement beyond the glass in the shadows of the room. She scanned down the side of the building and marvelled at Matt's skill to produce something as tangibly beautiful as this from his head and his ability to create a delicacy using bulky and ugly materials such as bricks and blocks. Her heart swelled with pride at his achievement. She brought her glasses back to the terrace, admiring the vivid colours of the bougainvillaea, oleander and hibiscus growing against the back wall of the terrace. Then, the movement in the room became more defined.

Marie saw a very brown-skinned man carrying a dark girl wearing a bright yellow T-shirt running out onto the terrace. The man's face was obscured by the girl who had her face buried deep into his neck. He then lifted her and as he lowered her onto his erection, Marie saw Matt's face perfectly clearly, his eyes half-closed in rapture.

A barely audible groan slipped from her mouth and her hands started to tremble. She wanted to run but forced herself to watch until they had finished making love and disappeared from sight into the pool. She let the binoculars slip to her side and looked at the inviting coolness of the sea and rocks 100 feet below her. 'It would be so easy to just close your eyes and slip off – after the first pain there would be dark, safe, impregnable oblivion.'

*

Marie had no idea how long she had been sitting in the tree. When she got up, she did not raise her binoculars any more and had the feeling that she would never smile, or even cry again.

She was able to return home that same day and called Stephen from the airport to pick her up. He was delighted when she told him that he could move in with her and that soon they would be married.

'However, Stephen, there are conditions. I have a fairly long story to tell you and you will never repeat it to anyone. I then have a task for you to perform and that will not be easy. You must promise, here and now, before I start, that you will do anything – and I mean absolutely anything – that I ask. If you love me, you will agree. Before you answer, you should know that I can set you up in your own business and you will be secure and independent from now on.'

Stephen agreed unconditionally without a single further thought.

*

Marie composed her letter with care and a calculated innuendo. Conscious of her involvement in crime and deceit, she wanted no references to point back at her at any time. She knew instinctively that Matt would not take this lying down. She also decided to tell a lie to punish him for his infidelity which she had seen for herself.

> 'Dear Señor Perez,
> Thank you for your letter inviting me to join you for a holiday in your new home. I do of course remember you, and from my recollection, you were a kind and sensitive man, a brilliant architect and a clever and astute businessman. My husband was exactly the same, but that man is now quite dead. I have accepted the fact that I can't possibly have him back and things will never be the same again.
> However, you will not know of changes that took place in the few months prior to his death. Over that period of time, he changed from the man I have already described to a bitter and vicious monster, intent only on exacting revenge and retribution

on those who had caused him harm. He was single-minded in his resolve, thinking only of reprisals, to the exclusion of everything else. He was definitely, at that time not the man that I had married.

You may also know that I was badly beaten and lost my baby and that my pet dog was killed. I blame Matthew for both of these tragedies and I will never forgive him for ruining my life for his own evil and vindictive ends. I am sure that you will read into these words a great deal of bitterness on my part. You are absolutely correct to do so – if he was alive today I would hate and loathe him!

In view of this, it would be quite inappropriate for me to join you in your new home. I really want to forget all about the past and anything connected with my late husband. That chapter of my life is best forgotten and I intend to rebuild my future without further thought of him.

Memories of his actions and the way in which he changed are poisoning my mind, and I must, for the sake of my health, wipe these thoughts from my brain. I hope that I am now succeeding in this resolve so that I will soon be able to smile again.

Fortunately my late husband, before his personality changed, took out a number of insurances so I am now very financially secure. I have no need of any help from you in this respect.

I understand from your letter that you secured a considerable sum of money for yourself recently, and this has enabled you to start a new life in Menorca. I am glad that you will be comfortable and although your letter does not even suggest the idea, I would have no intention of making any of my reserves available to you at any time. I hope that you are perfectly clear about this matter.

As I have said, I have absolutely no desire to see you again at any time and I trust that you will not bother me further.

I have rediscovered a friendship with a man that I knew intimately some time ago, and it is my intention to marry him in the near future and set him up to run his own publishing business.

Incidentally, you may be interested to know that I am pregnant again and I am looking forward to family life with my new man.

I must be honest when I tell you that I now feel no sorrow or remorse in writing to you in this way. My mind is firmly made up and I now have the power that wealth brings to impose my wishes. I do not expect to hear from you again.'

She signed the letter simply, 'Marie'. It was posted by Stephen the next morning and arrived in Menorca two days later.

*

'*Buenos dias, Señor Perez. Cómo está?*'
'*Bien gracias, Eduardo, y usted?*'
'*Muy bien, gracias.*'
The postman passed over a letter with a British stamp, postmarked Tonbridge in Kent. Matt recognized the writing at once.

He was sitting in the warmth of the early morning May sunshine, sipping a freshly pressed orange juice on the veranda, feeling very content in his imaginatively designed and beautifully built villa. He was conscious of his correct decision to make the nucleus of the villa the ancient circular stone watchtower. He thought the modern whitewashed building constructed around it provided an angular and visually pleasing contrast to the worn and weathered stone.

It overlooked the quiet, twin-beached bay of Cala En Turqueta. The contrast of the sparkling turquoise water fringed by a deep strip of pink-white sand and the various shades of green of the pine trees beyond was a constant source of pleasure to Matt. The deep hue of the Mediterranean beyond, under a pale blue morning sky, completed the panorama.

Matt usually collected his very small amount of mail addressed to Señor Perez from the *Lista de Correos*, the postrestante in Ciutadella. His mail consisted mainly of English architectural magazines. However, if Eduardo had a delivery to the big consular house at the head of Matt's driveway, he would always take the trouble to bring Señor Perez his mail in person, as he knew he would leave with a very healthy tip.

After Eduardo had departed on his rattly old motorbike, Matt pulled up a comfortable upholstered lounger, and sitting in the sun he began to read with great anticipation. It had to be important! Marie knew the rules and would not have written unnecessarily –

he had been awaiting a telephone call from her as arranged. The letter contained four pages of neat and stylishly small writing. As he read, his face slowly drained of colour under his deep tan. He read again urgently and he could not believe his eyes.

Although it was only half past eight in the morning, he went into the kitchen and took a bottle of Hennessey XO from the top shelf of the old-fashioned Spanish dresser. He took it back to the terrace with a freshly percolated jug of coffee and sat at the table.

How could she do this to him? They had planned and gone through so much together. He had been financially deceived in business three times before in his life. One of the cheats was in a wheelchair, another was in prison and the other one was dead.

He poured a sizeable measure of the amber liquid into a large balloon glass and with his freshly made jug of coffee at his elbow, he sat and started to think. Two hours later, he slowly sat forward and eased the muscles around his neck. A smile touched the corners of his mouth and he knew that his scheme could work. He carefully poured the untouched brandy back into the bottle and returned it to its place on the top shelf of the dresser. The coffee was cold. He tipped it away in the sink and set up a new jug on the machine to brew. Señor Alfredo Perez Gandia, né Matthew Ronald Du Bois had a plan ...

He thought that he might need help from people in England and he knew that he could call on three – Cathy, George Adams, and his brother James for assistance. However, he would need to arrange his reappearance carefully and sensitively. He had obviously hurt Marie more than he thought and knew now that he could never recover their relationship. Perhaps his three prospective allies would also find it equally difficult to forgive the deception and grief that he had caused them. He decided to wait for a few weeks to see if anything developed from Marie before putting his plan into operation.

She knew him well enough to know that he would not resign himself to being cheated without a fight. She would therefore have arranged protection for herself and her new man. She hadn't mentioned him by name but Matt was sure that it was

Stephen Murray. His fears all those years ago had been well-founded after all. Maybe he was well rid of the bitch! She would not keep his money though – of that he was quite sure!

Matt's brain was working fast and furiously, but he made himself take several deep breaths so that he could plan carefully and meticulously. He was in no rush, and he resolved to let Marie make the first move. He was sure she would. Perhaps he knew her better than she knew him.

Later that day, Matt contacted the electrical contractor who had worked on the house, to arrange for a sophisticated electronic security system to be installed around the villa. No expense was to be spared but it was essential that the work be carried out straight away.

Within three days, a system of harmless electronic laser beams surrounded the villa at a distance of 50 yards. When the installation was armed, if the beam was broken by anything larger than a dog, a series of muted audible and subtle visual alarms would be set off identifiable from anywhere in the villa. All of the doors unintentionally left open or unlocked would automatically be made secure.

Matt now felt totally safe, but as an added precaution he decided to arm himself. He applied to the *Gardia Civil* in Mercadel for a licence to own a shotgun, ostensibly to keep the rabbits down. He was told that the licence would take a week or two and that he could then purchase the gun.

19

Stephen Murray was in seventh heaven. He had at last got Marie. His patience of at least four years had been rewarded. Not only that, but she was very wealthy and had agreed to set him up in business. He had always wanted to be his own boss and was sure that he could run a successful publishing company, particularly if it was his own. He had not yet heard what his task was to be, but was sure that he could manage anything that she wanted.

On the evening of the day that he had posted Marie's letter to Menorca, Stephen was sitting across the dining table from her, awaiting her instructions.

'Stephen, an awful lot of what I am going to tell you may seem unbelievable. However, I can assure you that it is totally and entirely true. I will leave out nothing, even those parts of which I am utterly ashamed.'

Starting with a brief background of Matt's early business life and his amalgamation with Christopher, Marie told him the whole story. He listened quietly to her narration, which Marie delivered in a dull emotionless monotone. The impact of what had happened hit Stephen in a series of jabs as each new development was told. She explained how they had gone about framing Christopher and the detailed arrangements made by Matt, the Florida trip and his scheme to recover his money. Although he had already guessed as much, it still came as a jolt when Marie confirmed that Matt was alive and living in Menorca.

Marie explained that Chris's suicide had been unanticipated and she still felt a stab of guilt when she spoke of it. It was late into the night when she finished and Stephen felt worried and confused.

'I don't understand. Where does all this leave me, and why do you need to tell me? I am very touched by your trust that I won't run to the nearest police station, but if you're joining your husband as arranged, what about me? I don't think he'd exactly welcome me with open arms, do you?'

'Stephen, calm down!' Her voice was still devoid of emotion. 'I said I had a task for you. The only way for you to safeguard your position is to ensure that Matt doesn't reappear for any reason at any time. You need have no fears as far as my intentions are concerned. I wrote to Matt yesterday – you posted the letter, telling him that I don't ever want to see him again.

'However, he has already proven his ability to plan and plot and he won't take this lying down. To fully safeguard your interests and to ensure he never comes back, you must complete the job the police thought had been done by Christopher. You must kill him!'

At last her voice had developed some fire and her eyes were blazing with the release of this emotion. She had said it at last. She wanted the job done, not only for her and Stephen's protection, but for her own satisfaction. She wanted him dead! Stephen sat back in his chair, his mind in a whirl.

'I am amazed at what you have told me! The whole story is incredible, but I do believe you, of course. As far as killing Matt is concerned, that is totally out of the question. It is completely alien to me to hurt anything, let alone another human being. I'm sorry – it just cannot be done! There must be some other way. How about buying him off? Give him his share of the money. Anything except murder – I really cannot do it!'

Marie stared at him. 'Three things. First, you said that you loved me and would do anything for me. Well then, prove it. Second, before I told you this story, you agreed to do anything that I asked. That was only 24 hours ago. Well then, do you break your promises so quickly? Third, Matt knows about you now. If you don't kill him, I can almost guarantee that he will kill you! Do you want to be killed?' She glared at Stephen for a few seconds and then her eyes softened. She reached across the table and held his hands with hers.

'Look, darling, I love you and want to spend the rest of my life with you, but not living under a cloud of fear of what might be hiding in the shadows. I don't expect you personally to go and club him to death. Just organize it! I have plenty of money and I'm sure you can find someone to do the dirty work. I don't care how much it costs. Just make sure it is done properly. We will be in the clear. Who would associate us with the murder of a Spaniard a thousand miles away?'

Her persuasive tone was convincing and Stephen slowly relaxed.

'Yes, I see what you mean. Okay – I'll do it. Where shall we start?'

Having taken the decision, he now seemed quite enthusiastic and Marie was sure that his commitment was driven by fearing the possible dissipation of his newly found good fortune.

*

Michael Burford agreed to see Stephen Murray who had introduced himself over the phone as Marie's fiancé. He tried to keep an open mind, but quite naturally he viewed him as a potential fortune hunter. When Stephen explained that he had known Marie for over six years, he warmed slightly to him and decided to reserve his judgement, giving Stephen the benefit of the doubt.

Stephen explained that the reason he had made the appointment was that he was going to start his own publishing firm, and that he wanted some legal advice as to the best way to go about it. When their business was finished, Stephen turned the conversation round to Marie.

'She has been emotionally damaged by the whole sorry affair, but I am trying desperately hard to help her recover with a mixture of love, affection and compassion. In fact, I am slightly worried about her. I can't be there all the time and I know she is still very nervous when she is on her own in that big house. Probably a left-over from the attack by Marten. I am thinking of employing a minder for her. I don't want to just go to an agency,

I wonder if you know of anyone – tough and loyal; someone we can all trust completely.'

Michael thought for a moment. 'Actually, there is someone. I would describe him as a likeable rogue. I defended him on a couple of occasions for breaking and entering. He is very tough but he has never been done for anything violent, although he did box professionally for a couple of years. I'll introduce you to him. Marie will be as safe as houses with him. His name is Jerry Walls.'

The next day, Stephen and Marie interviewed Jerry and liked the look of him, so they engaged him on a trial basis. He would live in the house, work as a chauffeur and generally help around the house with odd jobs. He could still go to his gym in the Old Kent Road every Monday, Wednesday and Friday afternoon to help coach the junior boxing teams.

On the first Monday, Stephen went with him and while Jerry was putting two young Scots through their paces, he got into conversation with a seedy looking individual who seemed to have no job in particular there.

'We've just taken on Jerry Walls as a minder. Do you think he can do the job?'

The man spat into the sand-filled fire bucket that was littered with cigarette butts standing up like symbolic tombstones.

'Yers, 'e's okay. Good lad, Jerry. Bit too soft sometimes if you're really in trouble. Only uses his fists, don't like dirty fightin' with blades or dusters. Still, 'e'll be okay for yer.'

'What about if I need a real dirty fighter – a man who can teach someone a real lesson – cut 'em up a bit maybe?'

'Only one bloke for that, 'Arry the Pick, we call 'im – 'Arry Ewers. Lives down Millwall way, back of the Old Den football ground in Coldblow Lane. Ain't seen 'im about lately – he tends to flit in and out. Vicious bastard, but good to 'ave on your side in a fight. Did five years a while back for sticking a seven inch blade into a copper's arm.'

'Thanks for your help. I'll stick with Jerry. Here, have a drink on me.' Stephen slipped him a ten pound note.

The next morning, Stephen set off for the back streets of New

Cross and drove slowly down Coldblow Lane in Millwall. The XJS attracted the attention of four youths gathered around a lamp post at the corner of the road. Stephen tried hard to affect a cockney accent, but from the smirk that ran between the youths, he knew he was unsuccessful. He continued, however:

'Any of you know where 'Arry the Pick is?'

''Oo wants ter know?'

'I'm a mate. Got a few bob for 'im.' With his finger on the panic button that would lock all the doors and close the windows immediately, Stephen reached into his pocket with his other hand and brought out a large roll of banknotes.

'What's it worth?'

Stephen peeled off a 20 pound note. He wished he could remember if that was a pony or a donkey, or a monkey or something.

One of the youths snatched it and held it up to the light. 'Just down there on the right, number 27.'

Stephen pulled into the kerb, and with some misgivings he left the safety of the car. The youths were still eyeing him. He rapped on the glass panel of the front door which was right on the pavement. He tried again and saw a distorted shape appear through the dirty smeared glass. A voice sounded through the door.

'What yer want?'

'Is 'Arry the Pick in?'

''Oo wants 'im?'

'Friend – I got a little job for him.'

A bolt was released and the door opened only a sliver. An eye appeared in the crack and ran carefully over Stephen. He stepped back so as to give a full view and held both hands away from his sides.

The door opened fully and a heavy and very tough looking man poked out his head, and looked up and down the street.

''Ope you locked the motor,' he said, nodding Stephen into the dingy hallway. 'In there,' he said. Stephen pushed open the door to the rear room which was used as a kitchen and dining room.

A large black and white tom cat with notches in his ears uncurled enough to open one eye to look at Stephen before returning to the world of cat-dreams.

'Are you 'Arry?' said Stephen.

'I want to know what the job is, first.'

'Serious stuff, someone's been naughty and needs hurtin'.'

'Where? I don't do Mafia or any of the Wapping or Bermondsey crowd.'

'That's okay. It's abroad.'

'Right, if I do it, I want all expenses. For a little duff up and a few scratches around the chest, five hundred notes. If you want a bit more – like the face rearranged – it'll cost you a big one.' Stephen thought that this must be a thousand pounds.

'Okay, you've got the job. But I want five grand's worth.'

'Arry looked up sharply. 'You want someone topped?'

'Yes. There's no danger and it's remote. I'll be with you to make sure you've got the right man.'

'Arry looked him up and down. 'I generally work alone.' He felt Stephen's biceps through his jacket. 'Ain't much of yer – can yer fight?'

'I won't have to. That's what you're being paid for!'

'Okay – I'm on but it's fifteen grand – ten now and five when it's done.'

'No. Five – paid on completion.'

'You better fuck off, mate. I'm getting angry.'

'Okay, ten. Five now and five when we get back.'

'You're on. Let's see the money.'

'Wait here,' Stephen went back to the car and locked himself in. He then used his mobile to telephone the number on his notepad and booked two seats on Friday's charter flight to Menorca, returning one week later. They were for two holiday-makers, a Mr S Murray and a Mr H Ewers. Stephen gave his credit card number and arranged to pick up the tickets from the Air 2000 desk. He then opened the glove locker and extracted 5,000 pounds from a large brown envelope containing 25,000 pounds in used notes. He hadn't known how much he would have to pay.

Stephen returned to the house and passed over the money to 'Arry. 'It's all there, but count it anyway. You get the other five grand when it's done. I want you to be at the north terminal of Gatwick Airport at seven o'clock on Friday morning. Meet me at the Air 2000 desk and have enough clothes packed for a week. We're going on holiday, so look casual. If you need to buy any clothes or a suitcase, keep your receipts – I'll reimburse you later. Make sure you pack any equipment you need carefully. Sometimes they x-ray the luggage. Don't carry anything nasty in your hand baggage, and please don't be late!'

'You're the boss. Don't worry, I only use blades – I'll 'ide 'em so they won't show up as anything they're likely to be interested in. I'll see you at Gatwick on Friday.'

Stephen left Coldblow Lane, confident that his obligation to Marie would be fulfilled within the week.

*

On the following Friday morning, Stephen met Harry Ewers as arranged. He was pleased to see that Ewers was smartly dressed in a pair of light tan slacks, light shoes, a pale green sports shirt, carrying a light coloured reefer jacket. He read the slight surprise in Stephen's face and said, by way of greeting,

'Look mate, don't fink that just 'cos I don't talk nice that I'm a ficko! I'm a professional at my job and if you don't quit lookin' at me like that you can go screw yourself and get someone else to do the job for you. I 'ope I've made myself clear!'

'Okay Harry, relax! I'm sorry if I gave the wrong impression but I've only met you once, and at that time you must admit that you were unshaven, unkempt and wearing a ragged vest. Anyway, let's call it quits. My job is to identify the target and yours to do the business. I don't expect to interfere or get in the way. Come on, let's check in.'

Having made his point, Ewers became quite relaxed and allowed Stephen to take charge.

*

They stepped off the Air 2000 757 at ten o'clock local time and took their car hire voucher purchased with the air ticket to the Hertz desk. By pure chance, they were given exactly the same Renault Clio that Marie had hired a few days ago. Stephen was entered as the main driver. Through a contact of Marie's, Stephen had rented a small two-bedroomed villa at Son Parc, close to the golf course. They drove straight there and unloaded their luggage.

'Okay Harry,' said Stephen. 'We're holidaymakers. For the next few days we'll settle in and relax around the pool. Get to know our neighbours, maybe pull a couple of birds. I want us to be part of the landscape until we leave next Friday, nicely tanned and a few pounds heavier through a little too much San Miguel.'

Stephen led by example, smiling at the two couples on the terrace adjoining theirs. 'Hi,' he said jovially, 'Just arrived, my name's Stephen and this is Harry. Have you been here long?'

The tall good-looking man with grey hair said they had been there a week. 'It's been really super – unfortunately we go home on Monday. We stretched our week to ten days this time. Oh, I'm Richard and this is my wife Valerie and these are our dear friends Zöe and Ray – they own the villa. If you want details of some nice beaches or good restaurants, let us know – we've been coming here for ages.'

Having set the pattern, Stephen would ignore them as much as possible over the next week, except to ensure that the 'holidaymaker' image of a couple of randy bachelors on the make was impressed on them as much as possible.

20

While Stephen and Harry carried out their act at Son Parc, Matt was busily preparing his boat for use after the winter. He had purchased a 30 foot ocean-going speed boat with twin hulls, powered by two 250 hp Volvo marine engines. It could reach 40 knots in a good sea, and Matt had bought it partly to use as his taxi between Turqueta and Ciutadella and partly to pursue his scuba diving hobby, and thirdly, quite selfishly, to discourage anyone else from mooring at his landing stage. The sea was generally too rough for a comfortable ride in the winter, but now that the weather was improving, he was checking out the operation of the sophisticated radar that he had had installed and running over his scuba gear.

The tanks and regulators were working well and his own compressor in the plant room charged his tanks for him without the need to take them into town. He had three powerful gas powered spear guns suitable for use in deep waters. He checked them by firing a bolt from each into a large block of wood set up at the back of the villa. Each gun worked perfectly, and on the third shot fired from 30 feet, the 4 inch thick piece of timber was shattered. The energy that the gun generated was enough to force a 12 inch dart at a depth of 100 feet of water for 40 feet before losing momentum.

*

Meanwhile, Stephen and Harry had set off early in the morning, aiming at getting to Turqueta in time to get a good spot on the beach before the family groups arrived. Marie had explained the layout of the bay to Stephen and he had already climbed to the vantage point where she had told him he could study the villa garden. Harry had not taken Stephen's description as read and climbed to study the layout for himself. He noted every detail and guessed at the uses of the rooms, planning the best approach through the trees and memorizing any large and easily recognizable landmarks in the terrain. This would be very important in the dark.

They stayed on the beach throughout the day, eating and drinking from the supplies that Stephen had packed that morning in the large green ice box. Stephen had consumed the six cans of San Miguel through the day but Ewers had refused all alcohol, taking only small sips from a two litre bottle of mineral water. On Harry's second visit to the vantage point, he caught sight of Matt through his binoculars busying himself in and out of the louvred door next to the pool. He observed with a professional eye the apparent fitness of Matt's body and decided that his throwing knife would be the best tool for this job. 'I wouldn't like to get into close quarters with this 'Erbert, 'e looks a bit too tasty for me!'

When he returned to the beach, Harry told Stephen that he would need him to help later that night as he couldn't manage entirely on his own. Stephen paled at this idea but relaxed as Harry explained that his role would be strictly non-violent, that he would only be there as a diversion.

'Look, we can only see this part of the villa, so not taking any chances on coming across the unknown, we'll work from this side. I'll go up first and get in position. You give me a few minutes and follow on. I want you to knock on the patio door of the villa closest to the pool; it looks like the lounge. When he comes out, you will have stepped aside and I'll get him with my thrower in the throat. I'll only be about 25 feet away in them flowers, so I won't miss. I'll finish him off with this in a few seconds.'

Stephen flinched at the seven-inch long stiletto that Harry produced from his bag. 'Put it away for God's sake!' he almost shouted, looking around at the few remaining groups on the beach.

Harry smiled. This was his realm now and he was in charge. 'Okay, let's go – that bloke closes the bleedin' gate at six.'

They packed up and left the beach, nodding to the guard as they drove through the gate. No more than 100 yards down the road, they turned sharply left into a lane signposted Es Talier, and parked out of sight off the road beneath the pine trees. It was now six o'clock and they would make their move at ten o'clock that night.

Harry sat quietly, not speaking for the next four hours. His eyes were half-closed and he was breathing deeply and regularly. Stephen was getting more and more agitated in his position behind the wheel. He was drumming on the dashboard and looking at his watch every few minutes. Harry ignored all of this but reacted very sharply when Stephen opened the door to get out to relieve his bladder of the pressure of some of the beer he had drunk during the day. Harry whipped his hand across Stephen's chest and quickly pulled the door to.

'Fool! The fucking interior light will show for miles in this darkness!' There was no interior light switch on this basic car so Harry levered off the lens and popped out the bulb. 'Okay, get your pee now!'

When Stephen returned, Harry said that it was time to make a move. They had both already changed their beach clothes for dark tracksuits. Getting quietly out of the car, Harry brought his bag from the boot, closing the lid with only a slight click. He placed his bag on the bonnet, and using a small pen-light he removed three sheathed knives and laid them on the car. He took out a worn leather harness and strapped it across his chest, placing two of the throwing knives into its loops. He checked these and their ease of release and grunted, satisfied when they both slipped free, one by one into the palm of his hand. The third, the stabbing stiletto was clipped to his hip and now he was ready. He took his pen-light and handed a similar one to Stephen. Then, cupping his hand around Stephen's ear, he whispered quietly.

'Close your eyes for a few minutes. Our night vision should be good in this moonlight – only use the torch if you need to. Don't look up at the moon and keep your eyes on the ground just ahead of your feet. I'll lead until we get close and then we'll split up.'

Harry led Stephen slowly and carefully up the track to the big house which was in complete darkness. They turned right at the fork, and Harry examined the gate hinges for ease of operation and any alarm wires before quietly slipping through. Stephen followed.

Stephen had been nervous of these moments all afternoon, but now they were moving and his adrenalin was running, he felt a strange elation and excitement. He felt that his heart was pumping so hard that it would explode.

It took over an hour to cover the three quarters of a mile of rough track to the house. Harry kept carefully to the edge, wary of disturbing loose stones. When they were about two hundred yards from the villa's lights, Harry slipped quietly into the trees, picking a path carefully to avoid the many rocks and boulders strewn on the forest floor. Stephen followed quietly, stumbling only once when he took his eyes off the back of Harry's legs to glance in the direction of a scurrying movement, but it was only some nocturnal creature.

They skirted around the villa, keeping a distance of about 100 yards. When they drew level with the rear terrace, Harry stopped and crouched. Stephen followed suit and in answer to Harry's gesture he leaned closer. Cupping his hands around Stephen's ear once again, Harry whispered.

'I'm going in now. I'll be in position in about 15 minutes. Check your watch. You leave here exactly three minutes after me and gauge your speed to get there three minutes after me. Watch your step and don't make any noise. I've found no trip wires or alarms so he obviously doesn't expect any unwelcome visitors yet. When you get to the terrace, do exactly as I've told you. Is that all clear?'

Stephen nodded in the semi-darkness and giving the thumbs up, Harry slipped silently into the gloom of the forest.

Stephen counted his pulse for the first minute and wasn't surprised when it got to 130 before the second hand swept past the 12 again. In exactly three minutes, being as careful as possible and trying hard to gauge the speed at which he covered the ground to about six yards every minute, Stephen crept towards the house.

*

Matt was sitting quietly at the large desk in the study reading an old architect's journal and listening to a recording of Benny Goodman's *Ain't Misbehaving*. Suddenly, a high-pitched intermittent buzz sounded from the unit in the corner of the study, and a small red light started to flash above it. He heard the click as all doors locked automatically. He swung around quickly to a console alongside his desk and saw that the light beam had been broken on the seaward side of the villa towards the pool terrace. He immediately cancelled and re-armed the alarm and threw a switch that closed all of the drapes throughout the house simultaneously. He feared the worst, but his shotgun licence would not be due for another week, so he searched his mind quickly for another weapon. He ran through the kitchen to the staircase leading down through his wine cellar to the pool plant room, taking a radio control box no bigger than a packet of 20 cigarettes with him. He could control any of the electrical gadgets in the house with this from 150 metres via the central unit in his study. He had memorized all of the command codes with ease.

As Matt reached the plant room, the alarm sounded again. This meant one of two things. Either the intruder had gone back through the beam or there was a second intruder. He had no idea where the second beam had been broken. He punched in 180 to his controller and then 'enter'. The alarm switched off; it would be re-armed automatically in 20 seconds.

Matt grabbed one of his gas spear guns and pressed four bolts into the carriage. He checked the gauge and confirmed to himself that it was fully charged up. There would be enough energy to release 18 bolts.

He punched in 187 to his controller, and when he pressed 'enter', all of the internal lights went out except for those in the study. The underwater pool lights slowly came up to power. He slipped out of the louvred plant room door and stood quite still in the shadows of the terrace wall. He looked deliberately away from the terrace and concentrated on the zone of the surrounding forest where the beam had been breached. After about 5 minutes that seemed like 20, he detected a very slow but positive movement at the edge of the cleared area.

Yes – a man was definitely there, dressed in dark clothing and moving forward swiftly over the open ground at a silent crouching run. Matt could have picked him off there and then, but he needed to be certain of the range, and he was aware of the probable approach of a second intruder. He stood quite motionless, lost in the shadows and observed Harry Ewers stop at the base of the steps up to the terrace, flattening himself against the ornate classical stone balustrading. Harry waited for no more than a few seconds and then ran up the steps, three at a time, and skirted the pool to gain the shelter of the bougainvillaea.

Matt still waited, no more than 25 feet away on the other side of the pool. He tried to shrink back even deeper into the depths of the shadow. His patience was finally rewarded when a minute or so later he sensed further movement on the edge of the forest and Stephen appeared. Matt didn't recognize him at once and saw only a tall fair man creep towards the steps. Stephen paused, then straightened and walked briskly onto the terrace and approached the dining room door. He rapped on the glass and quickly stepped back a pace. Matt was watching the first man who had now stepped partly out of the shade of the plants and adopted a pose with one leg set forward, slightly bent, and the other straight behind him. He had a wicked looking throwing knife in his right hand which he was holding level with his shoulder.

Matt waited. Stephen glanced around at Harry who nodded slightly, the movement discernable in the glow from the pool. Matt felt for his controller and dialled 183, the code to bring up the whole of the outside lights. As he pressed 'enter', the small box slipped from his fingers and clattered onto the tiles of the terrace. Stephen jerked his head round but stood rooted to the spot. Harry reacted faster, and by the time Matt had recovered, seven inches of hard steel had pierced his right shoulder.

He screamed involuntarily and almost dropped his spear gun. Harry could now see Matt's outline, and his second throwing knife was flying towards Matt's head when Matt dropped to one knee and triggered the twelve inch bolt with his left hand. The knife bounced off the terrace walling and clattered to the ground. The bolt caught Harry squarely in the throat, ripping into his epiglottis and driving his voice box through the back of his head.

He uttered a gurgling sound and crashed to the floor, his legs thrashing wildly as his hands clawed at the bolt projecting three inches from the back of his neck. The stem of his brain had been completely severed and he was dead in two minutes.

Stephen whimpered and fell to his knees as Matt staggered towards him. Matt's eyes were swimming and the spear gun was wavering in Stephen's general direction.

'Turn round,' Matt ordered. The blow to the back of Stephen's head with the butt of the spear gun knocked him out instantly. Then Matt too slumped to the ground, having the presence of mind to raise his feet on the steps to get them above the level of his head. He lay there for about five minutes, finally plucking up courage to reach up and pull the knife from his shoulder. He dropped it onto the terrace, and moving as fast as his wobbly legs would allow, he recovered his radio controller and signalled for the doors to be unlocked. He moved to the bathroom and grabbed a large towel which he pressed against the wound in order to stem the bleeding. He then reached for his radio-telephone and called Claudia. She sensed the urgency in his voice and left her apartment at once.

When she screeched to a halt twenty minutes later, she rushed round to the terrace at the rear. She put her hand to her mouth at the scene that greeted her. Alfredo was sitting on one of the garden chairs, a blood soaked towel pressed to his shoulder. A spear gun lay alongside him on the table. A blond-haired man dressed in a black tracksuit was lying spread-eagled face down on the ground in front of Alfredo. As Claudia ran up the steps, he raised his head. Alfredo kicked the man's foot and growled in English, 'Keep still!'

Claudia then saw a grotesquely twisted figure on the other side of the terrace who was obviously dead, his sightless eyes staring at the moon, his wide-open mouth seemed to be emitting a soundless scream. A length of metal was sticking out of his throat and a large pool of blood was congealing around his head.

'*Alfredo, Qué paso?* What has happened?' Her Spanish was quick and urgent, and Stephen who was beginning to recover consciousness was unable to understand either Claudia or Matt.

'I will tell you later, *Cariña*, but first we must secure this pig. Please will you fetch some cord from the plant room. It's on the shelf above the boiler.'

When she did so, he ordered Stephen to put his hands behind his back and to raise his heels. Claudia tied him very tightly, and when she had finished Stephen was quite grey. The swelling on the back of his head was weeping blood.

'*Gracias*, Claudia, now can you please attend to me?'

Claudia removed the towel and was relieved to see that the bleeding had stopped.

'You need a doctor to look at this. I'll take you to Ciutadella straight away!'

'No, Claudia. We'll do that later. I must get these two goons sorted out first. Just get some of the anti-biotic powder from my First Aid chest and strap it up. The knife was very sharp – I don't think it damaged a major blood vessel. If I keep the cut clean, it should heal quite quickly.'

'But what's this all about? We must call the police!'

'No! That's the last thing I can do. I'll explain everything later, but for now, please trust me. I'm going to have to leave you with the one you tied up while I get rid of the dead one.

'I'm going to take him out into the ocean and anchor him to the seabed. He'll be eaten by the fish in no time at all. I know this seems gruesome but it has to be done.'

'You're in no fit state to dive – I can't let you do it!'

'Please, Claudia,' he kissed her gently. 'I feel fine now. It will only be a very short dive – I'll be back in not much more than an hour.'

Together, Matt and Claudia manhandled Stephen into the plant room, ensuring that his bonds were quite secure. Matt pulled on his wet suit with Claudia's help, and together they dragged Harry Ewers's body down the steps to the jetty. It took a further trip to get all Matt's gear together, and he was sweating profusely by the time he pulled away from the landing stage. It was gone midnight, and he would have to be careful not to run into any of the many small fishing boats that would be working through the night. He set course for a submerged reef that he had explored only a few weeks ago, six miles due south of Cala Galdana.

It took only 15 minutes by dead reckoning to find the ideal spot, which he had chosen because he knew that fishermen would not trawl over the rocks. He set a sea anchor and turned the boat into the wind. Then he rolled the body over and began the grizzly task of undressing it. He tried to remove the bolt from its neck, but it was wedged fast in the head and neck bones. As far as he knew, the bolt bore no identifying marks, although he did not expect it ever to be found.

Matt struggled into his tank harness with difficulty. His shoulder was now quite stiff and he thought that the wound had started to bleed again. He dragged the spare anchor from the cable locker and draped the body across it, attaching the arms and legs to it with stainless steel wire. When he was satisfied that the body was quite secure, he attached a rope to the anchor ring and pushed the body and anchor overboard. With a large splash, the gruesome bundle sank into the depths.

Matt paid out the rope, letting it run through his fingers until the slackness told him that it had hit bottom. He let out another 50 feet of slack and tied off the rope to a cleat. Pulling on his face mask and fins, he dropped off the back of the boat. Switching on his powerful underwater lantern, Matt swam down the line, checking the depth on his wrist gauge as he went.

He knew that the ocean floor was 60 metres deep at this point, the reef rising to within 28 metres of the surface. The body had wedged itself between the rocks at about 10 metres above the sea bed. Matt dragged it free and guided it to a fault in the reef that was several feet wide. He pushed the frightful mess of metal and flesh over the edge and swam down after it, wedging it firmly beneath an overhanging ledge. He was sure that it would not be washed out by underwater currents. While the stainless steel wire held the body securely to the 200 lb anchor, the sea would keep his secret. In no time at all, the creatures of the deep would destroy all evidence of this visit. Matt untied the rope from the anchor ring and started his slow ascent to the surface. By the time he regained the safety of the villa, he was totally exhausted and fell into a fitful sleep after Claudia had redressed his wounded shoulder.

The next morning, Matt awoke feeling stiff and unwell and knew that he was running a fever. He would not allow Claudia to call a doctor and asked her to work the anti-biotic powder into the wound and dress it again. He promised that if he was no better by the next day, he would go to the hospital, telling them that he had fallen on a spike during his building operations.

*

Matt took some water and a plate of cereal to Stephen, releasing him from his bonds so that he could eat.

'What are you going to do with me?' he asked.

'I know who you are. I know why you came here and I know who sent you. I also know that neither you nor Marie is clever enough to pit your wits against mine. I'm faster, fitter, stronger and more devious, and when necessary I can be quite ruthless. Your man will never be found and nothing will link me with him. I could kill you here and now with my bare hands if necessary, and no one would ever know, except Marie that is, and she wouldn't tell. I could imagine the policeman's face if she reported that the men she sent to kill her dead husband were missing!' He chuckled, and the sound sent shivers down Stephen's spine.

'Look, I knew nothing about any of this and tried to persuade her to leave things alone.'

'Of course you did, that's why you're here now! Don't treat me like a fool – you are well and truly involved. No, my friend, if you want to go free, I'll need some comfort that this sort of thing will never happen again. I can't spend the rest of my life looking over my shoulder. I have some serious thinking to do but in the meantime I'll keep you locked away here for a few hours. You'll have my decision by midday.'

Matt retied Stephen's bonds tightly and locked him up again. Stephen briefly considered resisting but discarded the idea at once. He had never been a physical person, and knew that he was no match for Matt, even in his injured state.

Matt then spoke to Claudia for over an hour to explain what had happened. He said that he had been involved in a building project some years ago that had gone sour. The contract had been riddled with bribery and corruption and he refused to get involved. He said he had reported the crimes to the police and several powerful men had been put in jail. These men had now come for revenge. He had been lucky this time, but if they struck again, he might not be so well prepared.

He was going to take the one they now held prisoner back to his bosses to persuade them that they would never beat him. He would be gone only a few days and when he returned, he would arrange to close up the house for a year and he would take Claudia travelling around the world. He told her that she knew that he was very fond of her, and that if they got on perhaps they could marry and settle down. Claudia was overwhelmed; her joy was beyond expression.

'*Cariño*, please persuade these men to leave you alone. What is done is done and hurting you will bring nothing back. I will travel anywhere with you – I love the idea. Now, I'll clear up the mess on the terrace for you.'

She danced out into the sunshine, her happiness and naivety causing a slight pang of conscience in Matt's heart.

*

By midday, Matt had decided on his future strategy. Claudia was convinced that he was the innocent party in a vengeance campaign and was willing to do whatever he asked. Her anticipation of their developing relationship over the next 12 months had completely overwhelmed her. The terrace had been cleared of blood, and the clothes that Harry Ewers had been wearing had been burnt in the boiler. After Stephen confessed to Matt where he had left his car, Claudia collected it and drove it back to the villa.

Matt asked Claudia to contact Señor Brechia and explain that she would be leaving her job soon. Claudia foresaw no problem; her cousin would step into the position. She then started planning her wardrobe for their forthcoming travels. She sparkled as she left, happy that Matt's shoulder was showing no further ill effects.

*

Matt left Stephen for a further three hours without drink or food, to soften him up even further. When he finally opened the plant room door, the heat rushed out, even though the outside temperature was approaching 26°C.

Stephen blinked, his eyes red-rimmed and sore as the beam of sunlight from the doorway fell across his face. He licked his cracked lips and tried to speak, but only a dry croak came out of his mouth. His legs and arms were painfully cramped and he had a splitting headache from the blow he had received the previous night.

'I've something to discuss with you,' said Matt. 'But I could leave you here to rot for a week if I wanted, and no one would know. You realize of course, that you are no match for me physically. Even if you were in the peak of condition, I could kill you in a number of ways with my bare hands. I am an expert in the martial arts.'

This lie tripped off Matt's tongue with ease and he knew that it would help to reinforce Stephen's fear of him.

'I will untie and feed and water you in a few minutes, but before I do so I can tell you that if you show the slightest sign of resistance or try to escape, I will kill you without compunction.'

Stephen nodded and Matt knew that he had him totally subdued.

'I'm going to tell you what I'm going to do. I will need your full co-operation, and again I'll remind you that there is no negotiation. What I say goes, and unless you agree, both you and Marie will be destroyed.'

His voice had lowered almost to a whisper and he leant close to Stephen's face. 'Do you agree?' The words were punctuated by a two-second gap. His eyes had narrowed and he looked menacing. Stephen nodded.

'Okay Stephen, just keep everything I've said at the front of your mind all the time. From now on, I will treat you and act as though we are the best of friends. Remember though, this will only be an act.'

Matt stood behind Stephen, and with two quick slashes he cut the nylon cord that had secured him for so long. Stephen grunted with pain at the release of his constricted circulation and lay still for a few moments.

'Come on, these things have to be done sometime,' said Matt

more gently, and he massaged Stephen's bruised and lacerated wrists. After a short while, Stephen rose painfully to his feet and allowed Matt to help him into the villa.

'The tap water is quite drinkable, help yourself and then take a shower in the bathroom,' said Matt pointing to the guest suite. 'There's all you need, including a razor. My lady brought your bag in from the car. Take your clothes and let me have your friend's.'

Stephen splashed cold water on his face and drank deeply at the sink. He went to the beach-bag and took his shorts and creased T-shirt. 'Thanks,' he mumbled and went through the door indicated by Matt. 'I can assure you that I won't give any trouble.'

Twenty minutes later, Stephen reappeared and placed his tracksuit in the beach-bag. Harry Ewers's gear had gone and he guessed that Matt had destroyed it while he was taking a shower.

'Okay Stephen, let's get to it. I can't have Marie setting me up with contract killers more efficient than you and your dead associate for the rest of my life. As I've said, I need a little insurance. You are going to give me a complete confession as to what has happened over the past year, and even earlier – and you will sign it. I will keep it in a safe place, and if I should die in suspicious circumstances, it will be released to the police. Now, how much has Marie told you about what has happened over the last year?'

Stephen decided that he had to be honest. 'I believe she told me everything. I don't know the full details of course, but she told me how your partner had cheated you out of about a million pounds. She said that you had devised an intricate scheme to recover it, which you did, and set up a number of sparsely hidden clues to point the police to his having murdered you after you disappeared. She said that you expected her to join you here after the dust had settled. Your partner's death wasn't part of the plan. Neither was her turning against you so violently. That's all I know. She didn't tell me your Spanish name or how you got your new identity – just that you were now a Spaniard.'

'Okay Stephen – I think I believe you've told me all you know. Come to my study – you have a confession to write.'

Stephen was taken to the desk, and a pad of A4 lined paper was set in front of him. Matt gave him his instructions.

'I will now dictate your confession. Write exactly what I say – don't change a word; I will be reading it over your shoulder. There will be times when you will want to protest, but forget it. Your survival and that of Marie depends on your total co-operation. Understood?' Again, Stephen nodded.

'Before we begin, I think Marie said that you were once married. Are you divorced or separated from your wife?' Stephen nodded again.

'Divorced.'

Matt started to dictate:

> 'My name is Stephen Murray, I am writing this to be opened in the event of my sudden or precipitous death. It is written of my own free will and without duress. No one except me is aware of its existence.
>
> Over the past five years, I have been emotionally involved with a former work colleague of mine, Marie Du Bois. I met her at my office and we became attracted to each other. After a short while, we had what we thought would just be a love affair. However, it developed beyond that and we both wanted to live the rest of our lives together. The trouble was we were both married. I divorced my wife but Marie said that her husband, Matthew, would never release her.
>
> After a while, she told me of a plan that she had hatched with her husband's partner. He, Christopher Marten, had made several passes at Marie and obviously fancied her physically. Once, at a party, they both got a bit drunk and talked hypothetically of how they would both benefit if Matt was not around any more. One thing led to another and they started to meet secretly as they planned an intricate and complicated murder.
>
> They decided that if they were going to do this, it should be worthwhile. Marie suggested to Christopher that the partners should increase their partnership insurance, and if Matt died, Marie would get £2m. and his partner £1m. They intended to have Matt murdered by a contract killer ... '

Matt paused, 'What was your friend's name, Stephen?'
'Harry Ewers. He lived in Millwall, London.'
'Continue.'

'... and made contact with a man called Harry Ewers. Marie asked me to do it, but I just couldn't.

However, it seemed that Matt stumbled on a swindle that Chris had been working on him, so he confronted him. In a mad panic, Chris killed Matt in his office. He phoned Marie and told her what had happened. She told him to get the body out of the office quickly and to get over to see her right away. He was worried in case the security guard at the offices saw him, so Marie telephoned security to keep him busy while Chris got the body into the car.

Marie phoned me, and we all met at her house later that night to discuss the next move. Harry Ewers was brought in too and he got rid of the body. I don't know where.

We all decided to just play it cool and see what developed. The police were too clever for us and found out too much about Chris. He was eventually arrested for murder but released on bail.

He was panicking badly and couldn't put forward a defence, so he got us all together at Marie's house for another meeting. He had been drinking, and said that he wasn't going to take the rap for everyone. He would involve us all, he said.

Ewers got angry and threatened to kill Chris. Marie said we should all calm down and took Ewers out in the garden to cool off. Chris had another drink and I just sat there – it was all a bit over my head. I just wanted to live with someone I loved.

When they came back, Marie told us that we should all support Chris, and that we should work out a plan to save his skin. She poured us all another drink and we sat down to discuss it. Then she gave me a signal not to drink mine. I noticed that Ewers wasn't drinking either, but Chris was drinking his, and as the evening wore on he got more and more drunk. Marie eventually said at about ten o'clock that she had a plan, and that Chris would have to get some papers from his office.

As he was obviously too drunk to drive, Ewers drove him to the office, but stopped around the corner. Chris would be okay to drive for that last 100 yards or so and he took the car on from there, with Ewers hidden in the back. When he arrived, he got rid of the guard and they waited for Marie and I to arrive.

When we got there, we went to Chris's office, and he didn't need to be invited to have another drink. In 20 minutes, he slumped over his desk, snoring loudly. Marie slapped him hard but he wouldn't wake up.

We carried him down to his car and rigged up a hose from the exhaust. Then we left him there. He was dead by the morning.

Ewers and I went back to Marie's and we decided we all needed an alibi. I drove to London and went to an all-night cinema, where I would have been at the time of Chris's death, if questioned. Ewers wasn't worried about alibis – he could get one anywhere.

After I left, Ewers had to slap Marie around a bit to pretend that Chris had been there earlier and she would file a complaint in the morning. But Ewers was too heavy-handed and beat her too hard. She lost her baby. She told me she would never forgive him.

She said yesterday that I would never see Ewers again. I've tried to contact him, but he has disappeared off the face of the earth.

Originally, the four of us were in a plot to murder Matt. We all killed Chris and now Marie has obviously had Ewers murdered. My fear is that I will be next. She is not the woman I fell in love with and I want to bail out now. I am afraid though that if I do, she will have me found and killed. Without her, I have no money and can't hide.

It is for this reason that I have written this all down, and it will be delivered to the police if I am ever found dead in suspicious circumstances.'

'Sign each page, Stephen, and make sure it's your normal signature – I'll check it with your passport later.'

Even in the air-conditioned study, Stephen was perspiring profusely. However, he did as he was told and sat back in the chair, his hands shaking. 'I've signed my life away – I've confessed to something I never did.'

'Stephen – your life was signed away when you first met Marie.'

21

Matt waited until late that night and had Stephen drive him to his rented holiday villa at Son Parc on the north of the island. When they arrived, it was all quiet, and Stephen and Matt parked in their allotted space before going quietly up the short flight of steps to the terrace. They unlocked the shutters and entered the villa through the lounge.

'Get your things packed. You're staying with me for the rest of the holiday. I'll put Ewers's stuff together. Also, leave a note for the maid; tell her you've met a friend and you're both staying with him for the next few days. Don't forget her tip!'

Stephen scribbled a note on the maintenance agency's paper 'Ancora Services'. He began with 'Dear Vanessa,' and signed it 'Murray' at the end.

They left after locking up and leaving the keys under a stone on the barbecue. As they were about to get into their car, a small Suzuki mini-bus bumped up the kerb and parked next to them. Matt turned his face away and got into the driver's seat.

'Hi Stephen! Had a good day?'

'Get rid of them,' Matt hissed between his teeth.

'Oh, hello, Richard. Valerie, how are you? You're late back – I'm glad we saw you – we're packing up early. Harry's found a Spanish girl with a nice sister over in Galdana. We're spending our last two days with them – enjoy the rest of your holiday!'

Richard winked perceptibly, with a knowing glint in his eye. 'We certainly will – you enjoy yourselves too! You lucky dogs!'

Stephen climbed into the car and Matt sped away without giving him time to put on his seat belt.

'Harry's in a hurry,' remarked Richard – 'She must really be special!'

*

The next morning, under direction from Matt, Stephen phoned the telephone number given on his holiday itinerary by the tour operator who had arranged his flight.

'Can I confirm my return flight tomorrow. It's on AMM555. My name is Murray, Stephen Murray.'

'That's confirmed, sir. Depart at 12.25, check-in at 10.25. I have two seats for you.'

'Yes, my fellow traveller is Mr Ewers, can you confirm both?' The seats were confirmed, and Stephen replaced the handset.

'Stephen, you were obviously going to let Marie know what was happening,' said Matt. 'Did you have a code?'

'No, I didn't.'

'Okay. Phone her now and just say this: "Stephen here – it's done," then hang up.'

Stephen telephoned Marie and left the message.

Stephen spent the whole of the day locked in the guest room, although he had no intention of trying to run. He was out of his depth here and knew he had to rely on Marie to get him clear of this mess.

*

Stephen and Matt arrived at Mahon airport in good time to check in for their return flight. Matt stood back while Stephen presented their tickets as well as his own and Harry Ewers's passport at the Air 2000 check-in desk. The girl looked perfunctorily at the passports, only checking that the date was valid. She didn't even look at Stephen's face to confirm his identify.

By the time Stephen and Matt, who had reverted to being Señor Perez had cleared customs at Gatwick, it was half past one, Friday afternoon. They then took a taxi and arrived at Marie's front gate just after two o'clock. Stephen cursed to himself as they approached the house, to see Jerry Walls in his car, travelling in the opposite direction down the lane. Then he remembered that it was Friday afternoon and Jerry would of course be on the way to his boxing club. He pressed the buzzer at the main gate, and simply said 'Stephen' when Marie answered.

The taxi swept up the driveway and came to a halt opposite the front door. Marie skipped out of the house, throwing her arms around Stephen as he got out of the back seat. Matt had already paid the driver at the gate and stepped out of the car on the other side, with their travel bags in his hands. The taxi pulled away. Marie was still embracing Stephen when Matt noisily dropped the bags on the pathway behind them. She turned, expecting Harry Ewers. The smile of welcome died on her lips and she paled, her hand going involuntarily to her mouth.

'Hello Marie,' he said quietly. 'You're looking good and also quite happy for someone widowed twice by the same man!'

'Stephen. Help me!' Marie turned to run into the house but Matt had seized her by the wrist before she made the door.

'I'm sorry darling – you've chosen the wrong man,' said Matt. 'However, you shall keep him.' She winced as he pushed her through the hallway and into his old study. A few changes had been made. 'I see you've made yourself at home, Stephen. Well, you're welcome to it! Marie, we have some business to discuss. Let me make myself absolutely clear. I don't want you any more, Marie. You and this man can do whatever you like together. After today, you'll never see me again. If, that is, you do exactly as I ask. I say "ask", just to be polite, but quite frankly, you have no choice.'

While Matt was talking, he switched on a small A4 copier that he had installed when he equipped his study. He took the four pages of Stephen's confession from his pocket and ran off one copy of each.

'Sit down quietly Marie, and read this.' He passed the photocopies over to her and returned the originals to his pocket. She glared at him, her hatred coloured with fear. She started to read. From time to time, she grunted and twice looked up at Matt and then Stephen. At last she finished and with a shriek, she screwed up the four sheets and ripped them up in anger.

'You bastard! I won't sign this. You can't do anything with this – I know all about you, remember?'

'Marie, I have no intention of doing anything with it – unless I have to. You don't have to sign it. You are sufficiently incriminated by what Stephen has said. The document can be proved to be authentic if necessary. No, Marie. It's my insurance policy. If the police saw this they would investigate. There's enough evidence to make them dig and there's nothing here at all that you can disprove. I'm quite clear. Although you know my Spanish name, I can disappear quite easily, certainly for the time it would take for you to be put away.

'So, my love, you can't try to have me killed again. That's the insurance value of these few pieces of paper. They also have a more tangible use. When our scheme was first planned, we expected to come out of this with about six million pounds; I have so far only had the two million that was rightfully mine anyway. I now want the rest.'

Marie's jaw set and she tossed her head back, glaring at him defiantly.

'Don't look like that, Marie. I said this is not negotiable, and I meant it. Michael Burford will have arranged a settlement for you from the practice – you can keep that as income. I only want the capital that you have got as a result of my death.

'I'll be generous – I won't take it all – just four million.'

Marie laughed. 'You must be joking – or mad! I'm giving you nothing. Do your worst!'

Stephen stepped in front of Marie. 'Darling, we're beaten! We'd never get on the same level as him – he's too tough for us. Look, from what you've told me, we'll be left with a very good income from the office lease and this house. We can be happy and build a new life together – you and I, and clear of any fear or worry. This will all be behind us.'

Marie glared at him, 'Shut up, you useless little fart! You couldn't even carry out one simple little task for me – even with the help of an expert! What makes you think I ever wanted to get tied up with you anyway? Fuck off!'

Tears of anger and frustration were streaming down her cheeks, and despite himself, Matt allowed himself a slight smile.

He had used those very words to an office spy when Stephen and Marie went off for the trip to Scotland all that time ago. He turned back to Marie, and reaching into his pocket he wiped the tears away with a fresh, clean handkerchief.

'Marie, don't blame him. He did his best. There are times when you must accept that there are no acceptable alternatives. If you refuse to pass over the money, I'll disappear, and then I'll have this confession delivered to Orpington Police Station. I read that the man investigating my murder was called Webb, he would find this fascinating reading, I am sure. Now, let's be sensible and practical. I want to get this finished today.' He glanced at his wristwatch. 'Do you still have your bank account in Sevenoaks? Good. Telephone the Manager and tell him you want a banker's draft prepared straight away, debited to your account for four million pounds. You want to pick it up in 30 minutes before the close of business. If he asks what it's for, tell him to mind his own business. As it's only a piece of paper, it can be done that quickly. It's not cash but as good as. Okay – do it now!'

Marie's shoulders slumped and all the fight seemed to have gone out of her. She didn't even shake Stephen off when he crouched in front of her and put his arms around her shoulders.

'My bag is in the lounge; get my cheque book, Stephen – I'll need the phone and account numbers.'

Stephen returned only a few moments later and Marie placed the call. The manager expressed some surprise, and although he didn't know Mrs Du Bois very well, he didn't have many customers with over four and a half million pounds on deposit. Her beaten and dejected tone hardened when he asked if he could enquire as to the reason for the large withdrawal. She smiled slightly at Matt as she said, 'No you can't! Mind your own business and just do as you're told. This is not negotiable and I will collect it in 30 minutes.'

Stephen drove Matt and Marie to the bank after Marie had spent ten minutes retouching her face. She was still beautiful to Matt and he wondered, but only fleetingly, if their relationship could have been repaired, but he discarded the idea immediately.

*

Matt was unable to get a flight that evening so he stayed overnight at the London Hilton. Stephen and Marie dropped him at Sevenoaks Station when they left the bank, and Matt told them that they would never see him again. He constantly felt the five pieces of paper in his inside pocket, but instead of elation he felt strangely empty. Somehow, he had a feeling of déja vu, that he had been here before.

*

That evening, Matt spent much of his time on the telephone. He first arranged a flight with Air UK from Gatwick Airport to Jersey, departing at 10.00 a.m. the next day and returning at 1.00 p.m. This connected perfectly with the Monarch Airways flight to Mahon which left Gatwick at 4.00 p.m.

He then telephoned Claudia and asked her to be ready to leave on the following Monday morning. She didn't need to bring anything apart from an overnight bag with her toiletries – they would buy everything they needed as they went along. He told her to tell her relations that she would be away for a year, and to arrange for Nicholás Brechia to have the house closed down and maintained while they were away.

Señor Alfredo Perez accompanied by his very pretty and shapely girlfriend Claudia, left Menorca on Monday 5 June. They had no forwarding address and would be travelling the world, maybe for a year.

On his trip to Jersey, Matt had increased his numbered account by 6,080,000 dollars, and cancelled his instructions for regular payment into the account in Mahon, until further notice. He had also set up a procedure for gaining telephone access to his account from anywhere in the world and he purchased a hundred 1,000 dollar travellers' cheques.

While he was waiting for his connecting flight to Mahon, Matt went to the post office in the North Terminal and mailed a package to Detective Inspector Webb at Orpington Police Station. He knew that he might be taking a slight chance but he thought it was so insignificant as to be ignored.

As a result, Marie and Stephen would be investigated, and he was certain that they would have no plausible answers to the questions that they would be asked. He had turned the tables on their little ruse very effectively. Without doubt they would try to implicate him, but what had a Spanish gentleman to do with this plot? Matthew Du Bois still alive? Rubbish! That just wouldn't be remotely plausible. He didn't think that line would be investigated, and he wouldn't even be around to be questioned. By the time he returned, the whole thing would have gone cold and he couldn't see the police hanging around waiting on such slim evidence from self-confessed conspirators.

Anyway, Stephen only knew half the facts and absolutely no real detail, and Marie did not know all the details in their full complexity. When they were interrogated they would not be questioned together, and their separate stories would not dovetail sufficiently for full corroboration. The risk diminished the more he turned it over in his mind.

If it transpired that he heard of any investigation starting, he would simply not come back to Menorca – he could afford to build a new home anywhere in the world! To hell with it! – It was worth a very small amount of danger to ensure that Marie and Stephen had absolutely no chance of trying their luck again at some later date. But, he could not be watching his back all of the time, and there were bound to be occasions when either he, or Claudia, come to that, would be vulnerable.

*

When they had dropped Matt off at Sevenoaks Station, Stephen drove Marie slowly back to the house, without a word passing between them.

Stephen's thoughts were bred mainly by the relief that it was all over. Perhaps he and Marie could now literally start anew. Her income from the office rental and the small amount of capital, relatively speaking, she had left, would be enough for them to survive in a great deal of comfort.

The experiences over the last few weeks had slightly clouded his opinion of Marie. She had exposed a nasty streak hitherto hidden, but then she had been through so much lately that perhaps it was to be expected. His deep love for her would override any doubts that might surface.

However, he did have the feeling that he needed to be more assertive, otherwise she would crush his personality completely. Nevertheless, his only desire now was to live happily with Marie, and to make her happy, even though this would, he knew, be a very long-term process.

While Stephen was thinking about the future, Marie, conversely, was looking back. She felt totally drained of energy and emotion and completely dead inside. Her shame at trying to arrange for Matt to be killed was profound, but it was almost exactly balanced by her deep hatred of him. Was it true that love could turn to hate so quickly and with such intensity, she wondered? 'Yes, damn it, it was true!'

She didn't know if she hated Matt because she had loved him and he had left her or if she hated him so much because he had turned the tables on them. Perhaps she hated herself because she hated the thought of still loving him when he hated her. That was possible too.

She shivered as she tried to arrest her thought process, and for the first time since this had all begun, her mind turned to contemplation of suicide. She now understood fully and clearly how Chris must have felt – empty, alone, devoid of ambition or enthusiasm and totally beaten. Matt had done that to him too. It was not until they stopped outside the house that Marie finally roused herself from the deep depression that she felt was enveloping them both. With a huge sigh, she turned to Stephen. 'A few weeks ago, I said that we would start again. I will be absolutely frank and honest with you. I felt at that time that I would still end up with Matt. That facet of my life is now, and I think I am pleased to say, completely finished.

'For you and I to have any chance, we must put everything that has happened behind us. We won't see or hear from Matt ever again, and now that he has his "insurance" in the form of the fake confession, he has no need to fear us. As a result, we have no need to fear him so can put him wholly out of our minds.

'We must try to build on what we have, although, in all honesty, our relationship seems at the moment to be a bit fragile, but we do have the experiences of the recent past as a link, and we must both try very hard to strengthen that bond between us. I promise you that I am now entirely committed to you, and as a gesture of my good faith, I am going to arrange for all of my assets, this house, the cars, my income and everything else to be put into our joint names. After Matt, it is going to be very difficult for me to trust anyone but this demonstration of commitment to you will, I hope, kick-start my ability to believe in anyone again. You, in return, will have the demanding task of restoring my faith in human nature. The following months, or even years, are not going to be easy, but if you are willing to try, so am I.'

Stephen had sat staring at her, holding her hands while she spoke, and it was only when she stopped and relaxed that he realized her fingernails had driven deep into the flesh on the back of his hand.

'Marie, I don't know how many times I've told you that I love you, and I still do, as much as I ever did. I will also be entirely honest. The events of the last few weeks have frightened me more than I could ever say. Not because of the physical danger and the pain – that hurts, but is only short term. No, it was the mental assault of seeing you as a different person that caused me the most pain, and my allowing myself to do things so alien to me that I know that I must have changed greatly as well. What scares me is that it all happened without my really knowing it until after the event.

'When I was lying tied up in that room in Matt's villa, badly beaten, exhausted and dehydrated, I thought I was going to be killed. At one time, I thought death would be a welcome release. It was then that I realized that I was in that position because I had allowed myself to be bullied into doing things utterly against my nature and character.

'I am willing, in fact, I plead with you, to allow me to start again with you from now, looking only forwards and never back. The past just did not happen.

'However, reverting to my fear, there is one condition. If I ever at any time find myself being coerced into doing something that I do not want to do, or that is alien to me, I shall walk away. I think we both know that you are a stronger and more dominant person than I am, but I don't envy that strength or feel less of a man because of it. I hope that we can recover some of our reciprocated gentle feelings of those early days at the office. I don't want to be the boss, but I won't be your lap-dog either. If you can accept that, we can try to build a new life from the rubble we are standing on now.'

For the first time in many months Marie felt a genuine smile of newborn happiness touch her lips and although he probably did not realize it, Stephen had just regained a little of the respect she had felt for him all those years ago.

They went into the house hand in hand, and over the next few days, their time was spent in animated and enthusiastic discussion about their future. At last, Marie was beginning to experience happiness again, and her resilience was showing through.

22

Inspector Webb could now close his files. Both the Du Bois and Marten cases had been satisfactorily resolved. He had sent his report to the DPP and the Inland Revenue about Marten's fiddling Du Bois and Bullock's knowledge of it, so it was now up to them.

He could at last turn his attention to a rape case that was causing some concern to the residents of the small housing estate in St Mary Cray.

Detective Sergeant Walker rapped on the glass of the inspector's open door, and entered carrying an envelope.

'Hi Roger. This came for you in this morning's post. It's been through the letter bomb check and contains only paper. As it's addressed to you personally, I brought it through. Another love letter? I don't know what you've got but it obviously works.'

He passed the letter to Inspector Webb who examined the stamp before opening it. The contents were quite bulky, and it had been posted at Gatwick Airport yesterday evening.

He carefully slit the top and removed four handwritten A4 sheets of paper. He put the envelope aside after checking that it was completely empty and began to read. After only a few lines, he turned to the last page and read the scrawled signature; the name 'Stephen Murray' was printed below it in the same handwriting.

'Graham!'

Walker was only a few yards down the corridor and returned almost at once, his eyebrows raised in query.

'Sit down – it's not all over yet!'

The inspector started to read again, but this time he held the pages only by the extreme edges, gripping them between his fingernails. He read carefully and passed the pages over to Walker one by one, as he finished them. Each had the same signature at the bottom. When Walker had finished the last page, he sat back and looked across inquiringly.

'Jesus, Guv'nor – what a can of worms! What do you think?'

'We'll check a few things out, and then we'd better talk to Mrs Du Bois. You know, I always had my doubts about her, mainly because she's the principal beneficiary from her husband's death, but this plot is so complicated we'd never have unravelled it.

'God! What an evil woman. If this is all true, then she conspired to have her husband killed, was involved with her accomplice's murder and probably had this Ewers bumped off too!'

Gesturing at the pages spread on his desk, he continued, 'I wonder where this came from? If Murray wrote it for his own protection, it hasn't done much good. Such letters are normally lodged with a bank or a lawyer to be opened only in the event of death, but it looks as though it didn't get that far. Anyway, let's look at what he's saying in detail, can you make some notes Graham?

'One. We can check if Murray once worked with Mrs Du Bois and see if any of the staff from that time are still there; they would have noticed something if they had been having an affair.

'Two. The increased insurance thing checks out – it was her idea and then Marten sowed the seeds with Mr Du Bois.

'Three. See what you can dig up on Ewers. If he was well-known enough for them to dig him out, he almost certainly has a record.

'Four. So Marten did kill Du Bois in panic. If they were going to get Ewers to do it, why did Marten buy the gun in the States? Maybe he felt in need of protection as he was dealing with real crooks now.

'Five. Marten's removal of the body from the offices and Mrs Du Bois's diversion of the guard with the phone call all ties up with our notes.

'Six. We know about Marten's reaction when he was arrested. She must have been planning his murder even then – what a witch!

'Seven. The getting him drunk bit, taking him to his office and his fake suicide also fits in. You took the security guard's statement that night, and he said he thought Marten was already drunk when he arrived. We now know why he wanted to get rid of the guard so quickly – his partners in crime were about to visit! He didn't know they were going to kill him though!

'Eight. The bit about Ewers beating up Mrs Du Bois – strange. If he was a real pro, he could have bruised her a bit without causing real damage. Maybe things went on that evening that Murray didn't know about. We'll see what she has to say about it when we question her.

'Nine. Ewers disappeared? Check that as well, Graham. If he has been killed, she would probably need to get someone to do it. She would have left clues somewhere.

'Well, this is fantastic. It all ties in. I think that Murray has moved into her house with her now, but we must question them separately. I would guess that she will have no idea that this has been written, so we can take her completely by surprise. He will only know that we have seen it if he has missed it. Okay, let's go!'

Webb took two copies of the letter and delivered the original to the Forensic Department for a detailed report.

The pile of files on the side of Webb's desk labelled 'ready for storing in the archives' would now remain open.

*

Marie and Stephen were in the middle of poring over a cashflow forecast of their proposed new business that Stephen had prepared. They were both quite excited and considerably encouraged by the progress that they had made in their plans to resurrect their old relationship.

The telephone rang and Stephen reached over to pick it up, his lips touching Marie's cheek gently as he brushed past. 'Stephen Murray.'

'Good morning, Mr Murray. Detective Sergeant Walker here, Orpington Police. Is Mrs Du Bois there?' Stephen handed the phone over.

'Hello, Mrs Du Bois. I wonder if I could ask you to slip down to the station to tidy up a few final points for us. We are closing our files now and insurers need a few release signatures. No, not urgent, but if you are around today or tomorrow it would be most helpful.'

'Certainly, Sergeant. I can come in later this morning if you like. I'll be there at about half past eleven.'

Marie replaced the phone and explained to Stephen what it was about, adding that he didn't need to come too.

*

Sergeant Walker nodded to Inspector Webb. 'She'll be here in an hour. If I leave at a quarter past eleven, I'll get to Murray just after she's left. I think it's safe to assume that he'll still be there. If not, at least you will have her on her own. I'll see you later. Meanwhile, I'll spend the next half an hour or so digging for something on Ewers.'

*

When Marie entered Inspector Webb's office, he was quite astounded at the change in her appearance. The last time he had seen her she had been drawn, pale and sour looking. Now she was bright, smart, very bouncy and extremely attractive. He would never cease to be amazed at how appearances could deceive – he had already, and unusually for him, made up his mind about her.

'Good morning, Inspector. I believe you have some papers for me to sign.'

'Yes, Mrs Du Bois. Before that, can we have a little chat? I would just like to clear up a few points that have been worrying me. I wonder if you can tell me anything about a Mr Harry Ewers?'

He was studying Marie's face very carefully and noticed her flinch visibly at the mention of Ewers's name.

'No, Inspector. I don't think I've ever heard of him.'

'I have it on good authority that you do know him, and that you employed him to do some work for you.'

Marie was fidgeting with her gloves and trying to act calm and collected without much success. This was a bolt from the blue and totally unexpected.

'No, there must be some mistake, I don't know him!'

'Very well, Mrs Du Bois – We'll come back to that. Can you tell me again what happened on the night of Mr Marten's death?'

Marie paled. 'God – do I have to go over that again! He got into my house uninvited; he killed my dog and beat me up badly. I lost my baby – or have you forgotten?' Her voice was shrill now and tears had welled up in her eyes.

Inspector Webb lifted the internal phone and asked for a woman police officer to come into his office right away. He sat quietly looking at Marie without expression, until a smart WPC tapped gently on the door and entered. He nodded at her to stand behind Marie and continued his questions.

'Mrs Du Bois. Is it not true that on the evening of Mr Marten's death, you and Mr Stephen Murray met with Mr Marten and Mr Harry Ewers at your house?'

Marie stared at him. Her mind screamed at her. Webb was relating what she had read only a few days ago in Stephen's 'confession'. Somehow Webb knew! She rallied and took on a belligerent stance.

'What you are saying is rubbish, Inspector. I have never had this Ewers man at my house and when Christopher Marten came, he came alone!'

'I also have it on good authority that you all then went to the offices, and having got Marten paralytically drunk, you then rigged a hose into his car and calculatedly and cold-bloodedly murdered him!' His voice had risen progressively and Marie recoiled at the venom with which he spat the last two words.

The realization that Matt had sent the confession to the police had dawned on her slowly, with relentless and irresistible pressure, forcing the blood from her head. Her heart was racing to restore it. Marie screamed once very loudly and then hysterically beat her hands on the desk, her feet stamping a tattoo on the floor. An incessant high-pitched wail pierced the quietness of the room.

Inspector Webb leaned sharply across the desk and slapped her hard once with the flat of his palm, careful not to harm or mark her. Marie stopped her screaming instantly and stared at the inspector with non-seeing eyes. The WPC had her arms around Marie's shoulders, partly to restrain and partly to comfort her. The policewoman looked at her superior for guidance, and he knew that he would get nothing further from Marie at this stage.

'Take her to a rest room and give her a cup of tea. Stay with her.'

The WPC helped Marie to her feet and led her from the room. He was convinced that she knew Ewers, and once her hysteria had subsided he was sure that she would confess. She was too weakened by events to resist further. He wondered how the sergeant was getting on.

*

Stephen was slightly surprised when Sergeant Walker announced his presence at the front gate. His immediate reaction was one of fear that Marie had had a road accident but the sergeant reassured him, saying he just had a few questions to ask. Stephen showed the sergeant into the lounge and offered him some coffee.

'I don't think I can really help you to clear up anything, Sergeant. I only came back onto the scene a few months ago after Mr Du Bois was killed. I was an old friend of Mrs Du Bois, and I got in touch again to offer my shoulder to cry on. Things just moved on from there.'

'Forgive me for saying so, but hasn't your relationship with Mrs Du Bois developed a little quickly after Mr Du Bois's death?'

Stephen reddened. 'Quite frankly, that is a personal matter between Mrs Du Bois and myself and of no concern to you.'

'Yes sir, of course. I apologise. Tell me, you say you were an old friend – did you work with her?'

'Actually, yes – for about six years until she left last June because of being pregnant.'

'Forgive me again, but was your relationship more than just friendship? In other words, were you lovers?'

'Really, Sergeant! This is too much – what are you getting at?'

'I won't pursue that line at the moment, sir. Could I ask you something else? Who do you think killed Harry Ewers?'

Stephen blanched. His mind was racing but couldn't find a safe place to stop.

'Let me make it easy for you, sir. Mrs Du Bois is at the station with Detective Inspector Webb and has by now almost certainly confessed. You are perhaps not quite as guilty as her, but you are an accessory to at least one murder, possibly two, and you were fully involved in a third.'

Stephen started to splutter.

'Don't deny anything, sir!' Sergeant Walker pulled a single sheet of paper from his pocket. 'Isn't this your signature?'

Stephen was now quite cold. There was no point in lying further – he would have to tell the truth, but out of loyalty to Marie he would try to spare her as much as possible.

'Very well. I'll tell you the whole story. I did write that, but only because I was forced to do so. Du Bois made me write it – he isn't dead! He's living in a villa in Spain. I've seen him. I went there with Ewers to talk to him. He ambushed us and killed Ewers. Then he made me write a confession.

'Let me start at the beginning. I only found out after Christopher Marten's death what had happened. It seemed that Marten had somehow fiddled Matt out of a large sum of money. Matt managed to get the money back and then he disappeared to Menorca in the Mediterranean. He left a number of clues to make it look as though he had been murdered by Marten. Matt had arranged all of this with Marie and they expected Marten to be sent to prison. Marie was then going to join Matt in Spain. It all went wrong with Marten's suicide and his attack on Marie. She lost her baby, as you know, and so much else that she turned against Matt – even hated him. That's when she asked me to go to Menorca with Ewers.

'That's the truth, Sergeant, and as much detail as I know. Marie knows more of course, but in her defence she was originally influenced and provoked by Matt's insatiable desire for revenge.'

'Well Mr Murray. That sounds most convincing.' The sarcasm was not lost on Stephen. 'I think you had better come back to the station with me; we will have further questions for you, I am sure.'

When they arrived at Orpington Police Station, Stephen was put into a small interview room alone with his thoughts, except for the constable standing guard at the door.

*

Sergeant Walker entered Webb's office and dropped into the chair alongside his desk without taking his coat off.

'What have you got, Sergeant?'

'Well, firstly I managed to check out Harry Ewers. His nickname is "Harry the Pick", and he has a record as long as your arm. He has been inside many times and even stabbed a copper a few years back. As his name suggests, he is a knife specialist and works entirely alone. He has some family in the Wapping mob and once worked with the Jamaica Road crowd in Bermondsey.

'He lives in a run-down house at 27, Cold Blow Lane, Millwall. He comes and goes as he pleases. It's thought that he has a wife somewhere in the Midlands. He hasn't been seen for a few weeks – that's not unusual, but he's never been away for more than a month at a time.

'As far as Murray is concerned, I've brought him in. He claims that he was forced to write that confession by ... guess who? Matthew Du Bois!' Webb smiled.

'He claims he's still alive and living on an island somewhere in the Mediterranean. He said that Du Bois disappeared, leaving a trail of clues pointing in the direction of Marten.

'Strangely enough, Murray didn't know how Du Bois got out of the country, how he made Marten buy the gun in the States, or how he made Marten drag the body across the office reception. In fact, he didn't really seem to know much about anything! How did you get on with the lady?'

'She threw a fit when I told her I knew what they had done. I've put her in the rest room to recover and then we'll have another go. I think she'll confess, particularly when we tell her that her boyfriend's written a confession implicating her, for his own protection. Let's see her again now.'

Marie was sitting on a couch, with her back propped up by a cushion and her feet up. The WPC said that she had not spoken for an hour, and that she had just stared into space the whole time.

She didn't even look up when Inspector Webb and Sergeant Walker entered the room. She just said, without expression, 'I will tell you everything.'

The inspector pulled up a chair and asked the sergeant to bring in a tape recorder.

'Alright, Mrs Du Bois. If you don't mind, we'll record the interview, and thank you for your co-operation.'

Sergeant Walker set up the machine, and the inspector switched it on. 'Interview with Mrs Marie Du Bois conducted by Detective Inspector Webb with Detective Sergeant Walker and WPC Jenner in attendance. Interview commenced 1.15 p.m.'

'Mrs Du Bois has agreed to this interview being recorded and is speaking of her own free will. Please Mrs Du Bois, could you tell us in your own words what really happened?'

Marie began in a clear but monotonous voice, devoid of any emotion.

'About eight months ago, my husband Matthew Du Bois discovered that his partner, Christopher Marten had been stealing money from him, earned through their practice. He had hidden the money away in a numbered account in the Cayman Islands in the Caribbean. Matt set about recovering the money, and then arranged to disappear, with the suggestion being that he had been murdered. He constructed a number of clues to point to Christopher being the murderer and we expected him to be arrested. Once the dust had settled, I was going to join him in his hideaway in Menorca. He didn't explain to me how he got around the customs and officialdom, but he has some documents that prove that he is a Spaniard, a Mr Alfredo Perez.

'One of the clues that he left was the gun that was supposed to have killed him. He brought it back from America in his golf bag. Then he disguised himself as Christopher to lay all of those clues, and I helped him whenever necessary. The scheme blew up in our faces when I lost my baby and I realized it was all Matt's fault. If only he had left it alone when he got the money back we would have been okay, but not him! He had to go on!

'Even then, I thought that we could get back together, until I went on a surprise visit to Menorca. I caught him fucking a woman in what was going to be my new home. I could never forgive him for that on top of everything else.

'I persuaded my friend Stephen Murray to get some help and go to Menorca to kill him – I hated him that much, but Stephen bungled it. The man that Stephen took with him, Harry Ewers, was killed and Matt made Stephen write a confession note, saying that he and I had set everything up. He said that he would keep the confession as insurance so that we wouldn't try again. However, the bastard just wanted to get us out of the way. That's why he sent it to the police. He's vicious, vindictive, and an evil, evil man.'

Webb interrupted her, 'Now Mrs Du Bois, can I ask you a few questions? If this is all true, why did Du Bois send us the confession – he must have known that you would tell us all this.'

'I don't know – perhaps he's flipped.'

'Everything you have said is based upon facts that we uncovered in our investigation of your husband's disappearance, except you've changed the emphasis. It is my belief that everything in Murray's confession is factual, and that it is a true sequence of events from beginning to end.'

Marie was not quite as unguarded as she appeared.

'If what you are saying is true, how would I know what is in Stephen's confession?'

Inspector Webb pondered for a second. 'Although Murray apparently wrote this confession so that it would give him some protection from you, it would only be effective if he informed you of its existence. Otherwise you would have no deterrent to not have him removed. It is also my view that you are a cunning and devious woman, and that you concocted this new story with Stephen Murray to tell in case the true facts ever came out. It is for this reason that you are both telling a similar tale. However, we are not deceived.'

He paused for a few seconds then went on. 'Marie Du Bois, I am arresting you on suspicion of murder, attempted murder and being an accessory before and after the fact. You need say nothing, but anything that you do say will be taken down and may be used in evidence against you. Interview closed at 1.52 p.m.'

Inspector Webb reached across and switched off the recorder, nodding to the WPC to take charge of Marie. Then he rose, and turning to Sergeant Walker he said, 'It is time to arrest Mr Stephen Murray.'

He smiled smugly to himself. He had them both now!

23

Over the next six months, Alfredo and Claudia roamed the world, exploring rough and little-known places, living at times in run-down and totally uncivilized accommodation, and at others in the lap of luxury, having rented a whole island with a staff of 20 to look after them.

They had seen the wild animals, plains, deserts and jungles of Africa, the unspoiled beauty of the Maldives and Mauritius, and the stark, beautiful brutality of the Icelandic and Greenland landscapes. They had skied in Canada, played in Florida and California, joined Jazz festivals in New Orleans and beer festivals in Germany.

They also sailed the Caribbean in a privately chartered ocean-going yacht with a seven-man crew. They stayed for several weeks when Matt revisited the Cayman Islands. On Cayman Brac and Little Cayman, Claudia learned to scuba dive under his expert tuition. They saw rays, sharks, barracuda and squid, moray and mantas, and every conceivable colour and type of fish available. Matt also scored a first in his life when they made love in 20 metres of water off the House Reef of Little Cayman. He later joked, 'To hell with the Five Mile High Club, we've just started the Sixty Feet Below Club!'

Eventually, when they had reached the Seychelles in the Indian Ocean in December, after a romantic dinner in their hotel suite overlooking Beau Vallon Bay, Matt proposed. They were married the next week at a ceremony organized by the Smuggler's Reef Hotel, and spent their honeymoon playing on the remote and deserted beaches of Praslin.

Throughout their travels, whenever possible, Matt had arranged for up-to-date copies of quality English newspapers to be delivered to his hotel rooms.

It was in Kenya, in his second week away, that he read that the wife of a famous English architect had been arrested with her boyfriend, on suspicion of a number of crimes including murder, attempted murder, conspiracy to defraud and for being accessories. The trial was finally set for mid-November, and Matt made sure that they were in civilized places for the next few months so he could follow the progress of the trial. Once Matt had established the date of the trial at the Old Bailey, he asked Claudia to do him a further favour. Under his close direction, she telephoned Cathy Steiner at her home.

After Matt and Christopher's deaths, she had resigned from MDB, knowing that both she and Wendy were somewhat superfluous. Tim and the other partners already had their own secretaries. Claudia explained on the phone that her boss, a wealthy Brazilian lawyer, had an interest in the Du Bois-Murray trial being a somewhat unusual case, and that he wanted the details of the court hearing for future reference.

As the trial was expected to last for two months, Claudia said that her boss would be willing to pay a fee of 10,000 pounds for Cathy to attend court each day, where she would take shorthand notes or tape recordings and prepare a full transcript of everything that was said. The transcript would be sent in serialized sections to various hotels, the locations of which would be notified later by telephone.

Although she knew that this would be a most demanding task, Cathy readily agreed as she needed the money. She also had a considerable interest in the case anyway. Cathy duly gave Claudia her bank details and Alfredo arranged for the 10,000 pounds to be deposited straight away.

Every week for the next nine weeks, Claudia received anything from 20 to 30 closely typed A4 sheets, sent to her at various hotels in Europe, Asia and Africa.

It was in January that Alfredo read in a day-old copy of *The Times*, that Marie Du Bois had been found guilty of several crimes and had been imprisoned for four terms of 25 years, 25 years, 7 years and 6 years, to run concurrently. Her accomplice, Stephen Murray, had been given three terms of 25 years, 15 years and 6 years. The complete seven-page transcript from Cathy arrived three days later.

Matt was very quiet all evening, and Claudia could not understand the fury and lack of compassion that he demonstrated in their love-making that night. It was almost as though he wanted to hurt her.

*

Alfredo and Claudia Perez, a wealthy and beautiful couple, returned to the house in Menorca in May, just in time to see the mass of spring flowers bursting into colour throughout the island. They had telephoned ahead so that the villa could be opened up and aired for them, as it had been shut up for nearly a year. When he heard of their planned return on the local grapevine, the inspector from the *Guardia Civil* Office in Ciutadella kept his promise and placed a telephone call to his English counterpart.

Detective Chief Inspector Webb had at last managed to persuade his superintendent to authorize a visit to Spain. 'A 120 pound fare to the Mediterranean is okay, but not 400 pounds for Disneyland!' he had said. It was a fantastic story that Marie had told, quite unbelievable really, but it was worth checking out for his own peace of mind.

Inspector Webb arrived in Menorca two days before the Perez's return, and with the co-operation of his local police contact he had had a chance to look around the inside of the villa. He had even managed to bend the rules and have a little forensic help.

When Alfredo and Claudia finally arrived at their house, their first impression was one of pleasure that the access track had been properly surfaced during their absence, and that the gardens and cultivated areas had been well tended. They were surprised, however, to see a strange car in front of the villa. They went round to the back and climbed the steps to the terrace.

A balding man, wearing a pair of grey trousers and an uncomfortably hot-looking shirt and tie was sitting in one of the loungers, his jacket on the back of one of the chairs.

'Who the hell are you?' Alfredo asked in Spanish. *'Esta privado!'*

The man looked up and raised his eyebrows. 'Can we speak in English please, sir?'

'What is it?' said Claudia in English. 'Who are you?'

'Perhaps I should show my credentials.' He rose and took his badge and warrant card from his jacket pocket. 'Detective Chief Inspector Webb. CID from England.'

Largely as a result of his success on the Du Bois-Murray-Marten cases, he had recently received promotion to Chief Inspector. He took a photograph from his other pocket and compared it with Alfredo's features.

'Could you remove your spectacles please, sir?'

Alfredo obliged. 'Please tell me what this is all about.'

The chief inspector looked at the picture again and saw similarities. He tried to imagine Perez without the well-trimmed jaw-line beard that he was wearing, and after Perez had removed his spectacles, he recognized a distinct resemblance to Matthew Du Bois.

'I have been told an amazing story, sir. Almost unbelievable in fact, so unbelievable that I think a lot of coppers wouldn't even have bothered to check it out.

'You see, a crime was committed in England and all the evidence pointed to a certain suspect. I was quite happy with the weight of the evidence even though it was only circumstantial. Then, to tie it all together, the suspect, we thought in an admission of guilt, committed suicide. The case was closed.

'Then, sir, blow me down if some new evidence didn't appear. It was in the form of a confession which had obviously fallen into the wrong hands and was sent through to me. Well, it implicated the wife, her boyfriend and a small-time London crook.

'We looked into it, and it was obvious that they were the real guilty parties; they had no plausible answers to the charges made against them ... except this fantastic story I mentioned. It implicated you, sir. It said that you were really the "murder" victim and that you had engineered the whole thing. Unbelievable really, although you do bear a physical resemblance to him. What do you think of all this, sir?'

'Amazing, Inspector. Quite amazing,' said Alfredo, his Spanish accent mingled in with his perfect English. 'My name is Alfredo Perez Gandia, and I have all of my identity documents to prove it. I can stand up to any scrutiny you like to instigate. I know, of course, the case that you are talking about. I knew Señor Du Bois from one of my projects – we were both architects. He was a good, if distant, friend. I saw both him and his partner just a day or so before his disappearance.

'However, that is our only link and this story has been made up by his wife and her lover to try to convince you of their innocence. I have had no other contact with these people. I have read in detail the transcript of all of the evidence presented at the trial. As you say, their story is quite unbelievable, and so you should not believe it! The jury didn't, they have both been proven guilty!'

'Yes sir, that's what I thought – a quite unbelievable story.' Chief Inspector Webb rose and picked up his jacket. He turned to go and then seemed to remember something.

'Oh, just one more small thing, sir. I wonder if you could tell me how it is that your fingerprints appear on the confession letter sent through to me, and why it is that Matthew Du Bois's fingerprints have been found all over this villa?'

Matt licked his lips, his gaze switching across to Claudia who was frowning, perplexed. He dropped into his chair, his expression blank. Then he smiled.

'Inspector, it is not Señor Du Bois's fingerprints that are here. It is my fingerprints that you found over there! As I said, I visited England the day before Matt disappeared. I had a meeting with Señor Du Bois and Christopher Marten. We chatted over old times and had several drinks. He even let me use his shower to freshen up, and he loaned me a clean shirt. I still have it somewhere in my wardrobe – would you like to see it?'

The Chief Inspector sighed. Either this man was immensely clever, incredibly lucky, or a mixture of both. If Du Bois alias Perez was guilty, what had he done? Nothing as far as he could see – to innocent people at least! If it was Du Bois, he had only hurt those who had tried to rob, harm, maim or to kill him. Webb had always thought that the laws related to self-protection were somewhat weighted against the innocent, and he had found this anomaly of justice unacceptable. There was a massive insurance fraud of course, but he was no great lover of insurance companies either.

Should he dig deeper? he wondered. Would it lead to further promotion? Also of course, if he had arrested the wrong people all along, he could possibly have his recent advancement to chief inspector revoked! He would almost certainly be suspended and he could even lose his pension and everything! He thought he was a good copper, but his devotion to duty was now being sorely tested against his desire for self-preservation.

Detective Chief Inspector Roger Webb rose from his seat. He held out his hand to Claudia Perez and shook it, without warmth or friendliness. 'Goodbye, Madam,' and turning to Alfredo, 'Sir. I would like to say that I can now close this case completely, but I think you will be seeing more of me very soon. I still have no explanation of how your fingerprints, or those of a dead man are on the confession letter. Yes, Mr Du Bois, if I may call you that, I have a feeling that you will certainly see me again!' He turned on his heel and left.

Matt went to Claudia and put his arm round her shoulders. They turned and walked to the edge of the terrace, and they both looked out to sea. The deep-blue sky on the horizon was streaked with red. Matt stooped and idly picked up a couple of small stones. He cast the first out into the sea far below.

*

He dropped back into his chair and stared wearily into space, wondering what move Chief Inspector Webb would make next. For once, Matthew Ronald Du Bois did not have a plan ...